Into the Way of
PEACE

by Karen Kelly Boyce

KFR
Communications, LLC

Into the Way of Peace

First edition copyright © 2006 by Karen Kelly Boyce
Published by Cloonfad Press, Cassville, NJ

Second edition copyright © 2010 by Karen Kelly Boyce
Cover art copyright © by Andrew Gioulis
Book design by Andrew Gioulis
Photograph of the author copyright © Andrew Gioulis

Published by: KFR Communications, LLC
                148 Hawkin Rd
                New Egypt, NJ 08533

Publisher's Note: This book is a work of fiction. Names, characters, places and incidents are either the product of the author's imagination, or are used fictionally. Any resemblance to actual events, or locales, or persons either living or dead, is entirely coincidental. The author and publisher have taken care in preparation of this book but make no expressed or implied warranty of any kind and assume no responsibility for errors or omissions. No liability is assumed for incidental or consequential damages in connection with or arising out of the use of the information contained herein.

ISBN-10: 0-6153-6895-6
ISBN-13: 978-0-615-36895-5

Printed in the United States of America

www.kfrcommunications.com

Dedicated to Amanda...A Dreamkeeper

On the edge of the world, ocean showers rise and seep
Ancient mist of hill hums, eternal bog black and deep
Peat smoke entwines through the strands of moonlight
Sons and daughters of love kept the dreams of the night
Dreamkeepers whispered memorywords of the sod
Celtic lovetales dreamcaptured, the touches of God

Memorieknots whispered, floated free clan to clan
Dreamkeepers like bogmist arose from the land
The dreams that they dreamed and memories they told
Burning lips, quick nightsilver weaved into daygold
Dreamkeepers spin, singing webs born of sod
Dreams they kept, cinder glowed, the touches of God

Timekeepers cold winds blew west over the land
Timekeepers kill dreams they don't understand
Dreamkeepers floated, golden beams, even in day
Timekeepers blew hard, blowing dreams from the bay
Dreamkeepers hungry, drifted far to cold land
Keeping fantasywords, dripping gold from God's Hand

In the light of new city on the shore of new world
Spinning childhood lovetales is a dreamkeeper girl
Weaving sweetamanda wordsongs, dust of the moon
Touching dreamkeeper children, sparking new whimsytune
Timekeepers rantweep, confused, still afraid of the dark
Far away from the sod, Dreamy moonstrands still spark

With special thanks to Father Brendan Williams, who answered all my questions with patience and kindness.

And thanks to Janet Fair for her wonderful editing skills.

One

Melchizedek, king of Salem, brought out Bread and wine, and being a priest of God Most High, he blessed Abram with these words: "Blessed be Abram by God Most High, The creator of heaven and earth; And blessed be God Most High, Who delivered your foes into your hand." (Gen.14:18-20)

The priest could hear the echo of his footsteps as he walked the empty hallway. Father Christopher D'Angelico's footsteps had gotten slower over the many years he had walked this stone floor. *Age has a way of slowing one down,* he thought as he reached for the large ring of keys jangling on his belt. The doors of both the rectory and the church were ancient wooden doors — heavy doors meant to keep people out. Not like the hollow light doors they make today. The old keyhole locks each had their own key. The priest had been at the parish for so long he knew each of the numerous keys by feel — he could find his way around here in the dark.

Fifty years ago, he'd been so anxious to learn his way around the church and rectory. He learned the rules quickly, proud of being assigned to this holy place. How pleased he had been with himself. It was a beautiful little church.

His mother was so delighted. She was the first to arrive that morning for his first Mass at Holy Rosary Church. Sitting in the first row in her best dress, the black dress that she wore to his fathers' funeral. She waved to him throughout the Mass. It was hard for him to keep from laughing. He couldn't stop her. Each morning sitting in the first pew, she grinned and waved throughout the service.

The small Italian woman delighted in being the proud mother of a son who was a priest. Only heaven could be better. Now, looking back, the frail priest was glad he didn't say anything to her.

Somewhere in his heart, he must have known she would not live long after his father died. The two were much closer than most married couples he knew. After her husband was gone she seemed to wither away. Within a year, she joined her beloved husband, Anthony. Having a son in the priesthood made her last year happy and after her death, he threw himself into his parish work.

When he first arrived at the city parish, it was a largely Italian community. Tucked on a side street of a largely Italian neighborhood, Holy Rosary was built with the pennies and dimes of immigrants. For the first ten years of his priesthood, it was a lively and vibrant community. He ministered to a large Catholic community of people who truly believed in the church and God.

As the next generation matured however, things changed. The children of the immigrants felt they wanted more out of life. They fought the war and the GI bill gave them a chance to buy homes of their own in the suburbs. Suddenly, they moved from the city in large numbers. They left the city and the old ways. They assimilated and became Americans, not Italians. They felt their parents were old fashioned.

Unfortunately, many of them also felt that their parent's faith was old fashioned. They became "Cultural Catholics." They followed the outward signs of the Church but not the beliefs. They enjoyed watching their children receive the sacraments like baptism and communion but they just did not believe in, or live, the true faith. It was too inconvenient.

Father D'Angelico became Pastor as the church community shrunk. For the next twenty years, the parish consisted of mainly older people. As the Italian community became a black community, church attendance declined, and now most of the neighborhood was largely black and protestant. The small parish now consisted of older Italians, some younger blacks, and a few Hispanics. Always a poor community, it had not changed. Yet the beautiful church, built with the pennies and dimes of the poor, was solid and graceful. The imported stone and marble grew ever more exquisite over the years as the patina of the stone added to the warm glow. The rarity of the smooth stone added to its grandeur.

The elderly priest scanned the small church as he entered the sacristy. This had been his home for most of his adult life. The glow of the candles reflected the glory of this house of God. It was a good life. He knew that Jesus was with him. He had no regrets.

As he opened the cabinet and donned the garments of his profession, Father D'Angelico thought about his life. His parents were poor yet proud and hard working. The son of Italian immigrants, he grew up in this very neighborhood. It was a tight knit community.

His father worked as a sandhog. The sandhogs - mainly Irish, West Indians, and Italian immigrants - did dangerous work building tunnels and subways. Modern New Yorkers took these tunnels for granted, yet each tunnel came with a heavy price—about one life per mile.

Construction accidents claimed the lives of many men, yet many more died of the effects of tunnel work. Much of the ground beneath New York is made up of hard rock. As the men blasted their way through the hard rock, small pieces of silicon were released in the dust and as the men breathed in that dust, the silicon became embedded in their lungs. As the amount of silicon grew in their lungs, they developed a disease called silicosis—the disease that cost the priest's father his life. Before he died he gave an inheritance to his only son. Being poor, the only thing the old man had to give was his faith. It was enough. It was all the young man needed to find his way.

The priest, now fully attired, left the sacristy and headed for the tabernacle. The Body and Blood of Christ were kept in this small golden box. Father D'Angelico bowed before His God, present in the form of bread and wine. He never lost the wonder of His Eucharistic Lord. The Presence of Jesus in the appearance of bread and wine was a great gift, given at the Last Supper. It sustained the people, as manna sustained the Jews in the desert. God fed his people and the priest never lost his wonder over the miracle of it.

The practice of adoring the Eucharistic Lord in the form of bread started in the Middle Ages. That's why this priest came to the church. Each Friday, from six PM to midnight, Father D'Angelico opened the church for Eucharistic Adoration. The church doors opened for anyone who wanted to stop and pray directly to the Lord in His Eucharistic Form. It was a quiet, personal time. The priest saw great miracles happen because of this, the close touch of Jesus.

Face down, on the floor before God, the elderly man prayed. His relationship with Jesus was one of the few relationships he now had left. Age and death robbed him of both his family and most of his earthly friends. It didn't matter, Jesus was all he needed.

"My friend, I am here again," the priest began. *"I love you. Please help all of those that you call here. Please send angels to them, to show them the way. Keep all evil spirits from interfering. My Good Friend, bless all the souls that reach out to you tonight. All seven of these souls are yours. I will love You forever. I will do your work for as long as You want me to. I long to come home to You soon."*

The priest felt the pain in his brittle bones as the coldness of the stone floor permeated his frail body. As Jesus touched him, those pains disappeared. The warmth of Jesus flowed through him. The love of God filled him with both peace and joy. As the winds of a blizzard blew outside, Jesus filled this church and this priest with His warmth and love.

Many years ago, after his mother died, Father D'Angelico almost lost his faith. He became so busy with the work of God that he forgot the God of the work. He spent endless hours helping the poor after starting a soup kitchen that was still feeding people. He also ran a shelter for the homeless.

As Jesus said, "The poor will be with you always" and He had not lied. There were so many in need, a seemingly endless crush of humanity, and Father D'Angelico emptied himself to them. It was good, but he forgot the most important thing. He didn't replenish himself with Jesus and he was quickly drained. Father D'Angelico couldn't give away something he didn't have. He had lost Jesus.

Slowly he stopped praying. His good works filled all his hours and gradually cut away all of his prayer time. It wasn't long before he stopped praying altogether. He never asked Jesus what His will was. The priest never asked Jesus if any good work was within God's plan for him—they were good works after all. He even found himself distracted at Mass as he planned his busy days.

Slowly, without even realizing it, he grew tired. The endless stream of the needy started to wear him out and he grew disgusted and unable to cope. It seemed that some of them were bottomless pits. They needed more than he could give. He grew irritable, even with the people he was trying to help.

Drained, the young priest lost his faith. His spiritual advisor and confessor counseled him to develop his prayer life. When he tried to pray, however, nothing happened. He then set about studying the prayer life of the Saints. He studied the contemplative saints. He lost himself in the wonder of the prayer castles of Theresa of Avila. St. Theresa's study of the different levels of contact with God, or castles as she called them, fascinated the lost priest. The poetry of the contemplative St. John of the Cross touched him deeply, and even caused him to weep. Yet, he could not seem to reach the God he loved in his own prayer life. Concerned, his spiritual advisor recommended the book, *Introduction to the Devout Life*, by St. Francis De Sales.

St. Francis De Sale was known for his work with the poor. Like Father D'Angelico, he devoted himself to the needs of the least of society. However, unlike Father D'Angelico, he led a very deep prayer life. The meditations in this book lifted him to a height of prayer that changed his life.

During the meditations, God Himself led the prayer. The thoughts were too exalted, the priest knew, to come from anywhere else. This sweeping sense of God's love was almost too much to bear. Father D'Angelico was swept away with the sense of The Almighty and His touch. So overpowering was the consolation of God, he would often be at prayer for hours without realizing it. The Creator ministered to his spirit in ways the priest couldn't even comprehend. As a result of that prayer, his whole life changed. His way with others better reflected Jesus. He became patient, kind, and gentle. His anxiety changed to a sense of eternal peace and joy. He never felt alone, always feeling loved. He grew without effort on his part. God, Himself, changed him.

He continued his prayer life with daily meditation on Scripture. Setting himself in the presence of Jesus, he learned to appreciate the recommended meditations as he allowed Jesus to speak to him. Sometimes just one verse of scripture would send him into ecstasy. He would flow in a conscious awareness of the closeness of God. He would be infused with a knowledge that was beyond his education or understanding.

Suddenly he could comprehend Scripture as he never had before. The Almighty, with his permission, took over his thoughts, soul, and spirit. Each time he prayed, he was changed. God infused him with knowledge, and virtue. God filled him with gifts.

Jesus had long ago filled this priest with special gifts. In his fifties, he developed the gift of reading souls. One Saturday in the confessional, he felt his first soul. It happened when an elderly woman entered the confessional and knelt behind the screen.

In a soft voice she began, "Bless me Father, for I have sinned..."

Instantly he felt as if a bolt of lightning had hit him. The force of electricity pushed him back against the wall of the confessional.

The woman continued with her litany of sins, "Father I have been unkind to my husband and less than kind to my children," she sighed as if frustrated by a continuing pattern of failure and sin. Father D'Angelico listened with interest as she turned in embarrassment from confessing the sin that truly burdened her.

Softly the priest spoke, "Is there anything else you would like to tell me?"

The woman gasped. The priest could sense the woman's tremors of fear, although she remained hidden behind the screen.

Father D'Angelico continued, "Wouldn't you want to unburden yourself. You have carried that weight for so long. Jesus wants to forgive you of the sin of adultery. Think of all the temptations you have resisted over the years since your fall from grace. Hasn't He seen and helped you through?" the priest paused. "Reach out to him for forgiveness. He is waiting for you with open arms."

The woman wept uncontrollably, unable to contain her emotions. Shock, relief, and shame struggled for dominance. A sense of peace finally won, as her weeping settled to a few breathless sobs.

Father D'Angelico had no idea what the woman in the confessional looked like. He felt a deep connection because he knew her soul. He saw her soul as God saw it. He could see the pattern her spirit had taken since her birth. He knew the sins she struggled with, as well as the virtues her spirit developed.

He could see the darkness of confusion that stained her

spirit. The abuse her father gave her as a baby caused dark shadows. He felt the shame of the sin she felt — the sin she had omitted from her list of offenses. The sin of adultery was part of a pattern of sin she struggled with all her life. At the base of her sin was a basic need, a need for her father's love.

"Turn to your Father in heaven," the priest continued, "Your Heavenly Father is waiting for you with open arms."

"How did you know?" she asked. The woman was stunned that he knew the sin. She cried as he gave her absolution for all of her sins. As she left, he knew that she would not be back. Her time on this earth was ending. The whole process left Father D'Angelico drained. He never felt such an intimate attachment to another as he had with this soul. Seeing the story of her soul, he found he could not help but love her soul. It was the first time the priest experienced the gift called 'the reading of souls.' As time went on, this God given gift grew more pronounced and fine-tuned.

Now the elderly man could read most souls just from casual contact. It was not always a pleasant gift. When he encountered a few truly evil spirits, it had been a horrific experience. Still, it helped him to know how to minister to people. It was a gift from Jesus for that very purpose. Jesus, through this infused knowledge, reached the people He loved.

It was how Father D'Angelico knew seven souls would come tonight. The younger priest, now in charge of the parish, had tried to discourage him from holding the Eucharistic Adoration on this night. The new pastor felt that it was a waste of the older priest's time. He was convinced that no one would come because of the storm.

Father Shelby, a patient and kind man, worried about the older priest and his health. Father Shelby had allowed the fragile priest to stay at home in the rectory long past retirement age. The blizzard was going to be a rough one, and he was sure that Father D'Angelico would be alone in the cold.

Father D'Angelico sensed the arrival of the first soul. He

knew there were others gathering outside, so he decided to open the church doors 15 minutes early. The sound of the wind drew him from union with his Creator and concern for the health of those outside in the bitter storm pulled him from prayer.

His body was stiff from the cold and damp. Painful joints reminded him of the body that held him bound. He longed for his soul to be free. Free to go home to his Father. But there were still many who were in need and Jesus still had work for him to do. He could tolerate the pain. Long ago, the elderly priest had learned he had cancer. It started in his bones, and had now spread to his lungs and liver. The pain had grown worse over the last few months. When the doctor first told him he had cancer, the physician was surprised by the older man's calm reaction. The priest already knew. He was too old for the strain of treatment.

Chemotherapy alone could not cure the cancer. Surgery would be too harsh on his aged heart. Besides the doctor said the cancer was aggressive and too advanced.

The priest had already outlived the date of death the physician predicted. It was up to God, not the doctor. The priest knew it would soon be over. He offered the pain up for the souls that would come here tonight. Like St. Paul in the Bible he united his pain to the pain of Jesus on Calvary.

Father D'Angelico didn't share his diagnosis with anyone. He didn't want to be sent to the hospital or the nursing home. The Lord still had work for him to do. When he hadn't said anything after his last examination, the young pastor just assumed the elderly priest was all right. Father D'Angelico would not have lied to him; he just hadn't asked.

The elderly priest was sure, as with everything, that Jesus was directing the situation. His trust in God was complete. The way it turned out was the Will of the Eternal One. Still, he was glad it turned out this way. He longed to finish his days in what had been his home for so long. The years that stretched out behind him were full and happy ones. His whole life centered on this little church. He wanted his life to end here.

Frankie the Bottle, as the children called him, ducked into the confessional as the old priest passed. He normally waited until the old man opened the doors but it was too cold outside. Frankie knew enough to slip in the basement window with the broken lock. A short set of stairs led up to the vestibule. He would just pretend that he came in after the priest opened the door. No sense freezing! The church was always warm and Frankie planned to stay for the night.

Father D'Angelico knew Frankie was there. It was all right. Jesus wanted to talk to Frankie tonight. The priest struggled with the large wood doors that opened the front vestibule. The wind was strong and the bitter snow blew hard, making it impossible to see more than just a few feet. It didn't matter. Four people waited on the steps of the church. And there were others. He could feel the young soul that hid in the bush. The seventh soul was just leaving his work on the other side of town. He smiled. Seven would come. Jesus had called seven.

The people waiting outside were bundled with scarves, coats, and hoods. It was impossible to identify any of them. Three of them rushed to escape the bitter wind that permeated the layers of clothing they wore. The fourth and oldest soul struggled on the stairs. The snow didn't slow her — it was the osteo-arthritis. She had grown used to it over the years and now she couldn't remember what life was like before the pain. The cold stiffened her knees. The priest smiled as he waited by the door for her. He could feel the pain she felt. As the others passed him, Father D' Angelico had strong, instant flashes of the spirits finding their way to the pews inside. As each soul moved past him, a flash, strong and as fast as lightning flowed into him. He understood now — Jesus had special work tonight. All these souls were in critical need!

Opening the tabernacle, he removed the Luna that

contained the Eucharist. The moon-shaped Luna contained a wafer larger than the communion host. The Luna was three inches in diameter. It fit perfectly into the monstrance that waited on the altar. The priest, with great reverence, placed the Eucharist inside the monstrance, and placed himself prostrate before the altar in prayer. The monstrance, gold and jewel encrusted, stood fourteen inches high. It was round and held the host in the very center. The golden branches that surrounded the Host looked like the golden rays of the sun. The warm light of the candles gave it a supernatural aura.

Kneeling before the monstrance containing the Eucharist wafer and the very presence of Jesus, he began to sing. He heard some of the people in the pews behind him join him in song. The priest raised his voice in the ancient hymn written by St. Thomas Aquinas. Although he himself was frail, his voice was not. The hymn filled the church:

> *"O salutaris hostia, Quae cae li pan dis o sti um*
> *Bel la pre munt ho sti li a, Da ro bur fer au xi li um*
> *U ni tri no que Do mi no Sit sem Pi ter na gloria,*
> *Que vi tam si ne ter mi no No bis do net in pa tri a*
> *O Saving Victim, op'ening The gate of heav'n to us below*
> *Our foes press on from ev'ry side, Your aid supply, your*
> *   strength bestow*
> *To your great name be endless praise, Immortal God head One*
> *   in Three*
> *O grant us endless length of days When our true native land*
> *   we see"*

The elderly priest struggled from his knees and made his way back to the last wooden pew. It was here he would spend the night. For the next six hours, he would be immersed in deep relationship with Jesus. Yet on another level he would still be aware of the people who prayed here tonight. And he would pray for them. His spirit would touch the Face of God. The pain of sitting in the uncomfortable pew for six hours would become pronounced. Nevertheless, he would not need the pain medication the well-meaning doctor gave him. He would not be in his body tonight. Father D'Angelico would be in union with God!

Two

During those days Mary set out and traveled to the hill country in haste to a town of Judah, where she entered the house of Zechariah and greeted Elizabeth. When Elizabeth heard Mary's greeting, the infant leaped in her womb. (Luke 1:39)

Little Megan Walsh stayed in her bed. It was too early to get up. Besides, it was a little scary. The shadows that played in the gray morning light made her room seem strange. She knew it was her doll on the shelf, but it looked like an old man's face. He seemed to be leering at her. She decided she wouldn't look at her doll until it got lighter. Megan often woke up before the sun. Sometimes she would get out of bed and play; she had to be quiet so she didn't wake her parents up. Grown-ups needed more sleep.

Sometimes, she would just take the tissues from her nightstand and if she twisted them just right, they turned into beautiful ladies in flowing white gowns. She could move them across the tabletop and pretend they were all at a big dance. She would hum the music as the tissue ladies danced.

She didn't feel like playing today. Today was a special day — it was her first day of school. It was her fifth birthday, too.

Given the choice, she would rather stay home. Megan didn't really want to go to this thing called school. The tiny girl kicked her feet in a flurry of strength. Her mother always tucked the sheets in and Megan hated to have her feet under the sheet. It made her feel trapped. She kicked the sheet off and the cool air tickled her toes. She decided to play with JoJo, her little stuffed monkey she had loved for as long as she could remember.

JoJo was right in the bed with her. In fact, she couldn't remember not having JoJo with her. She told him all her secrets and he always had time to listen. However, lately it seemed that everyone hated JoJo. Her Mommy wanted to throw him out. Mommy said JoJo smelled. Megan sniffed him and admitted he had a kind of sour odor. Megan didn't care! She loved him.

Her Daddy saved JoJo. He tried to sew the stuffing back in. Mommy laughed at the red thread her Daddy used. Megan thought it showed up real good, but the stuffing was starting to come out of him already.

Megan could finally see the morning light coming in through the window. The colors of her room brightened with it. With the light, her fear disappeared. She could hear her Mommy getting up in the next room. She cuddled with JoJo as her mother showered. Megan stayed under her covers until she heard the sound of pots and pans rattling in the kitchen. The sound of Mommy in the kitchen made her hungry. Megan loved breakfast.

Each morning she ate the same thing. Googees on toast! Googees were two sunny-side-up eggs, each placed on a piece of toast.

Her father would sing, "Barney GooGoo with the GooGoo Googally eyes. Barney GooGoo had a wife three times his size!"

Megan would always laugh at the same old joke her daddy sang as he looked at the two eye-like eggs staring out from Megan's breakfast plate. She adored her daddy!

Megan jumped out of bed and put on her slippers. Her daddy was up and he promised to give her a birthday present before she went to school. He wouldn't be there when she got home and would be gone for a few weeks. He was a truck driver and he drove one of those big trucks that carried things to stores all over the country. Megan was so proud of her daddy. He could do anything. She always missed him so much when he was gone. He explained to her that if he didn't do his job, then mothers all over the country wouldn't be able to buy food for their children. Yes, her daddy was a very important man. Megan knew that she couldn't be selfish and keep him all to herself. Skipping into the kitchen, Megan ran to her mother.

"What do you want for breakfast, Birthday Girl?" her mommy asked as she gave her a big hug.

"Googees on toast!" laughed Megan as she ran to her father. He was sitting at the table with a cup of coffee and the newspaper.

"I'm ready," the happy five-year-old announced as she reached the table.

Her father looked up, as if perplexed, "Ready for what?"

Megan laughed, "You know, my present!"

With an exaggerated look of puzzlement he asked, "What present? You were expecting a present? What for?"

Megan made a face full of exasperation, "My birthday!" Megan's father feigned surprise. "You mean today is your birthday?"

Megan started to worry. Maybe Daddy really forgot! That's when she spotted the gift hidden behind the paper.

"What's that?" she yelled.

Megan's father acted shocked to see it. "Why, it looks like a gift. Could it be your birthday present?"

"You know it is!" laughed the delighted girl.

Her father laughed as he answered, "Well then, I guess you'd better open it!"

Megan tore the paper with eager anticipation. She

couldn't wait to see what her daddy had gotten her. Last year he had gotten her a toy piano. Megan loved it. Each morning Megan would put on the television in the living room of their apartment. Mommy would do her cleaning as Megan watched her favorite show. When the large purple dinosaur played music, Megan would play her toy piano along with it. She loved music. Today she wouldn't be able to watch TV because she had to go to school — another reason she didn't want to go.

Megan tore open the box, and stood transfixed at what she saw. It was JoJo! No, it really wasn't him. The stuffed monkey in the box looked just like him, but was a different color. This JoJo was all new and fluffy. He didn't have patches of fur missing. His stuffing wasn't hanging out. Megan didn't know what to think. She looked at her father in wonderment.

"It's a new JoJo, just for you. It took me two weeks to find him. And I did it because I love you Megan, I wanted to give you something you would love."

Megan was stunned. She didn't want this monkey. She looked in his eyes. They were glass buttons just like her JoJo's, but they weren't the same. They didn't look back. They were just shiny buttons. They didn't love her. Why, they didn't even know her!

"Tell your father *thank you*," her mother said as she gave each of them their breakfast. Megan didn't know what to say. She didn't feel like saying thank you. What did it mean? Why had her daddy brought such a bad gift? Then it occurred to her that her daddy had gotten her a good present. Now JoJo would have a new friend. They could play together while she was at school. *Oh, Wow! Daddy thought of everything.* Now JoJo wouldn't be lonely while she was gone. Her Mommy told her she couldn't bring JoJo to school and Megan was not happy about that. So, Daddy had gotten JoJo a friend. It was a great present!

"Thank you Daddy. Now JoJo has a friend!" Megan saw

her mommy look at her daddy. That's when her stomach started to hurt.

"You know Megan, that old monkey has got to go!" Her mommy seemed upset. Megan's lip started to pucker. She didn't like the way this was going.

"Go where?"

Her mother didn't seem to know what to say.

Her Daddy answered, "Why, JoJo needs to go to the doll hospital. When little boys and girls get hurt, don't they go to the hospital to get fixed?" Megan thought hard about it. She had never heard of a doll hospital.

"Well," Megan sighed, "When Greg broke his leg, he went to the hospital."

Her daddy smiled, "Yes and didn't they fix him up and send him home all better."

Megan looked at her old JoJo. "I guess they could fix him up too." JoJo did look bad – only half of his fur and stuffing were missing and only one of his glass eyes was coming loose.

Daddy seemed happy with her answer. "It wouldn't be fair to keep JoJo like this. Why it seems that JoJo is just very sick and needs to be patched up. At the doll hospital, they could fix him like new. It must hurt JoJo to be like this."

Megan was stunned. It had never occurred to her that JoJo could be in pain.

"Will they send him right home?" Megan saw the look that her mommy gave to her daddy.

"Well, they might. However, doll hospitals are not the same as people hospitals. It's hard to say. Sometimes it takes longer to fix dolls than people. That's why I got you the new JoJo. He can keep you company until this JoJo comes home."

Megan didn't like the idea, but it made sense. She didn't want her JoJo to be in pain and if they could fix him it wouldn't be right for her to keep him.

Megan answered with trepidation, "Okay, you can take him to the hospital."

Daddy rubbed her head, "You're doing the right thing. Now go and get ready. I have to leave for work; I want to see you in your new dress before I leave." Megan gulped down the eggs and toast and started for her bedroom with her mother.

"I'll drop JoJo off at the doll hospital on my way to work," her daddy said as Megan's mommy slipped the fancy dress over her head. Megan didn't like the way the dress felt. It was all stiff and itchy. Mommy said it made her look pretty. Mommy braided her hair and scrubbed her face. After she put on the lacy socks and new black shoes she was ready. Megan didn't like the whole thing. It felt unnatural. Daddy loved it. He said she was the prettiest girl he had ever seen. Before he left, Megan gave him a big hug. She would miss him for the next few weeks.

Sometimes they, "the company" daddy called them, would send him far away. Megan's heart hurt whenever he was gone. Now, to top it off she had to leave home and leave JoJo behind. Her mommy walked her down the stairs and out the vestibule of their apartment building. Megan could see all the older children in their fancy school clothes playing on the sidewalk.

"Can I play for a while?" Megan asked hopefully.

Her Mommy shook her head, "No, I want you to stay nice and clean. Besides there isn't time. You don't want to be late, do you?"

"*Late,*" Megan wondered what that meant. There had never been anything called *late* in her small world. She wanted to ask her mommy what she meant, but she seemed in such a rush. Megan ran to keep up with her. They only had to go down two blocks to the school, yet Megan was out of breath by the time they got there.

The red brick building rose large in the sight of the small five-year-old girl. More children surrounded it than Megan had ever seen. She had seen children playing in the park her mommy sometimes took her to, but never as many children as this morning. It was so confusing. Then a loud bell rang and all the children just ran and got into lines. They seemed to know where to go and it seemed the big kids were all together and the little kids were all together too. It was amazing. Maybe school did make you smart after all!

Megan's mother grabbed her hand and led her to a doorway covered with crayon drawings. The smallest children were clinging to their mothers. Megan looked around. All of the kids were dressed up. The boys all had new white sneakers and fresh haircuts. The girls all had their hair curled and carefully brushed. Megan knew one thing all right, no one looked very happy.

Her stomach started to hurt. Maybe she shouldn't have eaten googies on toast this morning. She could taste the eggs in her mouth. Everything she ate for breakfast was rolling around in her stomach. She put her hand on her stomach as a sharp cramp came. Mommy was too busy talking with the other lady to notice. Then the strangest thing Megan ever saw came out of the school doors.

It looked like a tall lady. However, Megan never saw a lady dressed like this one. She had a big black blanket on her head; she had a long dress like the tissue ladies Megan made in the morning, but the dress was black. She had a sweet smiling face. *Why was she dressed this way?* Megan watched as the stranger went to the front of the line. She spoke first with each mother and then with each child. After the strange lady spoke to the mother and her child, the child was led into the door and the mother would leave. Megan couldn't see what was beyond the door. Her stomach was starting to hurt bad now.

Megan tugged on her mommy's dress, "I don't feel good. I want to go home!"

Megan's mommy just smiled at her, "Oh don't be silly Megan, you'll like school. You don't want to miss your first day. Look at all the new friends you'll be making!"

Megan had her doubts. The closer the strange lady came

the worse her stomach felt.

Megan watched as the little boy in front of her went through the door. *Oh no!* There she was, the lady in black and she was talking to her mommy! Her tummy began to really hurt. As the lady turned toward her, Megan tried to lift her face. But all Megan could see were the shiny black shoes the lady wore. At least she saw them for a few seconds before she threw up all over them.

For a minute, it was as if time stood still and no one made a sound, then the other children started to laugh. Megan's mommy pulled her away from the nun, but it was too late — the nun was covered with Megan's breakfast. Mommy seemed upset, but Megan actually felt better. Her stomach didn't hurt anymore and her head even stopped hurting as her mother kept telling the lady that she was sorry. One thing good seemed to come out of this, at least Megan's mommy was taking her home.

Megan noticed her mommy was very quiet as they walked home and if Megan was not so happy about going home, she might have worried about it. She did feel bad about ruining her new dress and would be glad to get it off. If they hurried, she would get home in time for Sesame Street. As soon as they got home Megan found out just how wrong she was. Instead of sitting down to enjoy one of her favorite shows, Megan was given a bubble bath. Usually Megan enjoyed playing in the bathtub, but she wasn't given the time. It was the quickest bath she ever took. "We'll put on your brown and orange dress," her mommy announced. Megan liked this dress better anyway. It was soft and comfortable.

"Why do I have to wear a dress anyway?" "You need to look your best, especially now." The full weight of what her mother was saying finally hit her.

"You mean that I have to go back to school?" This idea didn't sit well with Megan.

"Of course, from now on you'll be going to school every

day. And don't try getting sick again. It won't help. You can't stay home by pretending to be sick. There, you look fine. Let's go," her mommy said angrily.

Megan took her mother's hand and they headed back to school. Her mommy was upset and they walked in silence.

Megan wasn't used to the silent anger because her mother was so seldom irritated. The tiny girl felt it was all her fault — getting sick had embarrassed her mother. She had to admit the truth, she hadn't wanted to go to school. Megan was afraid, but now knew that she had to resign herself to going. *After all,* she thought, *all the other children have to go to school.*

The strange lady was called Sister Irene. She wasn't even mad at Megan and Megan figured this proved she was all right.

She liked all the toys in the big chests lining the wall of her kindergarten classroom. The middle of the room was crowded with long tables and little chairs. Each table seemed to be set for a particular activity. One table was filled with puzzles while the next table held large pieces of white paper and fingerpaints. Megan was delighted. She even made friends with a girl named Jessica who liked the same games as her. They stayed at the game table when all the other kids moved around to try other things.

Megan didn't like the twins who pushed their way into everything, grabbing toys from the kids who wouldn't fight back. They went to each table and took whatever they wanted without asking.

But, whenever Sister Irene came around they acted nice and sweet. *'Like butter wouldn't melt in their mouth,'* as her daddy would say. When the twins got to the game table, Megan wouldn't let them take the Chutes and Ladders game she and Jessica were playing with. They promptly reported Megan to the teacher.

Sister Irene put her arm around Megan and said, "Now Megan, we all have to share. I know you are used to being alone. The twins learned early in life that they had to share, because they had to share with each other. You will learn that too."

Megan wanted to spit. Share? Megan hadn't seen them share with anyone. They just took. Still, her mommy had told her to listen to the teacher. She let them have the game against her better judgment. She'd ask her mommy about this later.

The day turned out to be a good day and it actually went pretty fast. Lunch came quickly and with her stomach so empty, Megan was hungry. They were given trays filled with hot macaroni and cheese and hot dogs and a tiny carton of milk just like the large ones at home. Megan had never seen anything like this. She was hungry and had a good lunch with her new friend Jessica. Sister Irene spent the afternoon singing and she taught all the children new songs. Megan really liked singing – she only wished that she had her toy piano to play along. Megan decided school wasn't so bad.

Soon it was time to go home; she was glad to see her mommy at the classroom door. Maybe she would tell her new JoJo about her first day of school. Maybe if she were nice to him, his eyes would come alive. Taking her mother's hand, Megan waved goodbye to Jessica. She was glad she would be seeing her again tomorrow.

Megan was careful all the way home. She didn't step on any cracks. Jessica had taught her a new song today, "step on a crack, break your mother's back." Megan had never noticed how many cracks there were in the sidewalks around here. It was just plain good luck that her Mommy had never broken her back. At least not that Megan could remember.

Shouting made Megan look up from the sidewalk. As she raised her eyes she was shocked to see her mommy's face turn white. Megan looked at a crowd of boys shouting and throwing rocks at the pole that stood in front of their building. Mommy tried to pull her away, but it was too late.

Megan saw what they were doing and she started to scream.

They had her old JoJo tied to the telephone pole and were throwing rocks at him, trying to knock him down. Just as Megan started to react to what she saw, a large rock hit the JoJo she loved so much. He came loose from the rope and tumbled to the street. Megan didn't think. She knew that running in the street was not allowed. She forgot. She only knew that she had to save her JoJo!

Megan ran before her mommy, who reached out and screamed, could stop her. Her eyes were focused on the stuffed monkey she loved so dearly. Megan didn't hear the crowd shout at her to stop. She had to save him. He lay in the street with his stuffing hanging out. If he looked bad before, he looked worse now. The rocks had done their damage. Megan didn't stop at the curb. She ran between the parked cars and into the middle of the street. JoJo lay sprawled and crumbled on the painted white line waiting for her. Megan gently picked him up then started to pick up some of the stuffing that remained on the street.

Megan didn't see the car that was speeding down the street and the driver didn't see her in time to stop. He hit the brakes but it was too late. The screeching sound pulled Megan's attention away from JoJo. The crowd saw her look up at the car as it hit her. Megan's mother screamed as she watched the car plow into her daughter. Megan's small body was flung into the air by the force of the impact and flew twenty feet before landing on the street. The man behind the wheel sat numb and in shock after his car finally stopped. The crowd was sure the little girl was dead. Two men held Megan's mother back as she tried to run to her daughter.

Patricia Walsh struggled against the men who held her, collapsing in frustration and unable to reach her baby who lay limp on the cold September pavement. In the horror and confusion someone had the sense to call for help. The police arrived first and kept the crowd back until the ambulance came and took the girl.

For Megan the experience was different. As she looked up at the approaching car a glint of the shining metal gave off a blinding glare of light. In that light, Megan saw a woman dressed in glowing white clothes. The woman approached Megan with her arms out. She had the kindest face Megan had ever seen. Megan wasn't afraid.

The beautiful woman picked Megan up and held her in her arms. Megan never experienced such love. She felt completely safe as the woman smiled at her. It seemed to Megan that the car just stopped. The woman sat on the hood of the car with Megan in her arms. The nice Hispanic man in the car gave Megan and the woman a ride halfway down the block — it was so much fun.

Megan didn't feel any pain. Megan didn't hear the crowd scream, to her it sounded like applause during a parade where important people ride on the cars. The beautiful woman covered Megan with the flowing clothing she wore. Megan couldn't see the street anymore. It was dazzlingly bright as the woman carried her away. The light blinded her.

The woman opened her arms and released Megan. She found herself in a white room. She was feeling anxious. Where was her mommy? How did she get here? The room was bright and completely white. It had no furniture. There were no paintings on the walls. It was just plain white and filled with a foggy kind of white mist. The beautiful woman didn't talk although she was telling Megan not to be afraid. Somehow, Megan knew the woman would stay with her. It was as if she could talk in Megan's mind without moving her lips. The woman crossed over to the other side of the room. As the small girl's eyes grew accustomed to the brightness, she saw where the beautiful woman went.

The woman in white stood in front of a large black opening that looked like a door. Standing in front of the door, the beautiful lady seemed to turn into stone. It looked like she was standing guard, like a statue. Megan didn't like the sounds that were coming from the dark door.

The door was bad — she just knew instinctively. Megan pushed herself against the wall opposite the dark door as far away as she could get from it. As her eyes adjusted to the light she saw the staircase — on the same wall as the door — leading to another door. Megan was confused. She made herself as small as possible. Megan was afraid and wanted her mommy.

The police took Patricia Walsh to the hospital. People talked to her but she couldn't focus on what they said. She was in shock. She wanted to see her baby but everyone just seemed to hold her back. Maybe at the hospital they would let her near her daughter. She heard the people whisper that the little girl must be dead. It didn't connect in her mind. She just wanted to see Megan. She just wanted to hold her. Nothing else mattered. She longed to cling to the daughter who was her life. She knew that if she could just hold her and talk to her, Megan would be all right.

Patricia Walsh couldn't believe what was happening! Why did she throw the smelly stuffed monkey in the garbage outside? Why didn't she let David take it? Why did the boys decide to throw rocks at the old toy? Why? Why? It was all she could say. Dull shock numbed her as she was led into the Emergency Room's waiting room. The policeman stayed with her while she waited for the doctor to finish examining Megan. *The doctor will know what to do*, thought Patricia. He would make her well. He just had to!

Three

Listen, my beloved brothers. Did not God choose those who are poor in the world to be rich in faith and heirs of the Kingdom that he promised to those who love him? (James 1:2-5)

Frankie sucked in the dry, stuffy air. It was so close in here, like being in a coffin. He was relieved to ease out of the confessional as he heard people shuffling into the church. The over-large shoes on his feet were worn. They skidded loudly on the marble floor as he tried to slip silently into the back pew where no one would notice him. As he fell back on the smooth polished bench, his heart beat fast. He had outwitted the old priest once again. It meant a night in a warm place.

Frankie the Bottle, as he was known, spent each Friday night sleeping in the church. The old priest had a shelter, but Frankie didn't like it. There were too many others there — shiftless men that smelled of urine, sour men with grubby hands ready to rob the money Frankie made that day from begging. Sometimes, he made a lot.

Today, because of the snow he hadn't made much. Do-gooders hurried through the streets on cold, snowy days.

Pushing through the biting wind, they hurried to the warmth of their destinations. People didn't take the time to reach in their pockets on such bitter cold days.

Frankie recalled the afternoon. His stomach ached and growled. He had wandered down to the Golden Arches on Montgomery Street, drawn by the smell of grease and ketchup. It was the easiest place to find food. Frankie needed something to fill the aching emptiness in the pit of his gut. People wasted so much food. Half of what they bought ended up in the garbage.

Frankie was lucky today. There was a red-faced fat woman in a loud orange and white dress who screamed in a shrill voice at a whining brat. Pulling the child roughly by the hand, she threw his untouched happy meal and half of her Quarter Pounder in the trash. It was still warm when Frankie fished it out. Glad to have a full meal, he ate all of it before the surly manager spotted him and chased him away. He had a full fifth of scotch in his coat pocket and a warm night in the church ahead of him. Maybe there was a God after all.

The tall, sophisticated gray-haired man five rows up pealed off layers of cashmere and wool in the warmth of the church. The wind cried like a woman in labor outside. Frankie snickered. These do-gooders probably had heated homes, yet they came out on a night like this to pray to a God who didn't exist. He was glad these fools believed though, otherwise he would have spent the night curled in a ball in the corner of the cold bus station.

Frankie hated to spend the weekend in the bus station. There he had to sleep with one eye open, on the lookout for drunken teenagers. He would be safe and warm in the locked church. Frankie spent every Friday night in this church. Frankie had managed to fool the priest for years. He would just hide when the people left and the old priest would lock him in. He would sleep safe and warm, slipping out just before morning Mass. It was the best night of his long week.

Once alone, he would drink his bottle of scotch and fall

into a mindless sleep on the back pew. Frankie drank himself to sleep every night. It kept him from remembering. Frankie didn't want to remember.

Frankie watched the old man as he knelt before the golden monstrance and sang to his God in a loud and lusty voice. The old man seemed frail, his vestments looser than last week. Frankie noticed that the old priest had more difficulty getting off his knees. Was the old man sick? It was strange. Frankie couldn't understand his feelings. Even though he had never actually spoken to the old man he felt a kind of kinship to him. He watched as the old priest shuffled back past him to the very last pew. It was the aged man's habit. Frankie had a strange sensation as the elderly priest passed him. For the first time in all these years, he felt as if the priest was aware of him.

Frankie shook his head. The cold must be getting to him. No one ever noticed Frankie. It was one of the benefits of being one of the forgotten homeless. No one ever really saw him. He was one of the invisible people. He was invisible to do-gooders who thought they had real lives. They passed each day without seeing him. Oh, they gave him money because it made them feel better, but they never really looked at him.

Homeless people blended into the background and that suited Frankie just fine. He didn't want to be seen. He just wanted to blend. It gave him an advantage when it came to getting food and shelter. He didn't want the do-gooders to see him, or to try to help him. He just wanted to be left alone. Frankie wanted to be left alone to drink and to forget.

The priest was a do-gooder but he seemed all right. He never bothered Frankie. He never tried to reform him as so many do-gooders had tried in the past. Frankie appreciated that. He hated most do-gooders.

Frankie remembered the woman down at the shelter. She talked Frankie's ear off. She talked so much that Frankie wanted to hit her. He didn't though. He just smiled at her and nodded. It made her happy. It also made her give him money and the coat he was wearing. The money had brought the bottle that was in his pocket. The bottle that held the sweet golden liquid that warmed his soul. All do-gooders wanted to talk a lot and give you things. They thought Frankie was just waiting for them to come along to show him the light. Well, he had seen the light. He had lived in the light. He wanted no part of the light. Oh God, he had been thinking too much. It just made the memories come back. Frankie pushed them away. He'd concentrate on his surroundings instead. He'd fill his mind with other things.

Frankie looked at the people in the church. It was the usual odd collection. Frankie wondered what had brought them here. A fat, old woman with a cabbage face struggled from her knees, huffing as she sat. She probably had bad arthritis. Come to ask the silent God to heal her, to end her pain. Frankie thought that a good stiff drink would probably do her more good.

The rest of the cleanly pressed people didn't interest Frankie. Come to ask God for more money! They already had more money then they needed. They all looked like do-gooders. In Frankie's mind there were only two kinds of people, real ones and do-gooders. None of these do-gooders interested Frankie, but he didn't like the looks of the young man who had come in last. He was trouble if ever Frankie saw trouble, and Frankie had seen plenty of trouble in his life. Oh God! The memories were triggered.

Frankie reached in the pocket for the glass bottle of comfort that would drown the pain. Maybe a short sip would keep the memories at bay. He reached into the large pocket of the old wool topcoat the woman at the downtown shelter gave him. It was gone!

He frantically searched all the pockets of the enormously large overcoat. He searched the pew and the cold floor around it. No bottle! A chill ran through his body as a draft hit the slick layer of sweat that had formed on his body. He must have lost it outside in the storm. He would never be able to find it in the snow. He didn't know where he had dropped it. What was he going to do!

Frankie could go to the liquor store. He had enough money to get a cheap bottle of wine, but it was too late. The liquor store was closed by now. He had nothing, nothing to kill the pain. The thought of stealing the sacramental wine crossed his mind. He shook off the thought. He was no thief. He had no desire to steal from God, even if he didn't believe in him. He looked down at his hands as they started to tremble.

Father D'Angelico could feel the panic of Frankie's spirit. This soul was in so much pain. Tonight the Lord wanted Frankie's soul to feel this overwhelming pain. Jesus would be with him, helping him to work through the pain to the truth. A prayer whispered across the priest's mind as he felt the soul's needs revealed. *May the soul have the strength to accept the graces that Jesus wanted to bestow.*

Frankie tried to quiet his mind. He knew from experience that panic would make the need for a drink worse. He looked around the church he knew so well from his frequent stays. It was a beautiful church. A glow from the numerous candles reflected off marble statues and walls. Gold leaf gleamed in the flickering light. Frankie was always impressed with this little church. He knew. He used to do woodwork himself. He had been a carpenter. His basement shop had all the best hand tools.

Frankie enjoyed building furniture in his spare time. He took pride in building furniture without using power tools. Everything was fit together with dowels, not nails. He loved the smooth, warm feel of the wood. But, his union wasn't interested in a quality job, they just wanted him in and out.

During the day, he had to work with speed, at home he worked for the love of his creation. Home, oh God! He didn't want to think about the past. He tried to change his thoughts. He quickly looked around before the painful memories took over. If only he had a drink. The distraction of looking at the worshippers worked for a while, but then that young girl brushed her long hair with her hand. The soft, brown hair was so like *hers*.

Frankie had never felt anything as fine as the soft, silken feel of Jessie's hair, shining, caramel-colored hair that always smelled of shampoo. Jessie's beautiful face invaded his mind. The first time Frankie saw her was in the college bookstore where Jessie worked part-time. Frankie was sent by the union to put up some shelves. He had been in the union for a year when he met Jessie. When she looked up so shyly and smiled that gentle smile of hers, Frankie was hooked.

Frankie worked there every day for two weeks. His heart beat faster each time she came near him. He worked on whatever section of shelf brought him closer to her. He found himself thinking of her all the time. It took him two weeks to get up the courage to ask her out. Frankie was afraid that a college girl would look down on a tradesman, but he was wrong. Jessie blushed when he asked and agreed to meet him for dinner. They saw each other every day after that.

Soft as cotton, she wrapped him in her gentleness. Her wide brown eyes had no guile. Steady shining eyes that looked at the world full of hope, Jessie saw only goodness in the world. He wasn't called Frankie then. Jessie called him Francis. A soft smile kissed her face each time she called his name. The sound of her voice sent flutters through him. He had to hear her voice whisper his name each day. Separation was a little hell, an emptiness that ached. Frankie was with her as often as he could be. Not a day went by without contact.

She was studying to be a teacher. She loved children. It was hard on her because she had no family and was struggling with money. She juggled two part-time jobs, one at the college bookstore, and the other as a tutor. Even so, they managed to find time for each other.

Jessie had one more year of college before she could become a teacher. Francis was sure she would be the best teacher in the world. He wanted to help her with money. He couldn't stand to see the dark circles beneath those beautiful large brown eyes.

When he offered her money, her lips compressed and with her chin out, she refused. She had pride. Sometimes Francis would just watch her as she studied. He would ask her questions as she grappled for the answers. He loved her. They didn't need any fancy dates, as Jessie called them. He made good money with the union and could afford to take her anywhere, but Jessie just wanted simple things. A walk in the park was her idea of a perfect day. Francis was consumed. Within six months he asked her to marry him.

He cried when Jessie said yes. They made a small world of their own. Neither Francis nor Jessie had living parents and life had been so lonely before they met. Now it didn't matter. Francis and Jessie had each other.

They had a small inexpensive wedding with just a few friends and relatives. Jessie wore a white lace suit to the Judge's chambers. She was all Francis could see. His mind was filled with just Jessie, and she was enough for him. Francis never wanted anyone or anything more after he met her. She consumed his mind and his will. Francis couldn't believe that she loved him. He couldn't wait to be alone with her.

With his arm around his bride, Francis half danced, half walked, to their favorite restaurant where he treated all their guests to an Italian dinner. After spicy linguini and the last toast, he brought her to the small cape-cod home he had inherited from his parents. It was in northern New Jersey, just a ferry ride from downtown Manhattan.

Francis worked hard for the union and there was plenty of work, so now that they were married he wanted Jessie to quit her part-time jobs and concentrate on her schoolwork. Jessie's jaw clamped with stubborn determination. Shifting from foot to foot she patiently listened to Francis. Without the extra jobs, she would be able to finish school early. Francis wasn't going to give up until he finally convinced her and she finally agreed.

They started each morning leaving their soft bed to

share a hot soapy shower. The powerful engines of the ferry churned the deep water as the skyline of Manhattan beckoned. Sipping warm, creamy 7-11 coffee from carton cups, the salt-water spray of the Hudson River invigorated the beginning of each day. Standing by the chipped metal railing on the crowded ferry, Jessie shared her feelings with him. Francis would leave Jessie at the bus stop in front of the college library in the morning then report to his union job.

After working all day, he would take the bus to the college library and pick her up. She liked to do her work there. Some nights they would go to Mama Lucia's for a spaghetti dinner. Most nights they would take the ferry home to one of Jessie's simple but delicious dinners. As their life settled into a routine, Francis glowed with contentment.

Jessie blossomed under the protection of his love. As her confidence grew, her shyness lessened. Her marks improved when the financial burden she was carrying disappeared. She seemed happy.

"Francis, you're going to make us late!" she called nervously from the top of the stairs.

"I'll be up in a minute!" Jessie couldn't understand why Francis picked today of all days to run late. Today was her graduation day. If they didn't catch the bus to the ferry soon, they were liable to miss it! Francis seemed so proud. What was he doing in his workshop?

Jessie remembered how happy he was on the morning of their first Christmas together. When he opened the boxes of tools she had given him, he actually cried. It took her months of searching garage sales and flea markets to assemble the collection. Francis was ecstatic as he happily set up his woodworking shop in the basement.

"We're going to miss the bus!" She anxiously called again. This was so unlike him. Finally, Francis came up the basement stairs fully dressed. In his hands, he held a bouquet of roses.

"Oh, Francis!" Jessie cried.

"This is for the best teacher that ever lived!" Francis said as Jessie melted into his arms. The sweet smell of her hair filled him with desire. Jessie, always able to read his emotions, laughed.

"No time for that! Come on, we can just make the bus if we hurry."

"Okay! Just let me check something in the garage." Jessie was exasperated, but she couldn't bring herself to get angry with the man who was her life. Even if she missed the graduation, it didn't really matter. As long as she had Francis she knew everything was all right.

She couldn't wait to tell him the news. It would be her graduation present to him. Jessie followed Francis to the garage, knowing they just missed the last bus to the ferry. When Jessie saw the candy-apple red Mustang convertible with the oversized yellow bow, she froze. Francis laughed at her shock.

"Happy graduation, Baby! I'm so proud of you!" Tears of joy overcame Jessie as Francis hugged her. "Hop in. We've got a graduation to get to!"

Frankie shook himself hard. The memories were coming back. If only he could find that bottle. His hands were shaking. Maybe he dropped the bottle in the confessional. Frankie quietly left his seat to look. He didn't want to be noticed. No one seemed to look up as he tiptoed his way to the confessional in the back.

"Lost in their prayers, thank God!" He quickly slipped behind the red curtain that covered the confessional box. Down on his hands and knees Frankie prayed harder than anyone in the church.

"Where is that bottle? I can't stand it!" His callused and dry hands felt along the dark floor for the dark smooth bottle of comfort. Sweat beaded on Frankie's brow as his hands stirred up nothing but dust.

"Please, if you are there God, please help me find it!"

God didn't answer. Frankie felt like crying. The memories were sure to come back and he couldn't bear the pain that would swallow him.

He thought of just going out into the storm and letting the cold take him. He had thought about ending it all before. What kept him going he didn't know. This time too, as he left the empty confessional box, he made a decision to go back to his pew. He decided that when everyone left he would steal the wine in the back of the church. Until then, he would try to keep the memories at bay.

The fluttering of the sparrow against the stained glass window caught his attention. The bird was trapped, trapped in an endless circuit of trying to escape. There was always a bird flying around the church. Frankie wondered whether it was the same bird each week or just a new hapless prisoner. Frankie's tongue licked his dry chapped lips.

He watched as the young man slipped into the pew in the front. He didn't like the look of him. Frankie knew he was up to no good. He seemed to be trying to get closer to the old woman and her black purse. *Better watch out old woman, there's a wolf about.* The woman didn't seem to notice. That's the way it was with the do-gooders. They never watched out. Do-gooders were always surprised when something bad happened. She would never expect something bad in church. That would be to the thief's advantage.

Frankie closed his bloodshot eyes as he lay down on the pew. It didn't seem so hard after his many nights on concrete sidewalks. Sleep would close his mind. After they all left he would be able to get in the sacristy and the wine cabinet. His body trembled and his muscles twitched with longing. His gut ached as the happy meal returned to his throat. The salty-sour taste made him want to vomit. But the bulk of the meager meal had already been digested by his emaciated body. His stomach was already empty. His soul was even emptier.

As the unconsciousness of sleep overtook him, the dreams

began. It was Jessie's graduation day. Her smile as she accepted her diploma made his chest swell. It was after the hugs and the ceremony. Sitting in Mama Lucia's, with steam rising from her plate of spaghetti and meatballs, Jessie told him.

It was her present to him—they were going to have a baby. He spent the next six months in the basement making the cradle. It was ready just in time. Carved in the rosewood was humpty-dumpty on a wall, smooth as lake water for his daughter. As she grew that first year he made a highchair and a toy chest.

Amanda, as a chubby-legged toddler was full of giggles and loved to play in the sawdust as he worked. The smell of baby lotion and fresh cut wood invaded his dreams. The sound of Jessie humming upstairs filled him with utter joy.

That day, oh that day! He was making a little rocker for Amanda. She could sit in it and watch him work, as she liked to do. She loved to be with daddy in the workshop. Amanda was getting too big to sit on the floor but she was too little for the long pine bench that lined the workshop wall. The rocker would be just right. It was just about finished. He had the wood-burning gun on high. He was carving her name and some stars on the back.

Jessie called them to dinner. Frankie could swear he had unplugged the hot carving gun.

The smell of saltwater scented breezes flowed over Frankie's memories as he dreamed of leaving the house on a mission to buy more diapers. It was a quick twenty minutes to the supermarket. Jessie told him to take the Mustang. She would bathe Amanda and get her ready for bed. No, no she wouldn't put her to bed until Frankie got back. Not until he had time to read Amanda her favorite story.

Mission accomplished he hurried home. As he approached his home the shrill blare of sirens filled the air. Fire trucks blocked his way. As Francis left his car and started to walk toward his small home a sense of dread overcame him. Smoke filled his lungs as fear filled his heart. He started to run. He made it past the police cars with their lights flashing. Running, he reached his home. What was left of the small Cape Cod was still burning. Flames licked high into the black night. Two firefighters tackled him as he tried to run into the burning shell of the house.

Frankie couldn't believe what was happening. Smoke filled the sky, weighing down the heavy night air.

"Must be an electrical fire!" the reporter yelled into his cell phone. "One body, a woman, I think."

Frankie's heart seized up in his chest. He panted and gasped for air. In his mind the vision of the hot gun he had been working with in the basement filled him with pain. He wanted to scream at the reporter to shut-up, but fear caught his words in his throat.

"One child, I'm sure she's dead too! Probably smoke inhalation."

All the firefighters knew was that the man would not stop screaming. "Jessie-Jessie!" It didn't take the firefighters long to realize Francis was the husband and father of the woman and child. His pitiful sobs and screams made them all wince in pain. The paramedics wanted to sedate him, but first they had to restrain him.

"God damn it!" a young paramedic cursed.

Francis punched him in an effort to get away. It took four men to hold him down as the restraints were applied. The restraints were so tight that his hands and feet started to go numb. His fear had no outlet then. His heart beat so fast that he was sure it would burst from his chest. The blood drained from his head as his struggle to release himself failed. His head buzzed as his vision blurred. The paramedics lifted him on a stretcher into the awaiting ambulance. Strapped on the stretcher and immobile, they gave him a powerful sedative. Francis passed out in the ambulance.

Frankie woke with a jolt. The dream was always the same. Only drinking seemed to drown the nightmare. Repeatedly, the memories came back to him. Awake or asleep, Frankie couldn't escape them. Only the drink would drown them out. Frankie would pour the sweet scotch over the memory before he slept each night, numbing the wound and killing the pain that came with the dream.

The dream ended just where his memories ended. At least that is what they told him. He didn't remember the year he spent hospitalized. He was catatonic. That is what the doctor told him. Still, despite the doctor's protests, he signed himself out of the hospital a few days after he regained consciousness. He couldn't remember it. And he was determined to forget everything else. He became Frankie. The first night he took the ten dollars they gave him at the hospital and brought his first bottle. It killed both the pain and the memories.

Frankie learned the hard way to live on the streets. That first year was the toughest. He had to learn how to survive. He tried the shelters. They were the worst. The shelters run by the city were just deep black pits in which a man could drown, slices of hell on earth. Frankie was often robbed and assaulted. He quickly learned not to trust anyone. It was safer on the street. Frankie was always safer alone. You had to make them think you were crazy. They had to think you would do anything, even kill them. If they thought that, they usually left you alone. It wasn't hard to convince them he was crazy. Sometimes Frankie even convinced himself. He mumbled and leered at them to frighten them.

By the end of his first year on the street Frankie had a routine. He never stayed in the same place two nights in a row. That was dangerous. It gave them a chance to find you. The others could forcefully take what they wanted. They just wanted to take your stuff. Sometimes, despite Frankie's knowledge, they won. He was robbed of his few possessions on three occasions.

The do-gooders were worse. They wanted you. They wanted to take away your freedom. The do-gooders wanted to save you by making you remember. They came to you offering food, and warmth, pretending to really care. They were the most dangerous of all!

Frankie sat up in a sea of sweat. Shivering from the coldness of his body and from the coldness of his soul, his muscles twitched against the hard wooden pew. He knew where he was. He was trapped. Frankie had to hide until midnight. That was when the priest would lock up the church and leave by the large wooden door.

He held his abdomen as it ached with pain. His body cried in agony for the drink that was locked up in the cabinet of the sacristy. Even with blurred vision caused by the beads of wet-worry that cascaded from his brow, Frankie could see the clock. Only nine o'clock! Three hours until the priest locked up.

Frankie's hands trembled with need. He wrapped himself tighter in the large overcoat, as if to contain his need for a drink. The elderly priest felt the pain in the pit of Frankie's stomach. It was a reflection of the physical needs of the hiding man. Father D'Angelico prayed for the man whose body was now betraying him.

Four

"I will open my mouth in parables, I will announce what has lain hidden From the foundation of the world." (Matt. 13:35)

Frankie couldn't stand the pain. His muscles twitched and ached as his longing for a drink overcame him. His hands shook uncontrollably and his head pounded. Blurred vision was a bad sign—it meant that soon, if he didn't do something, he would start seeing horrible things that weren't really there. Frankie had been through this before.

Once, one of the do-gooders tried to help him, or so they said. They locked him up in a hospital. They said all he needed to do was to dry out. It was horrible. When the DT's came Frankie thought he had set himself on fire. He felt the flames, flaring up, burning his skin. His poor sweet Jessie must have experienced the same torture. He screamed for help but no one would help him. The do-gooders just belted him in the bed so he couldn't move. Frankie was so scared he peed himself. They just kept telling him to give it time and that he would feel better once it was all over. Frankie didn't feel better and left as soon as he could.

He needed a bottle. He didn't want to start seeing things again. Frankie would have to focus his mind until midnight.

He didn't want to lose control. Who knew what all these dogooders would do if Frankie lost control. They might even put him back into the hospital. Frankie forced his shivering body to sit up. He would have to regain control. Frankie would have to focus, at least until midnight. Then he would be able to gain access to the sweet red bottle of ambrosia that was locked in the cabinet.

Frankie pulled the wool coat around him as he sat up. Tightening the coat helped to control the tremors. He tried to concentrate on his surroundings. The same people remained. Only the young man that made Frankie uncomfortable was missing. Frankie wondered where he was hiding—he knew he had not ventured out into the cold.

Frankie noticed the old woman's purse was open. She probably wouldn't discover she'd been robbed until she needed her bus fare. It disgusted Frankie. He wasn't so disgusted that the young man had robbed someone—sometimes you had to do bad things to survive. It was the fact that he chose an elderly and frail woman. With all the rich looking dudes sitting here, he had taken the poorest. And it was all because she was the easiest. Well, Frankie supposed, she would be more careful with her old black purse in the future.

The old woman just sat and stared at the gold monstrance. Frankie couldn't understand it. All of these people came to pray, others stared at the round white piece of bread the golden rays of the monstrance surrounded. Some of the people brought Bibles to read, but most of them just sat there and stared at the bread. They seemed to be hypnotized. Frankie couldn't understand it. What was it that the old woman was staring at? What was so important that she couldn't see the boy rob her?

Frankie tried to concentrate on the bread. Perhaps it would take his mind off his need for a drink. He rubbed his eyes, which were moist with tears. His bloodshot eyes blurred his vision as he made a real effort to concentrate. The bread just sat there, the focus of his attention. There seemed to be something about it. Something warm touched him. Frankie sensed a yearning but not for a drink. He felt himself being drawn into the host. A strange sense of the supernatural hit him. He felt as if he was being called by the small whiteness, by a longing in his heart to reach out to his Creator, who he felt had rejected him long ago. He pulled away. *So what if this is really God?* Frankie thought. Frankie hated God! God had taken his Jessie and Amanda. Frankie would never forgive him! Never! Nonetheless Frankie felt the call of God. Then he actually heard it!

"Francis. Francis. Who do you say that I am?" Frankie the Bottle rubbed his ears. No one had called him Francis in years. He was just Frankie the Bottle. No one else in the church seemed to notice. No one moved. The voice was so loud. Why didn't they hear it? *Oh no*, he decided, *I must have imagined it.*

Once again the loud voice called. "Francis, Francis don't you know how much I love you?" Frankie looked up to the host and saw a bearded man in the center. The anger he had chased with booze for so long rose to his throat. Looking at the man in the host, he thought *this must be the God all these people came to see.* He supposed the man was that Jesus all the do-gooders always talked about. Frankie no longer felt cold as the heat rose to his face. His throat tightened as the veins in his neck protruded. His heart beat faster as a surge of energy flowed through his body. Frankie wanted to get up and smash the God that beckoned him. Only the fear of going to jail kept him in his seat.

Frankie vibrated with rising rage. Angry words caught in his throat. His mind screamed them. "Love, what do you mean love? What do you know about love? Jessie knew about love, and you killed her." Even as the words spiraled through his mind they caught in his throat, Frankie caught himself in the lie.

"No," his mind screamed, "I killed her! I forgot to turn the hot gun off! But you didn't save her! You're no better than me!" Frankie's mind roared with the anger he felt at the God he loathed. Looking into the bearded man's soft eyes, his mind bellowed, "Jessie and my baby are dead because you allowed it! I may have caused it, but you could have stopped it and you didn't. I hate you and I will always hate you!" Still shaken with emotion, Frankie couldn't peel his eyes from the face of Jesus.

"Look, Francis. Look at the truth!" The loud voice quivered within Frankie's spirit as the scene within the Eucharist changed. Frankie rubbed his eyes. Why was this happening to him? He was sure it was withdrawal. His mind was playing tricks on him again. He needed a good stiff drink.

Frankie decided if it didn't stop soon, he would just have to take the chance of breaking in to the sacristy with all these people here. The old priest was probably asleep anyway. Frankie tried to pull himself away from the host, but he couldn't.

The man, Jesus he guessed it was, melted away and now stood in a garden with a woman. Frankie found himself drawn into the landscape. It was as if he was sitting on the sideline, right there like watching a movie. Frankie the Bottle was in the garden. He was in the movie!

Jesus, wrapped in a white veil stood in a garden before a cave blocked by a large stone. A woman named Martha knelt at his feet and cried as others at a distance approached him.

Martha sat at his feet and she wept, "Lord, if you had been here, my brother would not have died. But even now I know that whatever you ask of God, God will give you." Jesus turned and, instead of addressing the woman, looked at Frankie.

"Your brother will rise." Frankie felt a chill run through him as Jesus turned back to the weeping woman who now stood before him.

"I know he will rise, in the resurrection on the last day."

Jesus told her, "I am the resurrection and the Life; whoever believes in me, even if he dies, will live."

Turning from Martha, Jesus' eyes searched Frankie's face. The piercing eyes studied Frankie. Frankie was in rapture, transfixed in the presence of his Creator.

Jesus spoke, "Do you believe this?" The moment hung, an eternity between the Creator and his creation. Frankie had never felt such a presence as he felt coming from this man. In the presence of this man, Frankie felt warmth and safety. His anger and rage melted away. A strange sense of peace flowed from the man to Frankie. Jesus smiled at Frankie and turned toward the woman who pulled her cloak tight around her and answered.

"Yes, Lord. I have come to believe that you are the Messiah, the Son of God, the one who is coming into the world."

Frankie watched as the woman got up and walked to a whitewashed house. She entered the house passing many men who tried to speak to her. She entered a courtyard and spoke to another woman.

"Mary, the teacher is here and is asking for you."

As soon as she heard this, the younger woman, Mary, rose quickly and went to him. Jesus had not come into the village, but was still where Martha had left him. The men who were in her house comforting Mary saw her get up quickly and go out. They followed her presuming that she was going to the tomb to weep there.

When Mary saw Jesus she fell at his feet and said to him, "Lord, if you had been here, my brother would not have died."

When Jesus saw her weeping he became perturbed and deeply troubled and He said, "Where have you laid him?" Jesus wept. So the men who had followed Mary said, "See how he loved him."

But some of them said, "Could not the one who opened the eyes of the blind man have done something so that this man would not have died?"

Yes! Frankie's mind screamed, *God could have saved this man, but he didn't.* Jesus could have saved Jesse and Amanda, but He didn't care! I hate you! Answer her question! Why didn't you save him? Why didn't you save my wife and baby?

Frankie shook with emotion. Frankie hated Jesus. He wanted to turn away and ignore the eyes that probed him. He could sense the love that this so-called God was offering and he wanted no part of it. He tried to disconnect and pull away, but it was impossible. Frankie had to watch—he was riveted as the scene played out before him. He was unaware of his surroundings as he entered into communion with his God.

Jesus came to the tomb. It was a cave and a stone lay across it. Jesus said, "Take away the stone."

Martha, the dead man's sister said to him, "Lord, by now there will be a stench; he has been dead for four days." Frankie sat spellbound. He agreed with the woman. It was impossible. Decay had set in. The dead were dead. How could it be possible? Frankie licked his dry lips as the scene before him continued. His fingers blanched as they gripped the back of the pew in front of him. What was happening? Once someone was dead, they were dead. Nothing could be done. Jesus smiled at the mesmerized Frankie and turned back to the woman.

He said to her, "Did I not tell you that if you believe you will see the glory of God?" So they took away the stone.

Jesus raised his eyes and said, "Father, I thank you for hearing me. I know that you always hear me; but because of the crowd here I have said this, that they may believe that you sent me."

And when he said this he cried out in a loud voice, "Lazarus, come out!"

The dead man came out tied hand and foot with burial bands, so Jesus said to them, "Untie him and let him go."

When Frankie saw the dead man walking from his tomb

he shook with fear! The man who had been dead now was alive. How could this be? Jesus turned to Frankie as the vision of the garden and the people faded away.

"Was he dead, Francis? Nothing I create dies, I am the Author of Life. The spirit lives forever."

Frankie tried to pull away. He did not want to answer the question. He closed his eyes. Even the pain, so familiar, was easier than this. Frankie was confused. What did this man, Jesus, want of him? Frankie covered his face with his hands. His hands no longer trembled. Frankie didn't notice. He tried to hide from the compelling force that called him. The call was too overpowering. Frankie opened his eyes to Jesus who called him. He wanted to cry.

Instead, Frankie froze. A woman remained kneeling before Jesus but the woman was no longer Mary. In her place, was Jesse—his Jesse! His arms automatically reached out to her but his body seemed paralyzed in the pew. Jessie spoke to the man just as Martha and Mary had done.

In the same words, she begged Jesus, "Lord if you had been here my Francis would not have died. But even now I know that whatever you ask of God, God will give you."

Who was she talking about? Frankie couldn't take his eyes off her. This Jesus seemed to be telling him that Jessie was still alive and with him. Was it possible? Jessie looked even more radiant now. Her soft brown eyes glowed with a special light, a peaceful light. Jessie's creamy white skin reflected the shimmering light of Jesus. Frankie became overwhelmed with a sense of joy. There is a God! And Jessie is with him. His heart overflowed with love. Frankie the Bottle wept as a sense of the eternal touched him. Frankie felt he couldn't handle any more emotion. Jessie turned and looked at him. Frankie suddenly realized that it wasn't just a dream. It wasn't just that he could see Jessie—Jessie could see him too!

The moment Jessie looked at him, Frankie felt ashamed. He knew what he had become. He wasn't her Francis anymore—

he was just a street person, a drunken bum. Frankie didn't want Jessie to see him like this. She had never known Frankie the Bottle. He became acutely aware of his old dirty clothes and his unshaven face. He reddened with shame.

Jessie's eyes blazed at him, showering him with nothing but love. Frankie felt humiliated as he dove behind the back of the pew in front of him. He couldn't look anymore! Why did Jessie have to see him this way? Frankie hid in his shame.

He no longer shook with a need for alcohol. He burned with embarrassment. Crouched behind the pew Frankie sobbed. Seeing Jessie was so wonderful. To know that she was alive in spirit thrilled him. There was a chance — a chance that he could be with Jesse again!

Frankie wept and wept until he could weep no more. He wept out all the pain, frustration, anger and humiliation that had built up in his soul over the four years since his family's death. At last the sobbing, which he muffled by hiding his face in the inside vest of his loosely fitting topcoat, subsided.

Frankie could still feel the call of Jesus in the Eucharist. Broken in spirit, he raised himself to a sitting position once again. Unable to resist the call of God, he struggled to open his eyes, eyes swollen from crying. Frankie looked up to the monstrance that held his Eucharistic Lord. The scene remained. Jessie, as lovely as ever, knelt before Jesus in the garden of Lazarus. Again, Frankie the Bottle watched as Jessie, kneeling before Jesus, asked the same question.

"Lord, if you had been here, my Francis would not have died. But even now I know that whatever you ask of God, God will give you." Humbled now, Frankie finally understood. Jessie was praying for him. Frankie thought in his limited understanding that Jessie died. Frankie had died!

In his mind, and soul, Frankie died. Frankie had allowed his pain and despair to kill whatever hope or faith he had. In his grief, Frankie turned away from the very God who wanted to console him. He died in the black pain of his spirit. The person who needed to be called back from the dead was not

Jessie, but Frankie.

The reality of it hit him hard. Jessie was aware of Frankie all the while. She had been and praying for him! Now her prayers were about to be answered. As Frankie watched the garden scene, Jesus turned to him. The eyes of Jesus were full of grief and pain for the man who remained dead before him.

With such tender love, Jesus called out, "Francis, come out!"

Francis responded. He reached out to Jesus. Jesus smiled and as he did, Francis felt the pain of separation and the chains of grief that held him bound to loneliness, guilt, and booze fall away. A sense of the perpetual peace of God overcame him.

Francis felt warmth and tranquility flow through him. The soul that was in turmoil for the last four years became still and alive, aware of the peace and grace of Jesus. Into that stillness and quiet, the Grace of The Ancient of Days flowed. His addiction was gone, his grief was healed, and for the first time in four years, Francis felt his interminable life force being restored.

Looking up into the eyes of Jesus, Francis felt freed. Kneeling down he started to pray.

"Lord, take care of my Jessie. Take care of Amanda too!"

Jesus smiled and looked tenderly at the now submissive man and said, "Jessie is with me for eternity. I will minister to Amanda through you."

Francis was confused, "What do you mean, Lord?"

"Look to the Truth. The Truth will set you free!" Francis was stunned as the scene before him changed once again. He was back at the fire. Francis didn't want to be here again but he couldn't tear his eyes away. The ambulance that carried him to the hospital had just left. Another ambulance was being loaded with a stretcher. The small form on the stretcher struggled against the oxygen mask as it was being applied. It was Amanda! She was still alive!

Francis watched as Jesus showed him a small girl, about five years old playing on a swing. The little girl looked so much like Jessie, yet she seemed so sad. A nun came and called her into the large brick-building characteristic of any city school. Francis was stunned. Shaking, he wept.

"But Lord, I thought I killed both of them!" Jesus just smiled again.

"Look Francis!" The scene returned to the fire. A fireman poked through the smoldering rubble. Bending down, he picked up a wire.

"Captain, the fire started in the back wall of the kitchen. The house had frayed wiring everywhere. A spark in the wall probably set it off and the fire must have spread quickly."

Francis sat in silence as the scene before him faded away. This was too much to digest. The hot gun in the basement didn't cause the fire. It was an accident. Francis had not killed his family. Could this be true?

Jesus showed it to him so it must be true. Sitting in the quiet church, Francis had trouble comprehending all that he had seen. He had no doubt he'd seen it. Suddenly his sense of the supernatural was more real to him than earthly worries. He would never doubt God again. A sense of truth permeated him. Francis felt a weight lift off him. He felt the weight of guilt, self-pity, and anger, lift. He hadn't started the fire that killed Jessie. He was free, finally free from the festering pain and remorse. His heart, chained for so long, now felt light.

Francis looked around the church. The same people sat in the same spots. Looking to the clock he was shocked. It had only been half an hour since he had looked to see when he might steal the sacramental wine. He couldn't believe it. In thirty minutes everything had changed.

For the first time Francis noticed that his hands had stopped shaking. His lips were no longer dry. Even the pains and aches had disappeared. Francis didn't have a desire to drink. In fact, the thought of having a drink repulsed him. It was a wonder, a blessing. God cared so much for him that

He even cured Francis's alcoholism. The sense of His Love surpassed Francis's ability to understand it. It filled him with peace. God loved him, and that knowledge set Francis free.

His Love was so profound he would never feel alone again. God loved him so much that He would always watch over him. No matter what happened in the future, Francis would always know God was with him. Francis realized both Jesus and Jessie waited for him to share an eternal life. The question left with Francis was, "What life?"

Frankie the Bottle didn't know Francis. Francis was just a memory. Frankie was the man he had been for the last four years. It had been a terrible existence, but it was the only existence he knew. Now that man no longer existed. So who was he? He was no longer a carpenter. He hadn't worked since the fire. He hadn't kept up his union dues. Would the union even let him back in considering the circumstances? Francis decided getting back into the local was something he had to take care of. He still had friends who might help him.

Francis actually felt happy at the thought of working again. He looked down at his hands, which no longer trembled with need and fear. *I can create beauty again*. His hands were a gift, a gift given back.

Plans for a new life flowed through his mind. *I have to find a place. I'll shower and get some new clothes. Once I'm cleaned up and have an address, I'll go down to the Union Hall. I'll just convince them that I've changed. I'll hang around until I get some work.* Francis started to get excited. The thought of starting a new life delighted him. He knew that was just what he needed — a new life.

He needed a home for Amanda. He would go and get her just as soon as he could but he needed to get a job first. It would take all of his strength to wait. He wanted to rush over to his little girl and hold her in his arms. He wanted to tell her that she would never have to be alone or afraid again. Francis knew better. If the social workers saw him like this he would never get Amanda back. For her sake,

Francis knew he would have to be patient but it wasn't going to be easy. He had to start from scratch and it would take time to save enough money, even if he got work right away.

Francis could feel the worry begin, but then he realized he was not alone and fell on his knees. Francis prayed to God, appearing before him in the monstrance. Francis could no longer physically see Jesus — faith alone permitted Francis to see Him in the small piece of bread. Faith was enough.

The grace of peace surged through his spirit. Jesus would help him. Francis knew he and Amanda would be together again. No longer alone, they would soon have each other. Jessie would watch over them. Jesus would help him. He was no longer full of guilt. Francis, the new Francis, wasn't afraid.

Five

So Faith, Hope, Love remain, these three; but the greatest of these is Love. (Cor. 13:13)

P eter sat still in the front pew of the quiet church. He had wandered aimlessly in from the cold. He roamed confused until the bitter winds made his walk impossible to continue. Just when he felt he could no longer bear the icy chill of the outside world, he saw the warm glow of the church. From the snow-covered sidewalk, Peter saw the inviting glow of the candlelight beckoning him as the old priest opened the ancient wooden doors. He followed the small crowd as they entered. Now that he was here, he was glad to sit. His feet felt like ice. The chill permeated his bones. The arctic wind left his toes and fingers numb. What had he been thinking? He was a physician, he should have known better. He could have ended up with frostbite.

Peter already knew the answer to the question. He hadn't been thinking. His entire spirit was numb. He couldn't think. He couldn't feel. Perhaps because the pain of what he would feel would destroy him. It struck him as strange. For the last year, ever since that day, he had been a boiling cauldron of emotion. Now he felt empty. He felt nothing at all.

It was all over. For a year, his brain had been consumed

with anger and plans for revenge. Peter wanted the lying bitch to pay for her betrayal! He plotted her punishment.

He'd would lay awake at night as he imagined scenes — scenes in which he would inflict sorrow and pain on Eva, but they never came about. Peter imagined her pain and shock as the judge handed her nothing. He relished thoughts of the judge kicking the whore out of the courtroom.

Peter's favorite vision was of Eva begging him to take her back. He took great pleasure in picturing Eva's tears as he rejected her plea. He pictured her weeping uncontrollably as she realized the judge was granting the divorce and that the marriage was over. On those long nights, he imagined — no he prayed — that she would collapse down dead from the shock of the judge's decision.

None of that happened.

The numbness of the cold and shock was starting to fade. Dr. Peter Caine could feel the familiar taste of hate-bile rise into his throat. With the rage of revenge in his heart, Peter had fought viciously to keep Eva from getting any of the marital assets. *That stupid judge, that stupid, stupid judge,* he thought.

Peter sat in shock as the court explained to him what his lawyer had already told him. The marital property would be split evenly — this was a community property state. He was granted a no-fault divorce. No-fault! What did that mean? Everything was her fault. She betrayed him. She destroyed him. It was only right that she pay. She was a cheat and a liar!

The first time he caught her in a lie was early in their marriage. Peter was in a rush one morning. Rummaging through the vanity draw looking for a razor, he discovered birth control pills. Why was she pretending to want a baby and acting so sad about not being able to conceive? He remembered the shock!

Until then, he believed everything she said to him. Why

had she lied? Yes, he wanted children. He had the means to support them. On the other hand, if she wanted to wait he would have understood. There was no need to lie. She didn't have to hide her birth control pills.

The whole incident stunned him. He never made the connection. It never occurred to him until that day a year ago that she might have another reason to lie.

Maybe he should have known, but he was just too busy to think about it. His cardiologist practice was growing rapidly and his work consumed most of his waking hours. Six months before finding the birth control pills he was so overwhelmed he decided to take on a partner. Vinny was an old friend from medical school. Peter decided that if he really needed a partner, and it seemed he did, then it should be his friend. It all came together so easily. The practice and their reputation grew and Peter was able to buy the larger brownstone his wife longed for.

Peter never cared about money. He had grown up poor and everything they had accumulated seemed excessive. Eva needed it. For some reason, her sense of self was linked to how much money she had. Nothing was ever enough for her. Peter was making great money yet Eva never seemed content.

When he first met Eva, while in college, he was stunned by her natural beauty and became tongue-tied. Eva worked as a recruiting associate in the guidance department. As word spread of the new girl in the department many of the male students suddenly needed guidance. Many just wanted to sit in the outer office and watch Eva work. A few even tried to get Eva to go out with them. She was steadfast in her refusals. Peter was smitten. He knew his chance was slim but he had to try.

One morning he finally got up the courage and approached her. With his heart beating at what felt like five times its normal speed, he simply asked her if she would like to join him for dinner and a movie on Friday. Her smiling approval stunned him.

Later, she explained that he was the only boy who was honest and direct. She was sick of all the bragging and the worn out, stale lines the others tried on her. He didn't care, whatever it was, she said yes to him. Eva and Peter became an item. He was so in love with her he couldn't see past her looks. She was so pretty that he overlooked most of her flaws.

Very early in the relationship she displayed a selfish streak. She connived and encouraged him to spend money on her, even if it left him strapped. One semester he spent his book money taking her to a posh restaurant she insisted on going to even though she knew it was beyond his budget.

Social status was all that Eva seemed to care about. She quickly pulled him away from most of his friends. She encouraged friendships with only the 'important' people. At first, Peter objected, but he soon found that fighting Eva was useless. She was determined to get ahead and she always won.

He was alarmed by her extreme vanity, but he was inexperienced with girls. He wasn't sure whether her behavior was normal and figured it probably was for gorgeous girls like Eva. She came from money and she took it for granted.

Eva never took the time to understand Peter's poor background. She only seemed interested in herself. Again, Peter dismissed her disinterest. He could only see her beauty. Thoughts of Eva, the young happy Eva, were painful.

Peter tried to distract himself. He watched as the elderly priest opened a golden box and removed a round object with great respect and ceremony. Walking with great deliberation, he placed the object in the center of a monstrance. It sat in the center of an ornately carved, white marble altar.

The gold and jewel encrusted monstrance was flanked by two tall gold candlesticks. His eyes were drawn to the warmth of the golden candlelight. It became the center of his focus. Amazed by the beauty of the altar and the monstrance, Peter studied them. The carvings were obviously a labor of love;

each of them intricately displayed scenes from the life of Jesus. Peter watched as the elderly priest circled and then knelt before the altar. He tried to remain focused but his mind burned with hatred and the past beckoned him.

Born in 1965, he had grown up poor. While the rest of the country flourished, the hill country suffered. Poverty was a part of his life for as long as Peter could remember, his father was a country doctor and as a child, Peter traveled with him on his visits through the mountains of West Virginia.

A real rural doctor, his father was known for his loving bedside manner. His patients were so poor that they rarely paid him in money, but mountain people had pride. If they couldn't pay in money they paid in food or services. One might fix the roof of the doctor's home, while another might deliver firewood for a month. The women would drop off eggs and home-smoked hams. Peter's mother always made them feel as if they had given too much. It was her way, words formed by charity.

In spite of their kindness, his mother barely made ends meet. She baked bread and sewed clothes for her family and for the poorest of the poor. Peter remembered her being up early and sweeping the worn wooden floors of his childhood home. As the rising sun glowed though the lead-glassed windows, he would try to catch the prisms of light on the floor as she swept. Such simple joy would make her laugh. Despite her needs, she laughed often. And at the end of each day, after the sunset, she still looked happy.

As she pulled the tattered blankets up around his chin to warm him from the drafty house she would always smile and say, "It's good! With the help of God we have managed!"

Peter loved to travel with his father. He knew all the families on the mountain. They'd leave early in the morning with lunches of leftover sausages and sandwiches. Most of the families would offer them food from their meager supplies. His father taught him mountain etiquette, "You have to eat.

Don't ever insult poor folks. But Peter, don't ever eat too much. Leave a lot untouched. It might be all the food they have."

Peter didn't think of himself as poor when he was young. Next to the mountain folk his father doctored, he was wealthy. Peter was never hungry like many of their children.

They pushed and prodded the old car through the rain and fog that wrapped the mountain on those cold mornings to the sick that needed them — the only other people Peter ever saw. The mountain people were tall and thin with dark, steady eyes. Dark, steady, and serious eyes that watched a world that seemed to rotate without them. The deep eyes of the mountain people watched a world that took little notice of them. They were quiet people who learned to live in their own world, a world apart.

Katy was part of that world. Peter's heart would pound faster as they passed her house. The youngest of ten children, she would often be out in the field and wave to them as they drove by. Peter sighed whenever he saw her with her bright red hair and freckled face. The whole day was worth one smile from Katy.

Peter loved Katy from early childhood and little changed as he grew. The love they had grew stronger with the passage of time. They started to date, mountain-style, as young teenagers. Mountain-style dating consisted of school dances and holiday picnics. Katy grew prettier with each passing year. They had their first kiss walking home from a Fourth of July celebration when they were just fifteen. By the time they were eighteen, they were planning marriage.

Peter wanted to be a country doctor, just like his father. He worked hard in school to get the highest grades. His parents didn't have much money but promised to help him as much as they could. It didn't matter. Peter won a full scholarship to college. The hardest part was leaving Katy.

"Don't cry." Peter held her gently on the day he left for college.

Katy sobbed uncontrollably. She clung to him as her body shook with sorrow. They had never been separated, and she couldn't stand the thought of being divided for so long. Peter didn't have much money, so the visits home would be very infrequent.

"I promise I 'll write each week. It'll be hard but the time will pass. And when I come back we'll get married and spend the rest of our life together." Peter hugged her and boarded his train. A quick goodbye to his parents, and he was off. He watched Katy as she ran behind the train with tears in her eyes. Peter truly loved her and intended to keep his promise. At first, he did write each week. Katy wrote each day. As Peter's workload became heavier, the letters became less frequent. Eventually, Peter stopped writing at all. Mountain life seemed so remote, so much a part of his past.

He was caught up in his new life. Peter hadn't planned on specializing but he became fascinated by cardiology. His original plan was to be a general internist, just like his father but the plan changed the first time he saved the life of a heart patient with his knowledge and newly acquired skills. He became hooked. The acclaim of his fellow students filled him with pride.

His instructor, a renowned cardiac surgeon, was impressed, "You have real talent, I'd be happy to recommend you for a residency in the cardiology department. I would love to see you develop your skills."

Peter applied for the three-year residency in cardiology without much thought of his promise to return and marry Katy. He hadn't seen Katy in years. He hadn't written to her since his second year in pre-med. Katy had continued sending him letters for months after he stopped writing to her, but he just tossed them. Things had changed. By then, he was seeing Eva.

Peter removed the cashmere scarf from his neck and the warm designer topcoat. It was cozy in the church. He heard the strong wind blowing outside and decided it was best if he stayed. Still, it was strange. He hadn't been in church in ten years and this church was very different from the church he knew as a boy. The mountain church of his youth was a very plain wooden building with simple wooden benches and a large wooden cross. There were no statues.

The preacher, Reverend Jonas, filled the near-empty room with his passionate sermons while Peter squirmed. The benches were uncomfortable and the sermons loud and long but he never missed church on Sunday mornings for two reasons: One, was because his mother was a faithful Bible-toting Baptist who insisted that her son follow the Lord and be saved and second, because Katy was always there.

She looked even better on Sunday with her hair pulled-back and her face scrubbed up and shining. Dressed in her worn hand-me-down dress, Peter was sure that Katy was the most beautiful girl God had ever created. He dreamed of having Katy as his wife. He dreamed of Katy all through the Pastor's sermons. Someday Peter knew he would be a mountain doctor and Katy would be his wife. A romantic boy, he dreamed of a house full of mountain flowers and mountain children but that dream died when he met Eva.

Looking around the church, Peter tried to pull himself away from those memories. What does it matter? That life was so long ago. He left that life. Katy was just a memory.

Peter watched as the old priest knelt before the golden monstrance. The people of the mountains had heard about Catholics. The word on the mountain was they worshiped statues and gave their allegiance to the Pope. They did whatever the Pope told them to do and gave him all their money. The people of the mountain thought it was sad that Catholics worshiped something besides Jesus. It was a shame that they were all going to go to Hell.

Peter felt sorry for the old priest as he watched him struggle from his knees. He could see the priest was in pain. The wrinkled man was suffering on his knees in front of a false god. A god made of bread and gold. Peter knew that Catholics believed the bread in the monstrance was the actual body of Jesus. It would be funny if it weren't so sad. Still it was interesting to watch their rituals. It distracted him from the painful thoughts of what happened that day. The day that changed his life.

A year ago, none of this would have mattered. A year ago, his life was going as planned, but it all changed in one day. That particular morning started out like any morning. The office waiting room was full of patients; Peter's staff complained about the workload. He loved the pressure. The adrenaline gave him a sort of high. That day was especially heavy because Vinny was attending a cardiology conference. Peter just worked faster feeling good as he watched the crowd in the waiting room shrink.

The hospital called at lunchtime with an emergency. Peter, as was his habit when his partner wasn't there, asked the office manager to cancel his afternoon appointments. These emergencies could take hours to resolve. As it turned out, the emergency resolved itself, before Peter even got to the hospital. He made the decision to go home.

Oh no, I don't want to think about that afternoon, thought Peter.

He tried to distract himself by watching the other people in the church. The old priest sat in the last pew, and seemed to have gone asleep. A younger priest should be doing this he thought — it was just too cold and late for an old arthritic man. Peter didn't like the way the old priest looked. His color seemed off. The slight blue around his mouth indicated a weak heart, which at his age that wasn't all that unusual.

Still, Peter thought the old man would be better off in bed. The rest of the people seemed like a mixed bag. Peter, as a doctor, couldn't help examining each person. After he had found a diagnosis for each one of them, and a proper treatment, his thoughts started drifting back to that day. The thoughts were not unusual, he had been reliving them for the last year. Now that the court settled everything, it should be over but the habit of replaying that day in his mind hadn't ended with the court decision. Despite the numbness, he felt after his day in court, the anger and resentment was still just below the surface.

The ride home from the office that afternoon was still vivid in his mind. Each detail carefully preserved. As Peter drove into the posh city neighborhood, he realized that Eva would probably be out shopping. It didn't matter, he decided he would relax for a change and wait for her to come home.

Thursday was the housekeeper's day off. The varnished wooden floor was silent. Peter dreamed of the day tiny feet would run across that floor to greet him. Peter dreamed of the love steps of children yet to be conceived.

The house spoke of emptiness. Expensive emptiness filled with the pricey trinkets of a woman who had no purpose in life.

Peter was halfway up the staircase to the upstairs bedroom before he heard her laugh. As he opened his mouth to call her name, he heard a man's voice. Her name stuck in his throat. The man's voice was so familiar. The sound of the creaking bed froze him.

Suspended in time on the staircase between illusion and truth, Peter's body began to shake. Reality physically hit him before it penetrated his mind. Leaping up the remaining stairs Peter broke through the unlocked bedroom door. The look of shock on Eva's face only made the contrasting look of derision and mockery on Vinny's face even more pronounced. Naked together in bed, Peter realized that they had just finished having sex.

Peter wanted to scream but he had lost his breath. It was as if he had been sucker-punched. He couldn't move; he couldn't breath! He felt the blood drain from his head as he became dizzy with shock. His life was being destroyed. All the blood in his body seemed to rush to his chest as if he was about to implode. That is until Peter heard Vinny's laughter, the deep mocking laughter of the man he thought was his best friend. Even Eva's head turned to the source of the sardonic, contemptuous laugh.

Vinny was casually dressing pulling on his socks as he sat on the side of Peter's bed. His face was full of scorn as he dressed without rushing. Vinny displayed no fear or sorrow. It triggered something in Peter.

Peter lunged at the man who had betrayed his trust. He punched the man who had shattered his marriage. Peter surprised him. Vinny was shocked by the attack and was quickly losing the battle despite his defensive moves. The heat of rage had Peter focused as murder flooded his very spirit.

Peter would have killed Vinny if Eva hadn't stopped him by hitting him. In defense of her lover, she hit Peter with a lamp. As the red rage faded to black, Peter could hear Eva comforting her boyfriend.

Peter awoke in the hospital as the nurse aroused him with a light in his eyes. She was looking for the uneven pupil dilation indicative of a concussion.

"Dr. Caine, can you hear me?" Peter could see, but his vision was blurred. He tried to focus.

"Yes, I'm awake!" Peter found himself waking to the nightmare that was now his life.

Peter didn't listen to his lawyers. He went from lawyer to lawyer, spending all his time and money on the hope of finding revenge. He spent so much time obsessed with getting even that he neglected his practice.

Vinny never returned to the office. With half of the money from their joint business account, Vinny opened his new practice across town. His following grew, while Peter's practice dwindled. Within a few months, Peter closed the practice. He was too busy trying to destroy Vinny and Eva in court. The legal fees he created in his quest for revenge drained him of almost all of his money.

Peter hadn't cared about the money. All he could think of was the smug look of disdain on Vinny's face as he stroked Eva's arm while sitting in the courtroom. The look of victory on Vinny's face almost destroyed Peter. Vinny's pride was just too much to swallow and Peter almost choked on it. His rage had been eating away at him for months — the divorce allowed it to consume him.

Peter felt cold, despite the warmth of the church. For a year, he burned with the heat of his anger. Now a strange coldness took over. He felt as cold as the marble around him. He looked around him. This church was so different from the court he just left. The court was full of polished wood benches, it was noisy and seemed full of papers that no one looked at. Before the court was called to order, people milled around, engaged in conversation paying little attention to their surroundings.

In contrast, the church was silent. An overwhelming silence that started after the priest finished his ancient songs of worship. No one here talked. Everyone seemed to be deep in the thought. Peter looked at the focus of that silence. The bread in the center of the monstrance drew each person to it.

Peter found himself staring at the altar, which held what was supposed to be the God of the Universe. It seemed to draw him. It took all his effort to pull himself away. He didn't want to talk to God. He only wanted to distract himself from the overwhelming pain that was flowing from his heart.

Trying to relax his tense muscles Peter stretched and looked up to the ceiling. It was ornate with a deep blue background and golden stars. The images of angels and clouds gave Peter a sense of the eternal. He had always been taught that images were forbidden but these images were beautiful. The glimpse of heaven comforted him. Somehow thinking of life as eternal made his troubles seem so small. Peter wondered if any of the faith he was taught as a child was true. *Probably not*, he decided.

In his pocket was an envelope with ten thousand dollars, all that was left of his practice and his life. All that was left of the money he had made. He couldn't blame the lawyers. They had warned him about all the money he was spending.

But the lawyers never truly understood. It was never about the money. It was about revenge! And as the heat of unrequited revenge inflamed his spirit, coldness filled the empty spaces. Peter was full of a frost that was destroying more than the fire of his hate. It left him numb. In that cold, pure and white like freshly fallen snow, nothing lived. The winter of his hate killed all. Nothing green or beautiful grew in that chill. The winter of Peter's soul had come.

Six

Then the Lord asked Cain, "Where is your brother Abel?"
He answered, "I do not know. Am I my brother's keeper?"
(Gen. 4:9)

With a deep coldness of soul, Peter looked around. His eyes were drawn to the false god, the god of bread and gold. *Why did so many believe such a lie?* he thought. Peter came in here to get out of the cold. These others went out in the cold to come here. Why? It was beyond him. He looked at the monstrance. Like the rays of the sun, its golden branches surrounded the simple round host. He wondered if he would see what attracted the others to come out in the bitter cold. He saw nothing and he knew why.

Peter finally understood. There was no God. The proof of his thesis was that there was no justice. How could any God allow such injustice in the world? Didn't he deserve better than what life handed him? How could any God allow such pain? It was unfair. It was proof there was no God. The angry man stared at the Eucharist in defiance. *I dare you. I dare you to show yourself.*

Nothing. Just as he thought, there was nothing. There

was nothing worth living for because life was too painful! Peter didn't want to live anymore. He had lived for revenge and now without revenge and hatred, there was nothing to feel, nothing to live for. Coldness numbed him. Coldness swept through his soul like a biting wind. The wind swept him empty. And empty, he stared at the host.

It started to glow, a warm glow steady and soft. It lit the church. The doctor was startled. The church surrounding the monstrance started to fade. The white marbled church began to fade as the lustrous light filled his field of vision. He looked around; no one else seemed to notice. How could they just sit there? Couldn't they see what was happening? He didn't want to look and made up his mind that this was just a trick. It had to be his imagination. He didn't want to see. The glow was so warm and felt so right. He was drawn to it. He couldn't resist. He stared into the warm pool of golden light.

A beautiful valley appeared in the host. It drew Peter in. He felt the grass beneath his feet. A gentle breeze caressed his cheek. It felt so natural that he felt the sun warming him from the cloudless blue sky. The air smelled of fresh grass, wildflowers, and soft spring air.

Looking around he saw a man come and walk up to the large flat boulder. Gray in the warm morning light, the boulder rose and from Peter's vantage point, it seemed to touch the horizon. The man, dressed in animal skins carried something in his arms. The doctor strained to see what it was.

Bowing before the large rock the man placed what he held on top of the boulder and stepping back stood motionless with his arms uplifted. It reminded Peter of something. It took him a minute to realize that it reminded him of the elderly priests' pose of worship before the monstrance. Of course, that was it. The man was worshiping before an altar.

He placed vegetables and fruits on the altar. The smell of overripe fruits perfumed the breeze. The smell was slightly nauseating in the cool freshness of the valley. Peter watched as the man just stood there. It looked as if he was expecting something, but nothing happened. Another fool! There was no movement because there was no God.

The man waited for a while as if expecting something, then stepped away and sat on a smaller rock behind a tree. He looked confused. Peter wasn't confused. It proved his point. The man was waiting, as so many people had, for a response from a God who never answered. What a waste!

He heard the sound of someone rustling in the bushes beside him and slipped further behind a scrub bush. The man he was watching apparently also heard the approach of another man. He too slipped behind a tree to watch. The second man, also dressed in skins, approached the table-like rock much as the previous man had. He bowed even deeper before the boulder and held his position of humility even longer.

Peter watched with interest as the second man placed his gift on the altar right beside the gift of fruit and vegetables. This gift moved. A pure white kid bleated as the man removed a sharpened stone dagger. Holding the tiny goat's head, with one swift movement the man poured the newborn's blood upon the altar. Stepping back, as the first man watched, the worshipper stood with uplifted hands. He lifted his hands in offering. Peter laughed to himself again. What a waste of time!

Suddenly a light glowed brightly and a glowing ethereal figure appeared. Light poured from the figure and flowed over the man who made the second offering. Peter couldn't believe his eyes! The radiant figure was so familiar. It looked exactly like Peter's concept of Jesus. Since childhood, he had a different concept of Jesus then the standard one. His image was very different from the one portrayed in the artwork he had seen.

Peter's Jesus was much more masculine. The sight of his imagined Jesus shook him. Peter never talked to anyone about his image of Jesus. He'd had a deep relationship with

Jesus when he was a child. Taught by his devoted mother, he prayed everyday as a young boy. This vision was the Jesus he had loved in his younger days. This was the Jesus he loved and trusted. Who was doing this? How could they know how Peter imagined Jesus? The figure turned toward him and spoke.

"Was it your imagination, Peter?"

He fell to his knees and tried to hide his face. It wasn't possible! Looking up to his God, he could taste the salt from his tears as they flowed into his open mouth. *Oh my God! This was all real!* Peter thought as he stared into the eyes of the God he had just rejected. The depth and love in those eyes hypnotized him. Peter could have spent the rest of his life just falling into those eyes so full of Love.

Jesus smiled as if sensing Peter's thoughts then turned back to the man in the scene. His light flowed over the man who had offered the goat. As the light flowed over him, he glistened. It was as if the man reflected the light of Jesus. Peter couldn't help but think of the word *grace*. A word his mother often spoke. That reflection must be grace! As the light brightened, the background grew darker.

Jesus stood steady looking with love at the second man and announced, "I am well pleased!"

The man fell prostrate in front of Jesus.

The man who had offered the vegetables, stepped out of the darkness just into the edge of the light. His head bowed and his arms folded across his chest. He stood with his feet firmly planted and seemed to refuse to worship. The stance was one of defiant anger. It reminded Peter of a child waiting for a punishment he felt he didn't deserve. Jesus turned to the first worshipper with a look of tender love. The first man watched suspiciously and appeared to resent the love that Jesus offered him.

Again, the powerful voice emanated from the Lord, "Why are you so resentful and crestfallen? If you do well you can hold up your head. If not, sin is a demon lurking at the door;

his urge is toward you, yet you can be his master."

With that parting word, the image of Christ disappeared. Both men stood before the boulder again in the cool morning brightness.

Peter lowered his head as his tears flowed freely. He knew what Jesus was trying to show him and he couldn't bear it. Peter was acting like the first worshiper. In anger at a God he doubted, Peter had defied God to prove His love. He had offered Jesus nothing. Peter realized that he offered God his leavings.

In his anger, he gave God nothing but the unwanted parts of his life. As the years went by Peter lost any sense of the Jesus he once loved. Soon, God was forgotten except as a target of his anger. Peter gave God all the bad parts of his life. He hadn't offered Jesus any thanks for the good, only the leavings. He was so ashamed. He didn't want to look up. Peter couldn't stand to see anymore!

Drawn into the garden again, Peter couldn't look away. He watched as the man who had offered the goat as a sacrifice rose. The first man approached him. "Abel, Abel!" Abel turned to the man that Peter now realized was Cain. A sick feeling nauseated Peter. He wanted to intervene but all he could do was watch.

Cain said to his brother, "Let us go out in the field."

Peter wanted to scream, "No," but he couldn't speak. He watched frozen as the two men walked. Peter saw them from the back as they walked away. He couldn't see their faces. Cain stood behind his brother and picked up a bricksized rock. As Abel looked to where Cain pointed, Cain lifted the rock up high above Abel's head.

Peter could feel the anger and jealousy that burned through Cain. It propelled him. It drove him. Cain could do nothing but act out the hatred that burned through his soul. Cain stuck a blow to the head of his unsuspecting brother. Blood sprayed everywhere as Abel fell forward. Abel's blood poured onto the ground as he died. Peter was horrified as he watched Cain let the bloodied rock fall from his hand. It landed with a muffled thud beside the lifeless body.

Cain stood transfixed. His shoulders seemed to collapse. Standing above the lifeless form, he could not believe what had just happened. Peter could see the muscles on Cain's back begin to twitch. Soon his whole body trembled. Cain let out a mournful scream, gripped with fear as he came to understand the reality of his actions. Cain ran. He ran in the direction of the boulder where he and Abel both placed their offering. Shaking he fell beside the boulder and hid.

The scene fascinated Peter. He understood how it had happened. Cain killed Abel in a fit of jealous rage. He understood because Peter could have killed Vinny that day when he was so full of jealousy. Until now, Peter was upset Eva stopped him. She had protected Vinny. Her actions then, as well as afterward, only added to his self-pity. Now, Peter realized how much worse things could have been. He could have actually killed Vinny. For the first time, looking at Cain's agony, Peter pictured himself as a murderer. Without Eva's intervention, he could have been just like Cain.

In this magical church talking to God, the shaken man realized for the first time through the haze of his anger that he was thankful. He had not felt gratitude for many years. His feeling about Eva took the slightest shift from pure hatred to gratitude. His gratitude to Jesus grew exponentially as he realized that, despite himself, he had been protected.

Drawn into the scene, Peter watched with profound pity as Cain, curled up like a ball, trembled in fear beside the altar. Darkness surrounded the murderer. Then as Peter watched, the light of Jesus appeared. As Jesus walked toward Cain, His light fell upon him.

Then the Lord asked Cain, "Where is your brother Abel?" Cain stood up. Peter longed to see Cain's face and the emotions his face would reveal but Cain's back remained turned to Peter. Gradually Cain seemed to stop trembling. His back stiffened as he faced Jesus.

Cain answered, "I do not know. Am I my brother's keeper?" Cain's shoulders squared as he faced Jesus with his defiant lie.

The Lord then said, "What have you done! Listen, your brother's blood cries out to me from the soil! Therefore, you shall be banned from the soil that opened its mouth to receive your brother's blood from your hand. If you till the soil, it shall no longer give you its produce. You shall become a restless wanderer on the earth. Cain fell to his knees before the Lord. Shoulders squared with defiance a moment ago now shook with sorrow and fear!

Cain said to the Lord, "My punishment is too great to bear. Since You have now banished me from the soil, and I must avoid Your presence and become a restless wanderer on the earth, anyone may kill me at sight." Cain, looking down, could not see the tender sorrow in the eyes of love.

"Not so!" the Lord said to him. "If anyone kills Cain, Cain shall be avenged sevenfold." Peter watched as Jesus reached out to Cain. He touched his forehead. So the Lord put a mark on Cain, lest anyone should kill him at sight. Cain rose in broken sorrow. He walked to the East as the Lord pointed. As he left the vision, Jesus watched him. He seemed so full of sorrow.

Jesus walked over to the field where Abel lay on the ground. Jesus knelt on the ground, and lifted the body. Peter watched in amazement as Jesus wept. Jesus wept and rocked in sorrow as He cradled the lifeless body of Abel in His arms. How much Jesus loved! Peter shook with emotion as he watched the display of God's love.

Jesus loved Cain, and He loved Abel. Peter trembled as he realized Jesus loved him, and he loved Vinny.

In a whisper, barely able to speak through the choking tears, Peter whispered, "Thank you Jesus, thank you for having Eva stop me from murdering Vinny!"

Jesus looked directly into Peter's eyes said, "Didn't you kill him! Didn't you kill Eva?" Peter gasped as the scene faded away and he was left sitting alone in the wooden pew.

Collapsing, Peter was stunned. His entire body trembled. He could no longer hide the emotions he'd kept in check all his life. Tears flowed freely down his cheeks. Peter dried them with his cashmere scarf but they kept on coming. The shock of such strong feelings overcame him as he tried to muffle his overwhelming emotions. Trembling, he could no longer kneel. Sitting weak and broken against the smooth wooden seat Peter sat in total fatigue. Lowering his head in his hands, he collapsed into a ball. Like Cain, he was weak from the truth revealed and he had no strength left. Rocking his body in grief, Peter leaned his head against the back of the pew. Trembling, he tried to hide from the other people in the church.

Jesus had spoken directly to him. Peter had no doubt about that. What did He mean? He hadn't killed anyone. However, even as he thought about it he realized he was lying to himself. A vague and distant memory came of Sunday school long ago deep in the mountains of West Virginia.

Something he memorized years ago in that Sunday school was coming back to him. It was a scripture reading, a reading from the gospel of Matthew.

Jesus was talking to a crowd of people from a mount, "You have heard that it was said to your ancestors, 'You shall not kill; and whoever kills will be liable to judgment. But I say to you, whoever is angry with his brother will be liable to judgment, and whoever says, 'You fool,' will be liable to fiery Gehenna. Therefore, if you bring your gift to the altar, and there recall that your brother has anything against you, leave your gift at the altar, go first and be reconciled with your brother, and then come and offer your gift.'

Peter trembled as the truth of what Jesus said hit him. He couldn't claim ignorance because as a child he knew. To hate someone was the same as murder. Peter hated Vinny and Eva. He committed murder in his heart and he tried to legally murder them through the court system. Peter looked up to the monstrance in desperation.

"Help me, Jesus! Teach me to forgive! I can't do it without you!" Lowering his head Peter felt a sense of peace. He knew Jesus would help him. He would trust in God from now on.

Peter felt himself being drawn again. The God of the Universe, the Eucharistic Lord, was calling him. Peter embraced his belief that the Jesus that called him was His God. Before Peter was a God who humbled Himself to walk as one simple man on the earth. He now came to Peter in the humble form of bread, as if to announce He was the basis of life. Here to feed his people he came in such a simple way. In His simplicity, as he walked the earth few recognized him. Peter recognized Him; the Love was so great that he could not resist the calling. Looking up, empty of tears, Peter could feel nothing but the twitching of his muscles reacting to the fear of what he would see. His stomach fluttered with apprehension.

Peter was again in the valley. A cool breeze touched his cheek. Peter watched two men offering their sacrifices at the altar. Why was he seeing this again? Had he missed something? Peter watched carefully. The Lord poured his love out to both men. Cain as before, drew Abel to the killing field. Peter watched as Cain lifted the rock above the back of Abel's head. Then suddenly the scene changed as he viewed now from a different angle.

Peter was in front now. He could see the hatred on Cain's face. He could see the rage that reddened his skin as the sneer of jealously distorted Cain's features. Peter recognized the face—it was his own! He couldn't look. It was just too painful.

Tearing his eyes away, he turned toward the unsuspecting face of Abel. Peter's muscles stopped shaking. He sat in shocked stillness. The face he stared at was the face of Abel. It was identical to Cain's face. It was Peter's face. Peter was both—Cain and Abel! Peter watched as the scene played itself out. He could not move in spite of his urge to leave. Peter didn't want to see. He wanted to run but remained frozen. He watched as he lifted the rock and killed himself.

The scene faded. The light disappeared and Peter was still sitting on the wooden pew. The silence of the darkened church reverberated through his mind. Peter sat still and silent in the church as his soul screamed. The scream rose from deep within him and took him by surprise. He could swear he screamed aloud but looking around at his fellow worshippers, he realized he had not. He looked back to the monstrance on the altar. Shining between the candles, the Lord betrayed nothing. Peter couldn't get the vision of what he had just seen out of his mind. He killed himself! What did it mean?

Peter couldn't understand it. He was alive. He hadn't killed himself. He never thought of suicide. What was God trying to tell him? Peter's heart fluttered with fear. He wasn't sure this was something he wanted to see. Even as he tried to slow his breathing he couldn't quiet his mind. Peter used the relaxation technique he taught his patients who suffered from anxiety attacks. He sat back and pictured each muscle in his body relaxing. Peter mentally pictured each muscle slowly relaxing. He slowed his breath, and made each inhalation just a little deeper. It relieved the shakiness but his fevered mind could not ignore the promptings of his God.

"Relax, relax," Peter advised himself. *Think, slowly, what does Jesus mean?*

I am Cain. I have been so full of hatred and jealousy. Eva loves Vinny. Do I even want her back? No! Do I want a practice with Vinny? Of course not, that part of my life is over so why can't I let it go. Why can't I forgive them and move on?

Peter understood how he ended up as Cain. Who was the Abel of his vision? Peter didn't understand. Abel was good and believed in God. Abel gave God the best of what he had. When had Peter done that? He suddenly heard a gentle voice.

"In your dreams, your childhood dreams," the voice whispered.

Peter couldn't see anything. The sighing voice was so low Peter wasn't even sure he heard it. He couldn't see the angel who stood before him but Father D'Angelico could see her.

"In your dreams, your childhood dreams!" The angel slowly faded from view. Father D'Angelico knew the man would find his way now. Peter wondered how the Abel of his vision could symbolize a childhood dream. His dream as a child was to join his father as a country doctor. He spent long afternoons pretending to treat the poor mountain folks. He dreamed of marrying Katy and living on the mountain.

Who changed that dream? He had. Peter was responsible for his own death as surely as if he committed suicide. He killed the Peter that God made. The realization of it stunned him.

As the truth dawned on Peter, a sense of peace filled him and he understood. He alone was responsible for the harm done to the little boy with the dream of being a country doctor. He alone had killed the little boy. Now that he knew, what was he going to do about it?

Feeling for the envelope that contained the ten thousand dollars which was all that remained of his former life, Peter laughed. If he kept this money, he would be the richest man on the mountain. Suddenly Peter's values changed and not enough was much more than it had been just a short time ago. Now it seemed like too much.

Peter already made up his mind. He was going home. If he were lucky his parents would help him. If he were blessed, Katy would still want him. He would become the Peter God meant him to be. He would live the life that would bring him true happiness. Peter would live a life of giving to the poor, a simple life. Dr. Peter Caine fell to his knees, lowered his head into his hands and wept. The coldness had left, Dr. Peter Caine was alive again!

Seven

Blessed art thou, among women And blessed is the Fruit of thy womb. (Luke 1:42)

The oversized clock that hung on the generic wall of the hospital waiting room screamed at Patricia Walsh. She wanted to scream back. However, unlike the pulsing clock, Patricia sat, her racing heart keeping time with the clicks of the timekeeper. Her mind was numb with fear. When would she see Megan? The doctor was taking too long. Still, Patricia took that as a sign of hope. She prayed Megan wasn't dead.

The memory of Megan's body flying through the air crushed Patricia's hope. How could anyone, especially such a small child, survive such a trauma? Patricia tried to still her hands as they shook with fear. She wanted to hold her baby. Patricia wanted to tell Megan everything was going to be all right. She wanted to smell the sweet warmth of her baby as she held her. Was that ever going to happen?

Oh, God, can you hear me? This is all my fault! Don't take my baby. All she wanted was her doll. She's so full of love. Love even for a ragged stuffed monkey. Don't let her die!

Patricia's face whitened as she prayed to an apparently silent God. People tried to comfort her but it was useless.

She prayed in silent desperation, as time stood still. Finally, a tiny glimmer of hope arrived with the doctor.

Dr. Puglisi was a small muscular man. Dressed in scrubs he barely filled, he had a large presence that filled a room. His confidence and knowledge gave his peace. Patricia gravitated to his spirit. Here was the man who knew all about her baby. Here was the man who would make everything all right again. Patricia looked for a sign in his dark eyes. Her own eyes filled with tears as fear gripped her heart.

"Mrs. Walsh?" the doctor said gently. Patricia nodded as he sat beside her. Ignoring all others in the waiting room, Dr. Puglisi took her hand. "She's alive and appears to be holding her own." Patricia collapsed in grateful tears as renewed hope washed over her. This doctor was the center of her world now. She hung on his every word.

"Mrs. Walsh, your daughter has had all her x-rays and blood tests. There is extensive damage, as you would expect from such a bad trauma. However, none of the damage seems to be beyond repair. She has a compound fracture of the right tibia that will need surgery to be repaired. She has three broken ribs, but thank God, none of those ribs punctured her lung." Patricia felt the hope rise up through her heart as the doctor continued. "We were, of course, most worried about head trauma. And there I am afraid we are not out completely of the woods yet." The doctor's face was set in grim determination. "Have you been able to contact your husband?"

Patricia nodded, "I called his company. They are trying to trace him down. They'll have him call the hospital as soon as they reach him."

The physician stood and calmly stated, "A nurse is going to come in and ask you to sign some papers. The papers are permission to take Megan into surgery. It's best not to wait too long. Are you ready to make that decision or do you want to speak to your husband first?"

There was no question in her mind. She had full confidence in this doctor and answered, "If you say she needs the surgery than I trust you. I know you'll take care of my baby." Patricia's face reddened and puckered with the tears she fought to hold back. "She's all I have, you know!"

Dr. Puglisi was touched, "I'll do my best to bring her home to you. You just pray." As the doctor turned to leave he heard the question he had been trying to avoid.

Patricia called out, "Can I see her? I just want to be with her before she goes to surgery!"

The doctor grimaced at the thought her mother seeing Megan who was still a non-responsive, bloodied mess. He hoped to whisk the small girl to surgery before her mother could see her.

"Of course, just follow me!" He had no choice even though he would have preferred to spare her this sight. Megan would seem so much better after surgery. This whole thing would be so much easier for this young woman to handle with her husband beside her. What the physician left out in his talk with this pretty mother was his concern. Megan had not responded to even painful stimuli. The mild concussion did not explain that despite his attempts to arouse her, she did not respond. Perhaps she would do so after surgery.

Patricia was not prepared for the sight of her daughter. She seemed so small and lost on the stretcher in the Pediatric Intensive Care Unit. Machines beeped and hummed around her. Her face was so bloody and swollen that Patricia barely recognized her. The nurse gave Patricia a chair so she could sit at her daughter's bedside.

Patricia sat in stunned silence trying to recognize her baby. It was a shock to see Megan this way. An IV pushed fluids through a machine that hummed and whirled. Glowing green lines moved and spiked across a screen above Megan's head. It took a few moments for Patricia to fully comprehend the situation. The shock of it numbed her.

As she looked at her daughter, her heart broke. She was

afraid to touch her at first, but she couldn't help herself. Patricia reached over and stroked Megan's hair. It was stiff with dried blood. Just a few hours ago, she had washed and braided her long silky tresses. Megan didn't move.

"Megan, Megan, it's Mommy. Can you hear me?" Patricia hoped for a response but there was none. "Mommy is here! Mommy won't leave you!" Patricia stroked the forehead of her only child. Megan didn't open her eyes. Patricia hoped it was because Megan had been given strong sedatives. *Well, of course, it was.* They wouldn't let a little girl suffer. The thought made Patricia feel better as they came to wheel her baby to surgery. She had no way of knowing that they never gave anyone with head injuries pain medication. She was better off in her ignorance. In her mind, she believed Megan was on her way to recovery.

Patricia kissed her forehead as they wheeled Megan away. She didn't want to leave her. Patricia didn't want to go back to that horrible waiting room. Dr. Puglisi explained to her that she would be waiting for hours. It was a lengthy surgery. Patricia prayed as she longed for David's arms to hold her. All of her neighbors who had come to stay with her meant well, but they couldn't really comfort her. They didn't feel the same as she did. Only one other person loved Megan as she did and that was her father. Patricia longed for him. Yet she felt an unnatural fear. What would he say? The accident was all her fault. Would he blame her? She dreaded telling him what happened. David doted on Megan. Would he hate her for what happened?

Why had she thrown that stupid monkey out? She never dreamed such a simple thing would have such serious consequences.

Questions blew through Patricia's mind like hurricane winds. Where was David? Would he hold her or reject her? She couldn't imagine anything but love. He had never shown her anything but love. Her own guilt condemned her. Would he?

What Patricia longed for, she feared the most. She could do nothing but pray. She took out her rosaries. Maybe everyone would leave her alone if she seemed deep in prayer. She wanted to be alone. She only wanted David and Megan. No one else could help her.

As she prayed, the mother of God flooded Patricia Walsh with the grace she would need to get through the trials that faced her. As she prayed she realized Mary, the Mother of Jesus would understand how she felt. *"Hail Mary full of Grace. Blessed art thou among women..."*

Megan rolled up like a tight ball against the white wall and hoped she was invisible. She closed her eyes. Perhaps if she didn't look no one would be able to see her. She cried for her Mommy until the tears dried up. She licked her lips and tasted the salt of her dried tears. Her eyes hurt. She had no more tears. Megan gasped for air as her sobbing subsided. Megan never cried so long without loving arms to hold and comfort her. Usually Mommy or Daddy helped her before she cried this long. But this time no one came.

I'm all alone! Megan could feel the fear as if it were a strange creature that sat hard on her heart. The fear was so heavy, unlike the white cool mist that surrounded her. She listened first in case something was there. When she couldn't hear anything, she decided to uncurl herself. Megan, for the first time in her life was aware she was alone. She uncurled her body and leaned against the wall. It took all her courage to open her eyes and look around.

It took a moment for her red and swollen eyes to focus. She realized the room was still covered in white smoky mist. To Megan it seemed like a dream, a strange dream. The room remained the same and she saw the beautiful lady who had carried her. The lady stood immobile like a statue people put on their dressers. Her mother had one on her bedroom dresser. But this lady was different. She had a large sword that she held straight up in front of her. It was as if she was waiting for a fight. She looked determined. Megan wished she would move. Megan felt safe in her arms before but now she didn't seem real. She didn't move or blink. Megan was frightened.

Behind the lady was a dark opening. It looked the same as before. As Megan stared at the dark hole, something moved in the dark. She could feel the terror seize her heart as she pushed herself back against the wall. Megan didn't want to look at the dark opening any more. She looked at the stairs that led up to a doorway although it was hard to see through the mist. Megan wondered if she should climb the stairs and try the door. Her fear stopped her; Megan couldn't move. She just sat there. Why wouldn't someone come and help her? Where was her Mommy? Megan's tears rose to the surface again. If only her Daddy would come. Maybe they didn't know where she was.

"Daddy! Daddy!" Megan screamed at the top of her lungs. The sound seemed muffled by the mist. The louder she called the more the mist collected around her. It frightened her. Megan lowered her head in her hands so she wouldn't see the mist that now blanketed her. It made it hard for her to see the statue lady. Then Megan heard a noise. It seemed to come from above her. It sounded like someone was moving in an upstairs room. Megan was used to hearing the people in the apartment above hers. It was a muffled walking sound like someone walking on carpeting. Megan strained to hear the soft sounds but the mist made it hard to hear. Megan heard faint blips like a machine. It was so hard to hear that she cupped her ear and pointed it toward the ceiling. Megan tried to still her own breathing as it too interfered with the soft sounds.

"Mommy's here!"

Megan could hardly hear the words but she instantly recognized her mother's voice. Megan started to yell. "Mommy, I'm down here! Mommy, Mommy come and get me!"

Did Mommy hear me? Megan strained to listen again. She heard nothing. "Mommy! Mommy!" Megan started to get up. *Mommy must be upstairs. I'll go up to her.* Megan walked through the mist toward the stairs. The fog grew thicker and she was breathing something that smelled very bad. It had a medicine smell like the doctor's office and it made her dizzy. She struggled back to the wall. Megan felt weak. She leaned against the wall, slid down to the bottom and fell asleep.

Dr. Puglisi waited for the anesthesia to take effect. Even though the girl had been non-responsive, he didn't want to take any chances. A memory of such pain might scar her for life. It took hours of intense work to pin and stabilize the tibia for it had been shattered badly. Much more than the x-rays revealed.

As Dr. Puglisi watched the attendants wheel the little girl into the recovery room, he hoped she would survive. It would be hours before the anesthetic wore off. He hoped she would wake up to her mother's voice.

Patricia noticed the crowd of well-wishers had dwindled over the many hours of surgery. Many of the women had to leave to go get their own children to bed for school the next day. Megan wouldn't be going to school. She wouldn't be playing with her new friend, Jessica. Patricia felt numb inside. She couldn't think about that now. She had to concentrate on Megan getting well. It was a blessing that Megan was still alive. Patricia prayed she would stay alive.

She waited, rosary in hand, for news from the surgeon. The nurse informed her that the trucking company reached David and he was on his way. Patricia longed for him. She wanted to fall into those strong arms that would carry her through this nightmare. David would make everything all right. That is, if he didn't blame her for the accident. Patricia feared this the most. What would she do if David rejected her?

Patricia was deep in prayer for over an hour when David arrived. He quickly spanned the room. His arms surrounded her, embracing her as she clung to him.

In a soft voice he asked, "Pat, how are you holding up? I'm so sorry I wasn't here to help you." Patricia wept as David apologized for his absence.

Patricia held her husband tightly as she answered, "David, I'm sorry. The accident was all my fault. I tried to stop her from running into the street. I just wasn't quick enough." She sobbed as David held her tightly. She felt she'd betrayed him by allowing their daughter to get hurt.

"Tell me what happened." David said. Patricia was burdened with guilt and talking was the best therapy. Sitting beside her, David listened to his wife.

"I threw that stupid monkey in the trash can out front. Megan didn't see me. I figured the garbage men would take it while she was in school. I can't believe what happened!" Patricia broke down in tears as David tried to comfort her. He held her as her sobbing subsided.

Patricia continued, "The boys must have fished it out of the can. They tied it to the phone pole for target practice. You know, you've seen them do it before. They tied it up with twine so they could hit it with rocks. That's what they were doing when Megan and I were walking home from school. I never expected it! The garbage hadn't been picked up yet. Megan ran so fast. The car couldn't stop. My baby is in surgery and it's all my fault."

David pulled away and looked deeply into his wife's eyes. Her eyes were so like Megan's. Putting his hand beneath Patricia's chin, David started, "I want you to stop blaming yourself. It was an accident. Not your fault. No one could have predicted this. Do you think it was my fault?"

Patricia was stunned. "No, of course not, what do you mean? How could it be your fault? You weren't even there."

"Exactly, I blame myself for not being there. It was Megan's birthday and her first day of school, but I was working."

"Oh David, you were just doing what you had to do!"

"Well, it is still my fault. I was the one who brought the new monkey. I talked Megan into the doll hospital. If only I had gotten rid of the monkey a month ago like you wanted to. I should have listened. This is all my fault."

Patricia couldn't believe David was blaming himself. It was ridiculous!

She hugged him and answered, "None of this is your fault. You couldn't have stopped the accident even if you had been there. It all happened so fast. The driver couldn't see her. He couldn't stop in time. The man cried. He said it was his fault even though he was going below the speed limit." Patricia stopped crying. She was sincere in her attempt to alleviate her husband's guilt.

"I'll stop blaming myself if you will. Everyone can find a reason for blame. Guilt is a waste. It was an accident, pure and simple."

Patricia realized that David was right. It was self indulgent to focus on what could have prevented the accident. "I know you're right. We have to concentrate on Megan getting well. She's in surgery. The doctor gave me a lot of hope that the injuries are temporary."

David gave Patricia a hug.

"Let's pray then. Prayer is the best thing we can do for Megan." As they bowed their heads in prayer for their daughter, she was being wheeled out of surgery.

Dr. Puglisi saw them praying as he entered the waiting room. Patricia introduced David to the doctor who then gave his report.

"The surgery went very well. The bone is pinned and should heal well. She's a very strong little girl."

"Can we see her?" David asked.

Dr. Puglisi smiled. "Yes, I think you will find her in much better shape than she was when she got here," he said as he led them to the recovery room. Megan was lying on a bed and cleaned up. Her leg was up on pillows and wrapped in a soft cast. Her color seemed much better. Patricia felt hopeful and turned to the doctor and asked, "When will the anesthesia wear off? Do you think she'll be able to talk soon?"

The doctor hesitated before he answered, "There is no way of knowing," he tried to stress the words. "It's different with everyone." Dr. Puglisi shook his head as he left the two parents at Megan's bedside. He prayed that the child would wake up.

Eight

For those who are led by the Spirit of God are children of God. For you did not receive a spirit of slavery to fall back into fear, but you received a spirit of adoption, through which we cry, 'Abba, Father!'
(Rom. 8:14)

Maisie Johnson sat toward the back of the church. She walked quietly on soft-soled shoes and the whisper of her presence could be easily missed. Not far from the priest, she sat without stirring. The silent worship of the night contrasted with the emotions that screamed through her mind. She was cold after walking the three blocks from the prison in tears. Her sobs went unheard covered by the roar of the Nor'easter.

The only other time Maisie felt like this was that night fifty-five years ago. She was only seven then, but she was a big girl.

She remembered her Daddy smiling, *"Maisie you're a strapping girl, a fine strapping girl."*

Maisie didn't known what *strapping* meant. Her daddy's smile told her it was a good thing. Maisie loved it when her daddy smiled. The memory of those hot molasses nights on the front porch in Alabama flowed over her.

The memory of her parent's love often conjured up

images of that old wooden porch. Early evenings, in the humid summer, her mama would sit and peel sweet potatoes. While Mama peeled, the children would gather around Papa as he told tales of long-ago times. The sharecropper's porch creaked years of neglect as the family shared precious moments. Laughter and memories of songs, happy nights that tumbled into one another until that night when Maisie turned seven.

That night no laughter rang on the front porch. The croaking of the bullfrogs filled the sultry night. A smothering blanket of silence covered the small home. A sense of imminent evil descended on the children as adult whispers filled the tiny rooms. Darkness called. When the light of the burning cross flickered through the window, Maisie knew evil had arrived. Men screamed outside, calling her daddy's name. Maisie's eyes widened as her daddy's body quivered. Kissing all of them, he whispered '*I love you*' in Maisie's ear. She wrapped her arms around his neck but they couldn't hide him from the evil. He held Mama the longest and last.

Standing by the door, Maisie watched his back straighten and his shoulders square as he stepped tall and proud onto the porch. Maisie watched through the window as the men, hidden in white robes and hoods, careened their pick-up trucks around the burning cross and turned for her daddy. Maisie screamed and shrieked at the men to let him go. She shouted as they threw a length of rope over the large branch of an old sycamore tree. Maisie howled as she watched the hooded figures drag her daddy from the porch.

Maisie shrieked into the night, "I know who you are! You're the grocer man!"

That's when her Mama slapped her. "You shut up Maisie. Stop your screams!" cried Mama as her dark hand covered her own screams.

Maisie never screamed again. She wanted to scream as Mama and the boys struggled to take her daddy's body down off that tree. She wanted to scream when the preacher talked of forgiveness as they buried her daddy but she didn't. Maisie grew quiet—so quiet her mama said she was the best child in the whole world. Maisie was no longer strapping. She seemed to stop growing that night.

How she did love this church. Maisie remembered the first time Miss Mona brought her here. She had been amazed to see both colored and whites praying together. Back home the colored had their own church and the whites went to a different church on the other side of town. No colored person was ever allowed into a white church, not if he wanted to live. Maisie remembered asking her daddy if Jesus was colored or white.

With laughing eyes, her daddy answered. "Maisie, I'm sure from the way he died he was one of us, but I wouldn't tell that to no white person if I was you."

Looking up to the crucifix hanging as the centerpiece of the ornate altar, Maisie thought her daddy was right. Only a colored man would be killed that way. Jesus was a good man who loved people just like her daddy.

Maisie looked around the church. She was the only colored woman in here. Now the word "colored" is considered a bad word, a racist word. When Maisie was growing up down south, they used much worse words. "Colored" was one of the kindest words. That's what the white men called her back then. That's what Maisie called herself now.

Ever since Miss Mona demanded Maisie take her to this church that Sunday morning so long ago she had loved this church. Maisie was mad, hopping mad as Mama used to say. Sunday was supposed to be a day of rest, a free day for Maisie. She usually went down to Mama's house to see the baby on Sunday. Now this old white woman was making Maisie take her to church on Sunday mornings. It cut Maisie's free day in half. Maisie was hopping mad at Miss Mona but she said nothing. She dressed up and with tight lips walked Miss Mona down to the little church tucked away in a corner of the city.

She was in awe. She'd never seen such a beautiful church. Gold-leaf glowed against the shining marble. Candles cast magical light and shadow. Murals told the stories of the life of Jesus.

Hanging in the vestibule of the church was a picture of the Black Madonna. The dark mother of Jesus, dressed in ornate gold and silver, stunned Maisie. Maisie was 22 when she first saw the icon. Torn away from the image by the grumpy complaints of Miss Mona, Maisie reluctantly left the picture. Entering the main church, Maisie again stood transfixed. At the center of the church, where all eyes were easily drawn, hung a crucifix. Both the cross and the man who hung upon it were a deep camel color. Jesus wasn't quite a black man, he was a mix. Just like her baby at home. Maisie was stunned. Both colored and white knelt before the brown Jesus.

Miss Mona made Maisie take her every Sunday after that, so Maisie didn't get to smell and stroke the mocha skin of her baby girl until afternoon. That baby was all Maisie had.

Work in Miss Mona's big brownstone never seemed to end. Miss Mona cried for this or that all day long. Between her cries, Maisie cleaned and cooked. The baby waited for Wednesday and Sunday love. Her baby waited at Mama's house.

Maisie blamed herself. She should have listened to Mama. The afternoon of daddy's funeral, Mama made all the children get on the train. Mama's sister lived in a city in the north that was much safer. The smell of hazy swamps was exchanged for the smoky scent of burning oil and salt water. The soft cry of bullfrogs, for the horns of clogged traffic. The family left for a new life of freedom that was supposed to be better.

Hatred was raw in the swamp. Alabama's hate hung in damp heat, coating the people. It kept blacks in their own schools and restrooms. It was brutally raw and never hidden.

In the north, it was concealed. Racism was covered in polite low pay and generous poor housing. Like a cold wind blowing through the cement canyons of the city, Maisie never really saw it. She never failed to feel it. Racism up north was cold and surgical, bitter and biting like the chilling winds. Racism was buried like the people in heavy coats and heavy lies.

The elderly woman knelt longer than she should have on her bony knees—knees that perpetually ached from years of scrubbing floors. No longer able to stand the pain, Maisie sat quietly on the long empty pew not wanting to disturb the others. Maisie opened her eyes. The darkness inside her was too deep to bear.

The old priest looked sick. His breathing was heavy, a deeper sleep would come to him soon. Miss Mona breathed like him for the two weeks before she died. Death, what was it really? Did Jesus come for you as the preacher always taught? Or did you just go to sleep and never wake up? Either way Maisie was ready for it. There was too much pain in this world and Maisie was tired of feeling pain. She didn't want to face what lay ahead. Maybe Jesus in His mercy would take her. Maybe He would even take her instead of her great-grandson, Johnny. Maisie prayed for that!

At her age death seemed like an old friend. She met him more than once over the years. The last time was when Miss Mona passed in the big pine bed in her upstairs bedroom. Miss Mona held Maisie's hand, clinging to the one who had shared these last long years of her empty life. Miss Mona died an old maid in a large and empty house. Maisie knew how lonely Miss Mona was. Miss Mona had a lot of money, but the money her father had left her was a curse instead of a blessing. The truth was that all of the people in Miss Mona's life loved her money more than they loved her.

Only Maisie seemed to know or care about the frightened little girl who lived inside the elderly woman, the little girl who longed for love that never came. Love never knocked on the door of the ornate brownstone and so Miss Mona left this world for a better life with Jesus. She left holding the black hand of the only person she ever trusted.

Miss Mona was remote, and yet a strange kind of friend. She believed in the old ways. Miss Mona maintained a wall of separation between herself and those who worked for her.

The passing of years, however, changed things. Shared experiences connected the two women and crossed all lines of separation. They shared a home and as that sharing spanned the decades, the closeness grew. Color or station grew to matter little as the heart learned to love. While the friendship between Miss Mona and Maisie blossomed, a strict decorum was still followed — an outer appearance of distance was maintained. In the eyes of others, the two women never crossed the line of employer and employee. In her heart, each woman knew better. Miss Mona reached out to her black housekeeper in her hour of need. It was enough to seal a lifelong friendship. Miss Mona reached out when Maisie needed it the most — the day Baby died.

Maisie had started housekeeping as a young girl after Mama got her a job. The work required her to stay at the house. She was lonely there, isolated from her family for the first time in her life. For the first few weeks, she cried herself to sleep on the small cot in the tiny bedroom off the kitchen. The large house was so different from her family's small home. No one smiled or laughed here. The house was full of expensive treasures, yet seemed so empty. Maisie worked hard to impress the white family, but felt as if she were invisible to them. No one ever talked to her except to give her an order. Mama warned her to stay away from the other workers. Maisie realized now that her mama tried to teach her the dangers of growing up too fast. "Watch out Maisie. Stay away from boys." Mama warned Maisie as the spring breezes of womanhood blew gently.

"Don't you look at the gardener's boy." Mama warned

her away from all the dark boys of the house. She never thought about the white boy. And in her loneliness, Maisie was easy prey for the teenage son of the white family. Maisie was swept away by the summer thrill of forbidden love on staircases and back rooms.

For weeks, their secret meetings were all Maisie looked forward to. She was in love. She was sure that he loved her even though he never acknowledged her in the presence of others. Maisie ignored that. She dreamed of the day they would marry. Maisie was sure it was eternal love. But the summer love only lasted until the winds of autumn blew, and with them the crushing consequence of that love: Love could not describe the household's reaction to Maisie's condition. The father of her child not only rejected any responsibility, but denied it. Maisie was dismissed from her job and from his life.

Baby was born in the early spring of Maisie's sixteenth year. Mocha skin and bright blue eyes foretold the girl's future beauty. Maisie named her Julia but everyone called her Baby. Mama took Maisie out of school and got her the job with Miss Mona. She took care of Miss Mona all week and saw Baby two days a week. It seemed like the best thing to do at the time.

Baby grew and thrived in Mama's house. Maisie loved Baby on the days she rounded the corner after the bus ride from uptown. But Baby called her mother Mama and that made Maisie cry; Mama didn't seem to notice. Maisie was more like a visitor to the child and Maisie couldn't blame her. Gifts and short hugs didn't replace long everyday love. Her Baby grew without her.

Mama died suddenly. Without warning she fell during one of Maisie's visits. Maisie watched the falling plate shatter as her Mama's heart stopped beating and her lips turn blue. Mama's heart never started again. Maisie hoped that Jesus took her to Daddy. She hoped that what the preachers taught was true. Baby came to Miss Mona's to live only because

Miss Mona decided it.

Sweeping into Mama's wake in her best wide brimmed hat, Miss Mona took one look at Maisie's brothers and announced that Baby would come live with her. Maisie was shocked but Miss Mona insisted. At the age of ten, Baby came to the big brownstone uptown. Miss Mona dressed Baby in pretty dresses and sent her to school. Maisie thought it was good for Baby to go to such a good school and live in a white neighborhood. But Baby never quite fit in. She looked white but the other kids knew she wasn't, and they never let her forget it. Baby grew hard and in a few years she became bitter.

Baby grew in the time of pride when blacks no longer asked but learned to demand. Baby grew out of dresses and into bell-bottomed jeans and tie-dyed shirts. The straightened hair Baby always wore grew natural and round. She became prouder of being black than the militants who were now attracted to her. Flames lit the city the night Baby ran away. She was old enough to be ashamed of Maisie for her lack of education and angry at the way Maisie waited on the solitary Miss Mona. Baby's anger burned like the city.

Maisie cried for Baby often during the dark nights of the next ten years. She longed to hold Baby, but could only hold her in whispers and rumors. Rumors of militant Baby who got involved with drugs and crime filled her lonely ears. She longed for Baby to give up her wild life and come home. Maisie grew tired and old while waiting.

One evening, ten years after Baby ran away, as Maisie poured Miss Mona's evening tea into the flowered porcelain cup, the phone that never rang sang out. Baby was in the hospital and needed her Mama. Miss Mona sent her chauffer and he rushed Maisie down to the poor county hospital in the rubble-strewn neighborhood.

Baby lay on the bed in the ward that reeked of poverty and despair. Ignored by the overworked staff, she received minimum care. Maisie sat by Baby's bed for days as her hope diminished. Miss Mona called the doctor. She let Maisie know how dissatisfied she was with his care. She begged Maisie to have Baby transferred. Miss Mona was sure that with better medical care Baby could survive. Maisie never asked for the transfer.

The drugs Baby took had paled her skin and slowed her breathing so much that she never woke up. Baby never saw her mama as she sat in her best hat and coat, holding her hand, watching the daughter she lost so many years ago slip away. Baby's anger was gone, numbed by the drugs that consumed her life. Baby left her mother and her lonely world without a whimper.

Miss Mona herself came to get Maisie and the little boy Baby left behind. Miss Mona walked with courage into the tenement to get the small boy. The only leftover of Baby's lost life screamed curses at Miss Mona who carried him down the broken stairs to his grandmother. The only gift Baby ever gave Maisie turned out to be the best gift she ever received.

It took a month for Miss Mona and Maisie to wash the drug den off little Willie. Lice and neglect consumed the first three years of his life. Obscenities, the only words he knew, turned to smiles. Maisie poured all of her pent-up love on Willie. Miss Mona watched with approval as Maisie finally found the child she lost in little Willie.

On the night that Baby died, Miss Mona became more than a demanding boss. On the outside, all was the same but her love became visible. It was during the first year Willie came to live with them that Maisie turned Catholic. Each week Miss Mona and Maisie would bring Willie to Mass and the little corner church became a home.

Maisie watched the drunk as he shivered in the pew across the aisle. He seemed so lost in his withdrawal. She heard the young white woman two pews in front of her sobbing softly into the endless stream of tissues that popped from her purse. Maisie looked to the Eucharistic Lord and prayed for both of them. There were so many troubles in this world, so much pain. Maisie couldn't stand the pain anymore. Could you take me home Jesus? Could you take me instead of my great-grandson, Johnny? I'm so tired of the pain. I feel the pain in my Willie's eyes. Maisie could drown in the deep brown pools of pain in Willie's eyes. The real Willie was lost in the sorrow.

The real Willie was joy. From the start, Willie was large, smiling, and joyous. Maisie thought he grew to look just like her daddy.

Miss Mona paid the bus fare to take little Willie downtown to the colored school. She didn't want him to get lost like Baby, in the whiteness of Miss Mona's world. Willie grew strong and blossomed as love poured all over him. Willie, and Willie alone, could make Miss Mona's face shine as he filled her life with tales of adventure. As a little boy, he sang songs of life and delight on Miss Mona's lap.

Maisie knew from the start that he was special. As a young man, he colored Miss Mona's secluded and darkened world with a light that gave a warm glow. Willie brought the love he received full circle. Miss Mona paid the tuition for Willie to go to the trade school were he learned the art of mechanics. He loved to work with his hands. Large black hands that fixed engines and lives with a turn and a smile. A strapping man, he filled Miss Mona with happiness until her death.

A big happy man with a big happy family, he had large rooms above his downtown garage. Those rooms were big enough for Maisie after Miss Mona died. Maisie moved in with Willie and lived with his wife and five children in happiness until two years ago—when the joy in Willie's house died.

Willie's five children were fine and strong and basked in

the love that filled their home. All of Willie's children grew up healthy and well, except for Johnny. Johnny was the baby with mocha skin and baby blue eyes, eyes that could often lie and deceive. Confused like Baby about who he was, he tried to make his own world.

In Johnny's world, he was a star. He dreamed of being a star on the stage or in the movies. He dreamed of the fame that would carry him to a world where he would be idolized and worshipped, a place so high that the mix of his blue eyes and dark skin wouldn't matter.

Johnny needed money. He didn't want to settle for ordinary acting and dance lessons—only the best was good enough for Johnny. He didn't have the money he needed to travel to the world he wanted to live in. Willie gave him what he could, but nothing was ever good enough for Johnny.

Johnny did whatever he needed to do to get money. He learned to bend the truth early and had no trouble bending life to make things reach his hands. Being an actor, no one knew when he lied—no one but Maisie. Maisie could tell because Maisie remembered Baby.

He lied about the crowd he ran with. He lied about the drugs that provided the money he needed. Maisie tried to warn Willie, but love refused to see. Johnny stole, dealt drugs and lied. Maisie could smell the lies on Johnny. The night the man at the corner store was shot and robbed for the cash in his register Maisie knew Johnny knew more about it than he claimed. Maisie knew he told the truth only when he said he hadn't done it himself.

The police looked amused when Johnny pronounced his innocence. Sold out by the true gunman who just wanted to deal his way out of the jam he was in, Johnny took the fall. Now, finally everyone believed Johnny lied. They believed it on the only occasion that Johnny told the truth. Only Maisie could smell the truth. Only Maisie was sure Johnny had nothing to do with the grocer's death.

The jury didn't believe him as he cried and professed his

innocence. The lost child wept in pain but the jury saw a murderer. One week over eighteen and in a city on a crime spree, Johnny became the poster boy of a tough new approach. The joy in Willie died the day Johnny was found guilty. The light of love in Willie's strong soul went out the day Johnny was sentenced to death by lethal injection.

Maisie knew Johnny was telling the truth. She had known from the beginning, but she knew he wasn't telling the whole truth. It took Maisie a long time to get Johnny to open up. He lied about his whereabouts and drowned in that lie during the trial. As others lost faith, Maisie's faith grew. Lost in the lies he told, Johnny continued to cry for his life. No one seemed to hear him and so he closed up. Maisie had to win his trust. Tonight he reached out to her. Tonight Johnny, through smudged glass, cried the truth. Johnny told Maisie of that drug-filled night and the friends who shared it with him. Friends, who after a night of abandon, took an early morning flight to Los Angeles. These two friends were the only ones who could verify Johnny's alibi.

Maisie left the prison a broken woman. She finally had the truth but it was too late. Johnny would sleep forever, because he told the truth too late. He was scheduled to be executed tomorrow.

Miss Mona would have known what to do. She would have called all the right people because she had connections. Miss Mona left all her money to Maisie, but she couldn't leave her power. Maisie used much of the money for Johnny's defense attorneys. The best in the city and they couldn't save Johnny from the prideful lies he told.

Johnny knew who killed the grocer, but he refused to rat anyone out. Almost proud of the notoriety of being convicted, Johnny kept silent. It was as if he was playing a part in a movie, and he played tough. Displaying his acting skills, he seemed unafraid. That is until the night the cold hard reality of his impending death crashed down upon him. With sweat on his brow and quivered lips, he cried the truth to

Maisie.

Too late, too late, Maisie's heart cried.

Her soul screaming in the pain of impotence, Maisie left the prison and came to the little church. Longing for a miracle that only Jesus could give, Maisie prayed. She couldn't look at Willie knowing the truth. Willie had accepted Johnny's lies and when they were exposed, he shrunk under the weight of Johnny's guilt. Johnny was going to die tomorrow. Maisie was sure of that. What could she do?

No one would listen to her, a simple old, black woman. Maisie was sure Johnny would die tomorrow. He would die an innocent man just like her father, and again she would only be able to stand and watch. Maisie couldn't stand to watch as the joy of her life, Willie suffered the death of his son. She knew the change that would overcome him. She had watched her mama's slow death after her daddy's lynching. Her mama lived for years after her daddy's death but in reality she died that night too.

On that night, the night her daddy hung from a tree in her yard, a light died in her mama's eyes.

"What can I do? Who am I?" Maisie softly whispered lost in a sea of pain. Drifting, Maisie heard a voice.

"You're right. You can't do anything. You don't know who you are."

Maisie opened her eyes. Who was speaking in the church? You were supposed to be silent. Looking around, everything seemed normal. The priest slept quietly in the back pew. The drunk seemed to have fallen asleep. The large white woman rubbed her arthritic knees as she rose from the kneeler and sat on the wooden pew. No one was close enough to Maisie to have spoken to her.

Maisie closed her eyes in prayer. She must have imagined the voice.

"Mary, Mary, you don't know who you are in Christ."

Maisie couldn't deny the voice any longer. Mary? No one called her Mary!

Maisie looked up at the monstrance. In the host, in the white host she saw someone. As the rest of the church faded from view, the vision in the monstrance defined itself. A bearded black man sat on a large rock. Dressed in a shining white robe, he looked at Maisie. The love in his eyes was deep and eternal. Maisie felt herself drawn in by the love in those black eyes.

"Mary, Mary you don't know who you are."

Maisie answered the man. She now stood right before Him as he sat on the large rock.

"I know who I am. I'm Maisie. What I don't know is who you are."

A wide smile filled the black man's bearded face.

"You don't know who I am because you don't know who you are."

Maisie wanted to argue, but the light of the man's face stilled her fears. "Who am I?"

The large black man rose and took both of Maisie's small worn hands in his.

"Your name is Mary. Why do you let people call you Maisie? Mary is your baptized name. I have a name special for you. The name written on your spirit is a name unique to you, one that I gave you when I created you. This is the name I'll whisper on the winds that call your spirit to Me at the end of days."

Maisie could taste the hot salty tears. "Jesus, you're Jesus!"

The Man smiled and His piercing eyes scanned the small woman before Him.

"Now you know who I AM. Who are you? All your life you've allowed others to tell you who you are and who you should be. You've lost who you are, the woman I made. You forgot who I called you to be. You allowed Mary to drown in fear. In fear, you became Maisie. Mary, the Mary I created, is a queen, a daughter of the Most High Father. I whispered that to you each day. You allowed your fear to drown my voice."

Maisie humbled before her Maker, wept, "Who am I? Tell me who I am then."

Jesus' strong hand cupped Maisie's chin.

"Look now. Look and see."

Nine

The Spirit itself bears witness with our spirit that we are children of God, and if children, then heirs, heirs of God, and joint heirs with Christ, if only we suffer with him so that we may also be glorified with him. (Rom. 8:16-17)

Maisie awoke sitting in the pew of the church. Nothing changed. What had just happened? Was it a dream? The man she saw, the man she thought was Jesus seemed so real. No one in the church seemed to notice. The bum across the aisle was asleep. The fat white woman sat quietly starring at the monstrance. Maisie noticed the young man sneaking around the pews. She would have to keep an eye on him — he looked dangerous. Maisie looked around but couldn't see the man she had just spoken with. *I must be losing my mind,* she thought. It didn't surprise her. She was so full of sorrow. It was overwhelming. She rubbed her throbbing temples. Johnny was going to die tomorrow. No vision of any imagined man was going to change that. Nothing could be done to change his fate.

The rich looking white man in the front of the church was crying. People carried so many troubles. Maisie started to ask Jesus to help him.

Again, Maisie heard the voice, "Why don't you help

yourself?"

'Oh no, that voice again!' she thought as she returned to her prayers and tried to ignore it. She closed her eyes.

Still, the voice came, "Why don't you pray for yourself?"

Maisie refused to open her eyes and look, though her mind answered the question: Because you should always pray for others, it is selfish to pray for yourself. God doesn't want you to be selfish.

Again, the voice answered her private thoughts, "You think that because you don't know who you are!"

Maisie recognized the voice of Jesus from her vision. She was afraid to open her eyes, afraid of what she would see. Maisie could feel the call of that overpowering love and it overwhelmed her. The pull was so strong. The compulsion to open her eyes and see overcame her desire to hide. Drawn by the eternal calling of her Creator, Maisie tried but could not resist.

Opening her eyes Maisie was pulled into the center of the Eucharist. Like a train speeding through a tunnel, the church around her passed away in a blur. Maisie found herself in a strange new land. The sky was dark and full of foreboding clouds. Cold and bitter winds blew though naked trees along a desolate plain. The roar of the winds echoed the rumbles of the land beneath her. Maisie stood alone and felt the ground groan beneath her. She felt a rolling sensation, a sense that the earth was heaving and about to rupture. Maisie felt dizzy. It was dark and lonely. A crushing sense of danger weighted heavy on her heart, evil was coming. She could taste it.

She heard a strange roaring sound different from the wind. A medieval groan of anger filled the sky above her. Maisie clung to the dark tree beside her as the awful roars in the sky above overpowered the sound of the wind.

In the sky two dragons appeared. The larger dragon cried out in anger as it clawed at the other dragon. Maisie shook with fear as the dragons struggled above her. The battle intensified the storm. Dark clouds swirled through the gray sky as the two monsters clashed in combat. The earth beneath Maisie heaved and broke as she clung to the tree on the darkened plain. Maisie cried out against the wind for help, sure that she couldn't be heard. Her heart pounded with fear and she thought she was about to die.

The two dragons rolled around the troubled skies as their rage tore through the dark clouds. Spitting fire and hatred they tumbled and then rose in combat. They were intent on destruction and oblivious to all else around them. The reverberation of their cries echoed off the land. Fear gripped Maisie's soul. Never was she so sure of her own impending death. The earth seemed to be dying, lost in the anger of the beasts above. She could feel herself being pushed and pulled by the strong gales of wind that blew against her. She was losing her grip.

In terror, she whispered a simple prayer, "Jesus, Jesus!"

Suddenly Maisie saw a tiny spring of water which started to grow in size. Large amounts of water began to pour from the spring. It turned into a stream and then quickly grew into a gushing river. Waves of foaming water rolled over the plain. The water swept everything clean. It even washed the dragons away. Maisie was sure she would be washed away too and she prepared to drown.

Then the scene changed. The plain was gone and as Maisie caught her breath, she saw an old man walking. Where was she now? The old man walked slowly, his long grey beard flowing over the torn rags he wore. A large walking stick supported him as he walked with great determination toward a large palace.

Maisie didn't recognize the land. It seemed ancient. The buildings were fashioned in the style of the ancient Middle East. Did the dragons destroy the earth? Is this all that was left? Maisie couldn't discern past or future.

The deep voice answered her thoughts, "There is no past or future to the Eternal God. I live outside of time."

Maisie pulled her eyes from the old man. The voice that

she recognized now seemed such a comfort as Jesus stood beside her.

"Where am I?" Maisie asked.

The dark man in the shining robe took her hand, "Watch Mary, watch and see. See who you are!"

Maisie turned back to the scene that was playing itself out before her. The old man finally reached the outer court of the palace. He walked back and forth moaning loudly in an ancient song of despair. His dark and ancient cries filled the air as he paced before the palace. Maisie recognized the cry: It was her cry that night on her front porch. The deep cry of pain that pierced the dark Alabama night as her daddy was murdered. It was hate and fear. It was a cry of helplessness and she recognized the mournful sounds that filled the air.

One of the servants inside the palace disappeared through the ornate dark wooden doors of the courtyard. In a hurry, he seemed to be carrying news of the man's actions to someone inside. The bald servant scurried through the long wide corridors of the large palace. Along shining floors of marble, his slippered feet barely made a sound as he wound the corners with confidence. Slowing, finally, before large ornate doors shaped in oval halves and covered with gold and jewels he hesitated for the first time. *'Should I disturb the Queen?'* he thought but quickly reasoned he had no choice. And so the Eunuch who served faithfully and without question softly knocked on the door before him.

A young servant girl covered in silk veils and satin cloth opened the heavy door. She led him through the private chambers to the queen. Large marble columns upheld the ornate carved ceilings that covered the steaming pools where numerous maidens waited to attend the needs of their queen. Large windows opened to interior courtyards revealing lush flowered gardens. The scent of the gardens drifted on the soft morning breeze and flooded through the open window with an intoxicating fragrance. The long walk through the queen's antechamber gave the servant pause to think. It was unusual for any servant to disturb the queen. He had done so only once and that was with a message from the king. This queen was compliant to the king's wishes, but his last queen, the one he served for so many of his years, had not been.

Vashti, the former queen was beautiful. Raised in a wealthy Persian family for just such a royal life, her manners and form were perfect. She carried herself with that air of confidence her state in life required. Beneath the beauty and the well-cultured etiquette was a strain of haughtiness and conceit that flashed in demands and a quick temper. Manners could not hide the selfish conceit of Queen Vasti. The queen managed to hide her defective personality for a short time, but on the day the King summoned the queen to his court, she made a fatal mistake.

King Ahasuerus summoned his queen to his palace after days of celebration and feasting. He demanded the Queen's presence in order to display her beauty. For the first time the King learned her true nature after her refusal to obey his edict. The servant realized the Queen thought herself too good for a drunken King. He watched fearfully as the haughty women in the Queen's inner circle laughed and remarked that her beauty protected her. Arrogantly they dismissed the thought that harm could come from her disobedience. They advised her wrongly which resulted in her loss of station. The King, with the approval of his advisors searched for a new, more accommodating queen.

This new queen now waited by the door to the gardens. In flowing veils of finest silks, her tiny feet shod in gold slippers, her slender arms covered with bracelets of woven gold and jewels, she stood tall and regal even among the ornate surroundings.

The servant announced his need, "My Queen, Mordecai cries at the palace gate. In torn and dirty clothing, he cries in mourning seeking the Queen's attention. His cries pierce the hearts of all who hear him. He paces as if in agony. With ashes covering his head and only sackcloth to cover him, he is a pitiful sight. His bitter cries rise up in mourning for the Queen's help. What is your answer to him, my Queen?

The Queen ordered the servant back through the corridors with fine clothing for Mordecai to replace the sackcloth he wore. Mordecai refused the offer. Hathach, the servant, questioned Mordecai for the meaning of his cries so he might tell Queen Esther. Mordecai told him all that had happened.

Mordecai told him the exact amount of silver Haman, who was in high honor in the eyes of the King, promised to pay to the royal treasury for the slaughter of the Jews. He gave Hathach the servant a copy of the written decree for the destruction of the Jews, which was promulgated in Susa, to show and explain to Queen Esther.

Mordecai ended with the pronouncement, "Tell her that she must go to the King on behalf of her people. For her people and mine are the Jews. Tell her to remember the days of her lowly estate when she was brought up in my charge. For I, as her uncle raised her after the death of her parents. She is queen only because of my instruction and tutelage. Esther must go and plead with the King on behalf of her people, for Haman, who is second to the King has asked for our death. Esther must invoke the Lord and speak to the King for us and save her people from death."

Upon hearing these words Hathach the servant again hurried through palace halls back to where the Queen waited. Maisie was lost in the story that played itself out before her. Hathach relayed his message the Queen.

Esther began to shake when she heard the news. Fine silks could not cover the fear that overcame the young queen. She answered with a trembling voice, "All the servants of the king and the people of his provinces know that any man or woman who goes to the king in the inner court without being summoned suffers the penalty of death unless the kings extends to him or her the golden scepter, thus sparing their life. And I have not been summoned."

The servant again ran back to where Mordecai continued his wailing.

Tired, he ran back to the frightened Queen with Mordecai's reply, "Do not imagine that because you are in the king's palace, you will escape. You are a Jew. If you now remain silent, relief and deliverance will come to the Jews from another source but you and your father's house will perish. Perhaps, it was the hand of fate that put you in the royal house at this time."

Maisie, who had been lost in the story, suddenly became aware of the dark man beside her. Jesus spoke, "Mary, do you understand now?"

Maisie shook her head back and forth. What did all this have to do with her? These were royal people in ancient times. She knew nothing of royalty.

Jesus spoke again, "Mary, you still do not know who you are? You are like Esther, the daughter of the King of Kings. Yet you go about in fear. You are afraid to speak up for yourself and your people. Unaware of the power of your spirit, you lose the very purpose of your existence. You must learn who you are and speak up to save yourself. Watch, Mary and see!"

Turning to the scene, Maisie gasped as she watched Queen Esther remove the gold and silken veils that hid her face and body. Donning sackcloth and covering her head with dirt from the royal gardens, she looked up and cried in prayers. Maisie could feel her muscles tremble at the sight of Queen Esther's face. For it was her face. The face clearly held all her features, yet they were different, proud. Maisie suddenly understood. Esther, in her beauty, was large and well formed and full of a sense of her own power. She was, for lack of a better word, "strapping." She was as Maisie was meant to be before the fear of that evil night changed her. Before her, Maisie saw a brave and strong woman, a woman Jesus had created. In the pew was a tiny fearful woman that a lifetime of fear had carved.

Maisie covered her face as tears flowed down her cheeks. Her body shook with the power of knowing the truth. She was old now. She saw her life of fear spread over the years gone behind her. She never questioned Mama about raising Baby. She never questioned Miss Mona about the best way to raise Baby. She hadn't left Miss Mona to follow Baby and drag her back and away from those people. Worst of all she let Baby die in the hospital. Why? Because Maisie never asked for anything; Maisie never demanded anything. The night her daddy was lynched Maisie lost the person she was meant to be. With her mouth covered in fear, Maisie never screamed.

The pain of truth overwhelmed her. Maisie wept with the knowledge of her loss in her life. She had been too passive. Maisie allowed life to overwhelm her because she was afraid. Fear consumed her. She thought she would suffer if she ever stepped up and asked for her rights. The very fact she never asked at all caused all the pain in her life. No wonder Baby left her. No wonder she was ashamed. Baby at least had some fight in her. She fought for human rights until the pain of racism drew her to a life of drugs. Who knows what might have happened if Baby had her mother's support. She may have avoided the drugs. Maisie wept as the truth seared her soul. *It's too late,* she cried as she realized she had sinned gravely. Maisie leaned forward and wept with her head bowed over the back of the pew in front of her.

In a whisper she cried, "Help me Lord, I wasted my life and now it's too late."

Maisie's heart cried out to Jesus. She couldn't see Baby who stood before her. Baby was holding the hand of Maisie's daddy. Her face was full of love and compassion for the mother who wept before her. Maisie couldn't see Baby as she reached out and stroked the cheek of the mother she had forgiven long ago. Maisie didn't know it was Baby touching her cheek. It felt like a soft breeze calling her from her profound grief.

Father D'Angelico could see the two souls as they faded slowly from view. He could feel the presence of Jesus waiting to minister to the wounded soul in need of healing.

Jesus spoke, "Mary, Mary, look up. Lift your head and see."

Maisie raised her head expecting everyone in the church to be looking at her. No one around was staring at her. Maisie was surprised at herself. Suddenly it didn't seem to matter to her if they did stare. Maisie only cared about Jesus. He wanted to show her something important. The others sat quietly, lost in their own thoughts and prayers. Drawn again to Jesus, Maisie was drawn to the monstrance and the Eucharist which it contained. She was again drawn to the love that beckoned.

Esther now washed and perfumed herself in the marble courtyard with the help of her maids. The finest silks were wrapped around her as her shining hair was brushed and styled. Her dark curls sparkled with jewels. Her eyes betrayed the fear that coursed through her body. It was likely that she would be executed for entering into the King's chambers without being summoned. Her muscles trembled as she made her way with two handmaidens. Esther could taste the fear in her mouth.

Her heartbeat quickened as she entered the King's court. The fluttering of her heart stole her breath and she felt dizzy from the lack of oxygen. At the head of the court on a large golden throne sat the King. His face turned red with anger when he realized Esther had entered his chamber. The king's enraged face made her knees buckle in fear. The two handmaids held her up as she nearly fainted with anxiety.

Seeing her fear, the King softened and immediately lifted his golden scepter and pointed it to Esther. This gesture announced to the whole court that he welcomed his Queen.

With courage renewed, Esther made her request to the King to join her in a banquet. She had full intention of pleading for her people with the King in his best and most gracious mood.

Queen Esther treated the King to two banquets. She also invited the enemy of her people. Haman was the man who out of jealousy of Mordecai ordered the death of all the Jews in the land. He was unaware of the Queen's nationality and felt sure he curried her favor.

The King sat well satisfied after his second banquet. He looked at Queen Esther and spoke with great affection, "Whatever you ask, Queen Esther, shall be granted to you. Whatever request you make shall be honored, even for half the kingdom."

Esther smiled, "If I have found favor with you, O King, and if it pleases your majesty, I ask that my life be spared, and I beg that you spare the lives of my people. For my people and I have been delivered to destruction, slaughter and annihilation. If we were to be sold into slavery, I would remain silent. But my enemy will be unable to compensate for the harm done to the King."

"Who and where," said King Ahasuerus to Queen Esther, "is the man who has dared to do this?"

Esther replied, "The enemy oppressing us is this wicked Haman."

The King, in anger, went to the garden to think. Haman begged the Queen for his life. The King saw Haman throw himself on the Queen. The King was furious at the assault and ordered Haman's death on the very gallows he had just built for Mordecai. The King issued a decree saving all of the Jews from destruction.

Mary, on her knees, watched in amazement as Mordecai, dressed in royal robes cried in thanks to God for his people's deliverance.

Mordecai cried, "This is the work of God. I recall the dream I had about these very things and not a single detail has been left unfulfilled. The tiny spring grew into a river, the light of the sun, the many waters. The river is Esther, whom the king married and made Queen. The nations are those who assembled to destroy the Jews, but my people are Israel, who cried to God and were saved.

Mary shook with the power of what she had witnessed. The power of God flowed through her.

Father D'Angelico watched as Mary's spirit, which had been curled up in a tiny ball, seemed to unravel. Like a rose, it blossomed and grew larger and brighter as the soul reached up to God. The priest praised the Father for the miracle he was witnessing. Mary Johnson started her prayer.

"Father God, I am your most royal daughter and I beg you to save Johnny from death. I don't know how you will do it, but I know You will because I have asked You. You will save him if it falls within your Will."

Mary Johnson sat back on the wooden pew. Somehow, she knew Johnny wouldn't die tomorrow. She was confident and unafraid. Mary had a sense of who she was now. She knew that she was the daughter of the Most High King. She would never be afraid to ask her Father for anything again. Struggling from her knees, Mary Johnson sat. Sitting up, she seemed larger.

Ten

See to it that no one captivate you with an empty, seductive philosophy according to human tradition, according to the elemental powers of the world and not according to Christ. (Col. 2:8)

B obby Myer couldn't tell if he was shivering from the cold or the adrenalin that coursed through his body. He could hear the police sirens. *Damn fools, let 'em look!* He wasn't afraid. Bobby Myer wasn't afraid of anyone or anything.

He felt the dry branches of the evergreen scratch his arms as he moved to a more comfortable position. No one could see him hidden in the bush. Not the police, not the stupid people who waited on the church steps above him. He was safe. He had fooled them all. It was so easy because they were so stupid.

The cold wind blew hard; the thin shirt he wore didn't protect him from the cold. He had ditched his jacket, a Versace leather jacket costing over a thousand dollars, his father had bought him. His father would buy him another, what did he care? He needed to change his description quickly. The police were on his tail. He wanted to cry out in victory. It was so close. He had once again defeated them. This was the closest call Bobby ever had. The cops had heard the gunshots. Then he slipped in the Chinaman's blood. Blank dead eyes stared at him as he fell on the body.

Bobby was quick. Pushing his hands against the dead body, he rose to his feet and ran. Just as the cop was breaking into the front door Bobby narrowly escaped out the back. Out into the cold blizzard he ran into the howling wind. The fat old cops would be too tired and lazy to run after him. They'd go back to get their heated cars, giving him just the edge he needed.

He ditched the jacket and the bag of stolen money in the dumpster, and ran. High from the rush, he ran until he was out of breath. Rubbing the handle of the pistol with his shirt to wipe away any fingerprints, he threw it into the sewer and continued to run. The cops were right on his heels. *What a rush!*

As he rounded the corner, he could hear the sirens growing louder. They were right behind him. Tossing himself into the evergreen bush, he felt the sucking warm wind of the police cars as they careened past him, spinning for grip on the icy snow beneath them. It was exhilarating. This was the closest they had ever gotten to catching him. He tried to hold back his laughter as he thought of how stupid the police were. He didn't think the people on the church steps could hear him above the howling winds, but it didn't make any sense to ask for trouble, so he covered his mouth. No, no sense at all when he could still hear the police sirens in the distance.

He would wait here. These fools must be waiting for something. They were out in this freezing cold for a reason. They seemed to be waiting for the church doors to open. It was perfect. Bobby could get out of the cold and the police would never think of looking for him in a church. Perfect, yeah, that's what Bobby thought. He started to relax, confident he had gotten away again. Moreover, this time it wasn't just robbery. Bobby's heart swelled with pride as he realized the chink must be dead. He had shot him in the chest twice.

He had shot Sam in the head in the chink's bathroom. He smiled. He got away with murder, twice!

The storm had protected him and given him cover, but it was now making things difficult. The small bush was no protection from the biting cold. He shivered as the melting snow saturated the knees of his jeans. Just when he felt he couldn't stand the cold any longer, he heard the heavy wooden doors of the church open. He let the bundled crowd start up the stairs and, looking to blend in, he joined them as he scooted into the warmth of the church. Unnoticed, he felt safe.

Bobby was grateful for the warmth of the church, even though he didn't like the feeling he got as he crossed the threshold. The old priest gave him an eerie feeling. He felt as if he could see through him. Bobby didn't like it. He grabbed a seat in the middle of the church and watched as the old man in the elaborate robes preciously carried something to a gold stand. He could hardly contain his laughter as he watched the ridiculous rituals. The contortions of the old man amused Bobby as the priest sang stupid foreign songs to his God.

Bobby wasn't completely ignorant of what the old man was doing. His father was a Catholic. His father was so stupid that he went to church every morning. He probably went to pray for his little lost son. What a waste! Bobby didn't buy any of this God stuff. People are weak, and weak losers need to have something to lean on. They were so stupid in this life that they dreamed of another. Bobby laughed to himself. Wait until his father died—then he would find out just how big a loser he really was. There was no God. The only thing that counted in this life was strength. Whoever was the smartest, richest, and strongest was the winner. Bobby laughed, as he looked at all the pathetic losers around him. He could clearly see that he was the strongest and the smartest there.

Bobby watched a homeless bum come out of the

confessional; he watched the old fat woman in the worn cloth coat struggle up the aisle. She held her purse too tightly, a little too close to her body. Bobby decided he would look into that as he considered the money he would need to get home. A timid black woman sat in the back by the priest. A rich looking dude sat up front. He looked angry and on edge. *Better stay away from him,* thought Bobby. The whole crowd looked like losers to him. Bobby always seemed to be able to spot them.

His old man was the biggest loser of all. His old man had plenty of money, a big house, and a wife who doted on him, but he was still a loser. Ever since he was adopted as a small child, Bobby felt the old man was a fool. He was too stupid to figure it out and that's what made him a loser. From the beginning, the old man tried to teach Bobby to be as stupid as him, but Bobby was too smart for that.

He dragged Bobby to churches just like this one and tried to convince him that the fool who died two thousand years ago on the cross was the one true God. How stupid! Even the God he picked was a loser. Imagine God—if there was one—allowing himself to be killed.

Bobby looked at the large beige crucifix with the dying figure of Jesus on it. What a loser! He was a criminal dying a criminal's death. *Some God,* he got caught. Bobby was smarter than Jesus was, he never got caught.

He started small. That sunny day in the classroom, Bobby impulsively stole the quiet, mousey girl's lunch. He enjoyed watching her search for it. He enjoyed tricking people. He feigned sympathy for her and even shared part of his lunch with her. She was so grateful she gave Bobby his first kiss. For the next few days, Bobby could think of nothing else. Her lunch was right there in his desk all the time. It was too easy to fool people and Bobby felt the buzz.

At first, Bobby just stole small things. Charlie's homework was next. Charlie was the teacher's pet with his hand always in the air first. Bobby could hardly contain his mirth as

Charlie squirmed and tried to explain to the teacher he had lost his homework. What a sense of power! What a rush! Bobby couldn't get enough and missing homework and lunches soon lost their excitement. Before long, Bobby moved on to bigger things.

The young blond teacher cried when her pocketbook containing her first paycheck went missing. That would teach her to ask Bobby for his homework in front of the whole class. She never suspected it was him.

Still, he found he needed a bigger rush. It wasn't enough just to steal. It was even better to set someone up to take the fall. Bobby knew they would search the classroom first so Bobby placed the teacher's purse, minus the paycheck, in the black boy's desk.

It was all so easy. Earl cried in denial. No one would believe him. The evidence spoke for itself. Bobby took no chances. He hid the wallet in Earl's rubber boots. When they found it there, without the money, Earl's guilt would be obvious. It gave Bobby such pleasure. He fingered the money and the paycheck hidden deep in his pocket as Earl sobbed. Earl's mother came to get him. Upset by the accusing stares of the white people she slapped Earl when he denied stealing the purse. Bobby was joyous as she dragged him from the classroom. Earl never came back to school. Bobby never knew what happened to him, nor did he care. It was such a rush, such a victory.

The best was when he fooled his old man. The old man was a holy roller and he made Bobby sick. Each morning he would get up early and have the chauffer drive him to church so he could attend morning mass. Bobby couldn't believe how stupid the old man was.

The first time Bobby stole some of his old man's money, he never even noticed it was missing. That really irritated Bobby.

Bobby decided to steal something his old man did care about, so he took the cheap Timex his grandfather, a bricklayer, gave his old man on his graduation day. It was engraved, "To my son, I am so proud." The old man's father died soon after that. Bobby's old man never took the watch off. He couldn't believe how sentimental his father was. Imagine wearing such a cheap watch when he could afford so much more.

Bobby knew his father only took the watch off while he showered. It was easy to slip into the steamy bathroom and snatch it. Hardly a challenge at all! Bobby couldn't look at the old man as he searched the house for the old watch. It wasn't because of guilt but because Bobby was sure he would start laughing. His old man was really a fool. He never suspected Bobby was a thief.

Bobby was adopted as a small baby. He was given to the old man's first wife, who was unable to have children of her own. Bobby barely remembered her. What he did remember was that she was sick — she was weak and unable to spend much time with him before she died when he was in the first grade. Bobby remembered the sobs coming from the old man's room for the next two years.

After that, the old man spent most of his time working. Bobby, however, was never neglected. He spent all of his free time with his little son. He took him everywhere. Museums and ballparks, camping and fishing, even a few trips to Europe. He spent quality time being a father to the boy. The problem was that Bobby didn't want a father. Bobby found the old man boring. It was no fun being with someone who spent all his time doing good. Bobby got bored easily.

The old man appreciated the simple pleasures of life. Maybe because he grew up poor and worked for everything he had. Bobby was never poor. He had all the material things he wanted and they bored him. His problem was that he only felt good when he hurt others. For as long as he could remember, he thought of himself as different. Bobby felt superior to others. His old man tried everything, gave him everything, and it didn't work. Bobby knew what the old man wanted: He wanted Bobby's love but Bobby wasn't about to give it to him.

Bobby would sometimes let the old man think he was reaching him. Bobby loved to string him along and as his father talked to him about love, respect, and the meaning of life, Bobby would listen and nod. The old man would get all excited thinking that he was finally reaching Bobby. Then, just at the critical moment, Bobby would verbally castrate him. The old man would fold like a broken accordion. Deflated he would walk away. His father never seemed to give up! That's what was so funny. It was so easy to make a fool of him.

A loud bang drew Bobby from his thoughts. Even the young woman three rows up turned to look. The vestibule door banged shut as a dark-haired, well-dressed man tried to hold it against the howling wind. It pulled away from him and banged shut again. He genuflected before he sat in the last pew on the opposite side of the church. His expensive silk suit gave his status away. Bobby thought he looked like a younger version of his father. The careworn face was etched with lines of kindness. A lifetime of giving left its mark on what was once a handsome face. The dark hair was heavily touched with gray at the temples. His hair was perfect, as was his pressed Italian suit and topcoat. The man knelt quietly in prayer, lost in his own thoughts. Bobby was relieved when he saw this—at least he wasn't one of the cops who were looking for him.

Bobby looked around. This church was older and a little more ornate than the church Bobby's old man attended. Bobby figured that years ago people were even stupider than they are now. Poorer than they were now, they gave too much of their meager funds to the church. The church built pretty places like this to get them to give even more of their money. You had to hand it to the church, it knew how to rob people better than any thief did. The best way to rob people was to fool them into giving you their money. And these fools even felt good when they handed their money over to the church.

Bobby pulled himself away from his thoughts. He needed to concentrate on the moment. The black purse lay unattended on the wooden pew she sat in, two feet away and just behind the crippled fat woman. She was lost in prayer and Bobby was never one to miss an opportunity. Quietly slipping down the pew he had been sitting in, he slipped down on the floor. Crawling silently, he took his time, his senses heightened like an animal's. He stopped and started listening carefully to the silent church. The rush of excitement quickened the blood that flowed through his body. Like a cat, he prowled up the side aisle. On hands and knees, he moved up, always aware of the others in the church. Sensing their distraction, he continued until he reached the pew directly behind the old woman.

Slicing along the pew, Bobby moved silently. Keeping his head below the back of the pew, he moved undetected. The young woman with the pocket full of tissues was the one he had to watch. She sat with her eyes open just three pews behind him. Bobby could feel his sense of superiority as he reached his destination with no one aware of his presence.

The old woman was directly in front of him, her black purse beside her. It was all so easy, too easy. In the stillness, Bobby did not betray his movement. He reached over the back of the pew in front of him, unclasped the purse and reached inside. The old silk lining was torn. He could feel the comb and compact. A lipstick rolled around the bottom. This wasn't what he wanted. He could feel the soft leather of her wallet. Quickly reaching inside, he removed the single ten-dollar bill inside and stuck it in his pants. This was too easy. The old woman, mesmerized by the altar in front of her, never noticed a thing. Unnoticed, Bobby returned to his pew, enjoying the rush that came when he was getting over on someone.

However, there was always that letdown afterwards.

The need for more peril grew over the years. It was harder and harder to maintain the adrenaline high. Bobby was as addicted to that rush as a heroin addict was to his fix. He needed it. Life was a bore without it. Robbery was no longer good enough. Tonight he had taken the big step. Bobby had killed.

He had decided years ago that he would have to kill the old man. Now he wished he had done it sooner. The old man eventually remarried and Bobby now needed to kill his stepmother, otherwise she would inherit all of his father's money — Bobby's money. He had no interest in school and the thought of work just bored him. He had to maintain his life style. Bobby understood that for a long time. Tonight had been part of the planning.

Sam came to him with the scheme a month ago. Bobby met Sam a few years ago while fencing jewelry he lifted from a guest at one of the old man's parties. Sam and Bobby had little in common. Sam was from the wrong side of town.

He cased the Chinaman's store for weeks. He knew he kept the week's money locked in the back apartment of the store and would take it to the bank each Saturday morning. That's why Sam planned the heist for Friday night. On Fridays, the man's wife went to visit her sick mother. Sam laughed about it. People were such creatures of habit. Sam thought he was smart asking Bobby for help — two were stronger than one and it was worth the split. But Sam had made a fatal mistake. Bobby didn't care about the money, and didn't care about Sam. It was an opportunity. Bobby wanted to see if he had it in him. Bobby wanted to kill someone.

They waited until the woman left and then they entered the store. The man cooperated easily with a gun pointed at his head. He closed and locked the store and readily handed over the money. But the Chinaman saw something Sam did not — he saw murder in Bobby's eyes. He tried to escape after he rang the silent alarm but Bobby didn't let him. Holding the gun to the kneeling storekeeper's head, Bobby let the man beg for his life, enjoying the sense of power. Sam begged him to just tie the man up and leave with the money but Bobby didn't care about the money. In fact, in the end, Bobby dumped the money with his jacket, just in case the police caught him. He wanted to test himself. Could he pull the trigger? Sensing that Bobby was going to kill him, the man got up to run but barely made a step.

"No witnesses!" Bobby shouted as two bullets ripped through the storekeeper's chest. Turning to Sam, he could see his face change. Sam finally understood and ran, but he didn't get far. Trapped in the small bedroom, Sam knelt and begged for his life. Sam's fear invigorated Bobby. He shot him execution style just before the cops started banging on the door.

Sitting in the pew Bobby looked at the paltry ten dollars he had stolen from the old woman's wallet. It wasn't much, but it was enough to get him home. He had proven himself. Now he could plan his parents' death. He wasn't afraid, he was looking forward to it. Bobby was about to leave the church when he heard sirens. *"Better wait,"* he whispered as he laid down to rest. The police were still looking for him.

Bobby couldn't see the dark spirits that swirled around him. The evil whispers of the dark spirits were only heard by his darkened soul. Father D'Angelico could feel them. Whispers of ancient evils spilled across the priest's ears as the demons swirled around Bobby.

The elderly priest prayed, "In the name of Jesus Christ and by the power of the Holy Spirit, I bind all of you evil spirits and send you to the foot of the Cross to be dealt with as the Father sees fit." The priest fell to his knees as he repeated his prayer three times. He could hear the spirits screaming. They didn't want to go, but because of the Power of Jesus, they had no choice. They swirled and screamed in agony, rolling repeatedly in the air. Rolling into dark burning balls, they spun through the air and landed, bound at the foot of the altar. Unable to move they pulsed in anguish beneath the altar.

Jesus, at the request of his priest, held them bound beneath the monstrance.

Jesus reached out for Bobby, calling to him in antique songs of everlasting love. He called from Spirit to a darkened spirit in primordial waves of longing. Bobby's spirit, because of the binding of evil, responded. Unable to rest, Bobby sat up. Looking to the Host in the golden monstrance for the first time in his life, Bobby heard the voice of God.

Eleven

Then I saw thrones; those who sat on them were entrusted with judgment, I also saw the souls of those who had been beheaded for their witness to Jesus and for the word of God, and who had not worshiped the beast or its image nor had accepted its mark on their foreheads or hands. (Rev. 20:4)

Bobby was suddenly afraid. Music beyond any memory of sound filled his ears. The music flowed so seamlessly and with such longing and majesty through the air that it overwhelmed him. The music flowed over the dark spirits with such power that the flaming balls of evil screamed in agony. Evil could not stand the painful sound of the Truth. The notes of truth sang out in worship to the Creator of the Universe. The song of angels cried, "Holy, Holy, Holy. Worthy is the Lamb!" Music of the soul called Bobby. It was the eternal song of beauty that musicians since the beginning of time have tried to capture in vain. Curving smooth sounds cascaded from the Perpetual Word in waves of undulating rhythm. The reverberation of Life touched Bobby's soul. The music awakened him to the Presence of the Host held in the golden rays of the monstrance. The Eucharistic Jesus called Bobby.

Compelled to answer the voice of God, Bobby sat up.

Looking into the whiteness at the Center of the altar, he watched, spellbound. The whiteness spun as the waves of song flowed and surged around the spinning orb. The Host pulsed in an eternal heartbeat calling to a heart blackened with sin. It was too bright! Bobby had to close his eyes to shut out the light. The song continued in strings that tugged like golden strands at his heart. Bobby could feel himself moving forward toward the source of the song. Bobby felt himself moving to the Eternal Father, flying smoothly over the bands of ethereal music. Try as he did, he could not resist the call.

Opening his eyes, he found himself far removed from the church, standing in front of an open door. The waves of music calling him, cascading from beyond. Bobby wanted to defy the call, but he couldn't. He stepped through the open door and found himself in an immense space. The space was so immense and unending that he lost his bearing. The light before him was so bright that he had to look down as it burned his eyes. Looking down, Bobby noticed specks of blood he hadn't noticed before. The blood was all over his clothes and dripping from his hands. He felt filthy and longed for a bath. This light revealed too much. He felt dirty and soiled.

Beneath Bobby, a floor made of crystals sparkled, reflecting the light. Bobby had never experienced such beauty in his entire life. He felt as if he were standing on a diamond that glowed in surging ribbons of light.

The light pulsed in time with the music, which continued to call him forward. Bobby walked looking down at the clear floor as his eyes slowly adjusted to the light.

Suddenly, as his eyes began to adjust to the brightness, Bobby stopped. He was standing in front of a golden chair, no, it was a throne. It glowed in the light, forged of the purest gold and encrusted with sparkling jewels that dazzled his eyes. The throne was huge. Bobby reached the height of the leg of the magnificent throne. He felt small in the immense space before the glowing throne. As his eyes continued to adjust, he could see the man who sat upon the carved chair.

The man was clothed in a dazzling white robe tied at the waist with a golden sash. His head, covered with thick white hair, was crowned with heavy jewels. His face was powerful and partly covered with a thick white beard. A sense of power and majesty flowed from the man who held a golden scepter. Bobby's knees started to shake and before he could stop himself, his knees buckled beneath him, and he found himself kneeling before the throne of God.

Around the throne, a halo glowed like a shining emerald. Now kneeling, Bobby could see 24 other thrones where 24 elders dressed in white sat surrounding the throne of God. The elders had gold crowns on their heads. Bobby shook with fright as the man who Bobby now recognized as Jesus looked at him. From the throne came flashes of lightning and rumbling thunder. Seven flaming torches burned in front of the throne. They are the seven spirits of God. In front of the throne was something that resembled a sea of glass that sparkled like crystal.

Bobby felt insignificant and dirty in the bright light. He wanted to run and hide but he couldn't move. Frozen in awe and fear, he knelt and watched in terror. In the center and around the throne were four living creatures with eyes covering their front and back. The first creature resembled a lion, the second was like a calf, the third had the face of a human being, and the fourth looked like an eagle in flight. Each of the creatures had six wings. They continuously cried out, "Holy, holy, holy is the Lord God Almighty, who was, and who is, and who is to come."

The 24 elders threw down their crowns before the throne, exclaiming, "Worthy are you Lord our God to receive glory and honor and power, for you created all things, because of your will they came to be and were created."

Bobby trembled uncontrollably. The vast space overwhelmed him. The sounds of the praise the four creatures produced was overpowering. The creatures were so huge they frightened him and he was sure they would turn on him. He felt unable to protect himself. This feeling of impotence was new for Bobby. He had always felt in control, and superior to others. Frozen, he knelt for what seemed like an eternity. The crashing lightning and thunder that flashed behind the shining throne overpowered him. He covered his ears but nothing could shut out the roaring power of the throne of God.

Bobby didn't think he could contain the fear that seized him any longer. His stomach cramped in panic as beads of sweat flowed from his forehead. His muscles trembled in rolling spasms of terror. Bobby never felt more frightened — until the eyes of God turned toward him and the thundering voice of the Lord spoke in ancient tongues of power. It was then that he almost passed out.

Jesus called out from the throne, "Look at the man who thinks he controls the Life I created!"

Bobby collapsed beneath the weight of the accusation. He was sure he was going to die. Instead, a deep silence followed. In time, Bobby looked up. The Lord remained steady, looking deep within his soul. Bobby had a sense of being probed by the "knowing" eyes of the Lord.

"Look!" the thundering voice shattered the silence as the King of Kings raised his scepter and pointed to the sea of glass before Him. Bobby could do nothing but obey. The lights beneath swirled forming scenes that came together like movies. Bobby was unable to look away and watched as the scene unfolded.

He lost all sense of where he was as he watched a man driving a garbage truck in the early morning light. The black man silently pulled and tugged at the barrels of trash; the large, soiled truck squealed as the small thin man fed the refuse into the back of the grinding truck. Bobby was confused. Who was this man and what did it have to do with him?

Bobby suddenly sensed a presence beside him as he stood

on the sidewalk in the wet morning dew. Turning he saw a different Jesus. Beside him stood a gentle Jesus appearing as he had always been portrayed. Bobby thought of him as weak.

The gentle Jesus spoke, "Do you see? Can you understand?"

Bobby was annoyed. His fear left him and in arrogance he asked, "What does a black garbage man have to do with me!"

Jesus looked at Bobby, "Don't you recognize him. You went to school with him. Don't you recognize Earl? He's the little boy you set up. You made him look like a thief. You changed his life. Haven't you ever wondered what happened to Earl?"

Bobby grinned and tried not to laugh. No, he didn't care. He never cared what happened to Earl. He was entertained for an afternoon by Earl's troubles. It killed the boredom that plagued him. Nevertheless, he decided to play along. He didn't want to end up back in front of the throne.

Trying to keep a straight face he answered, "He became a garbage man. Well, that's not too bad. It's a union job and he probably makes enough to live pretty well."

Jesus looked at Bobby. His extended stare didn't reveal any feelings in response to Bobby's callous answer.

Jesus spoke, "Earl is a good father and husband. He has four children who will always remember him as the anchor of their lives. Nothing, even what you did to him, can kill the good spirit of Earl. And no, there is nothing wrong with being a garbage man. It's just that it is not what I intended Earl to be."

Bobby decided to bite, "Oh, and what was he supposed to be?"

Suddenly the scene changed and Bobby found himself in a hospital. The doors of the hospital room were decorated with vibrant pictures of Santa Claus. Children of various ages played in a corner that was set up with toys and books. Nurses measured medication in pediatric droppers. Bobby watched with wonder. What could this have to do with him? He watched as the elevator door opened. To his surprise, Earl stepped out wearing a white lab coat and a stethoscope around his neck.

As soon as the children saw Earl they shouted with joy, "Doc Earl, Doc Earl, come over and play!"

Dr. Earl laughed as the children ran up to him. Scooping the smallest one up in his arms, he praised and petted the heads of the children who surrounded him. The scene faded and Bobby found himself back on the morning sidewalk watching Earl pick up another trashcan instead of a child.

Jesus continued in a soft voice, "I gave Earl the wisdom and desire to be a physician, a pediatrician. He was given a special gift. He would have saved many children's lives; touched so many families hearts."

Bobby couldn't keep the sarcasm out of his voice as he answered, "So what went wrong? He didn't have the money?"

Jesus stared at Bobby for a minute and continued, "No, he didn't have the support. After he was accused of being a thief, he was sent to an insignificant school. Whenever anything went wrong, Earl was blamed. It changed him. He no longer believed in himself. It took all the spirit he had left to become the good man that he is. He lost himself in the pain of false accusation. He lost who he was supposed to be."

Bobby wasn't impressed. What did he care? It seemed to him that all of this was a waste of his time. So what if Earl didn't become a doctor. So what if he didn't save some children. They were nothing to Bobby. He kept his thoughts to himself. There was no need to share them with a bleeding heart God. Bobby had the feeling that Jesus could read his thoughts. There was something in his eyes. It was the same uncomfortable feeling he had when the old priest looked at him. Bobby didn't like the look in God's eyes—the look of disappointment.

Jesus pointed ahead and said, "Look over there, Bobby."

In a flash Bobby found himself back in the apartment of the shopkeeper he had murdered. The man he thought he killed was still alive. Sitting on a flowered sofa and holding his wife's hand, he looked seriously concerned. His wife was telling him something important.

"The doctor said that there was a small chance that the baby would not survive to be born full-term. But we've waited so long and tried for so long. I can't believe that God would let anything happen to our only child." The man held his trembling wife who glowed with the news of her pregnancy, "You'll have to take better care of yourself. No more long hours at the shop, I want you to take the weekends off. Go visit your mother. We have some money saved, we'll manage."

The woman looked concerned, "No, it would be too much for you. It wouldn't be right for you to work all those long hours without help. I know how much work it is."

Hugging his wife, he said, "The most important thing is that you spend the next six months taking care of yourself and the baby. This may be our only chance to have a son or daughter."

She hugged him. "I will listen to you and the doctor. I want this baby to be healthy. I want him to grow up to be as good as his father."

The scene faded and Bobby found himself standing alone with Jesus.

Jesus spoke first, "Tonight a policeman will visit Mae Woo at her mother's and she will find out that the husband she so loves has been murdered. Murdered for the paltry amount of money he'd made that week. But we both know that isn't why he died. He was murdered because you wanted to see if you had what it takes to kill. You needed a victim and you decided he was expendable. Your action will result in terrible consequences."

Bobby just wanted to get out of here. He was sick of all this nonsense. He decided to play along, "So what happens? Does she lose the baby?"

Jesus looked at Bobby, "No, I will answer Mae Woo's

prayers and the baby girl will be healthy and born on time, but she will be born without a father to love and guide her. Mae Woo will have to work long hours to support the girl. The girl will grow up lonely and fatherless all because you wanted to practice murder."

Bobby was really getting annoyed now. What did he care about any of this? He just wanted to be left alone, "So I hurt a lot a people. I even killed people and I know that I'm evil. I guess you want to tell me I'm going to hell. There's nothing I can do about that. I can't go back and unkill the man or take back all the bad things I've done. If I'm headed for hell, well, so be it! Just leave me alone. You made me and I'm evil. You can't forgive someone as bad as me, so stop torturing me!"

In a flash Bobby found himself back kneeling before the throne of God. The music, which was so beautiful before, now sounded like nails screeching on a chalkboard. He covered his ears but the sound of praise was like torture. His ears shrieked in pain as the elders threw their crowns in praise of the Lord of the Universe. Doubled over with the crushing, horrific sound, Bobby screamed and suddenly the music stopped. Catching his breath, he looked up at the powerful enthroned God. Bobby had always been indifferent to the thought of any God. Now he was starting to hate him. He knew that he was in God's power now and his sense of survival told him to keep his feelings hidden. Those all-knowing eyes continued to probe him.

Bobby raised his bloodstained hands up to cover his face and screamed, "Leave me alone. I have done evil. I am evil. I'm unforgivable!"

The sound of total silence frightened him. Looking up Bobby could see Jesus looking at him. The King pointed his golden scepter at the sea of glass before Him.

Bobby screamed, "No! I don't want to see any more."

Colors whirled and Bobby, despite himself, was drawn into the kaleidoscope. Bobby found himself standing in a field before a large colorful tent. The tent sides billowed as gentle gusts of wind kicked up sand, which sprayed against the red and white striped tent. The golden tassels that hung on the sides and top of the tent swayed with the gusts of wind. It was the largest tent Bobby had ever seen. Around the large tent were smaller tents that filled the small valley. It was a desert climate, dry and hot.

The gathering of the small village of tents seemed to be on a green oasis. Lambs bleated and cried for their mother as large herds of sheep and goats sauntered up and down between the tents. Dressed in long cotton robes and veils, men and women walked with purpose. Some carried earthen vessels, others rudimentary farming tools. All seemed busy with a purpose and direction. Bobby tried to speak to them but they ignored him. Running from person to person for help, he realized they couldn't see or hear him. Still seeking help, Bobby entered the largest tent in the center of the small gathering.

It took a moment for his eyes to adjust to the dim light. The tent was full of servants who scurried back and forth with food and drink. The outer circle of the tent was bustling with activity. Amid silken pillows and lush curtains sat an old man with a grey beard. Dressed in the finest silk and adorned with thick golden jewelry, he reclined while a servant fed him. Grapes and other fruits, pastries and spiced meats lay before him. He showed no interest in the fare, as his full attention was taken by the young man who sat before him. Again, Bobby tried but failed to capture anyone's attention. To those present he didn't exist. He sat in frustration beside the young man. The unfolding scene captured his attention as he listened.

"Father give me the share of your estate that should come to me." The young man addressed the older man. Bobby laughed to himself. The kid was smart. Why wait for the old man to die. He might as well have the money now while he was still young enough to enjoy it. Bobby figured the old man would never go for it.

To his surprise, the old man agreed. This kid was brilliant! Maybe he could learn how to manipulate his own father by watching. *No harm watching this kid in action,* he thought. Bobby watched as the young man collected his belongings and all of the money he would have inherited upon his father's death. The kid was leaving and Bobby intended to go with him. This place was as boring as hell anyway.

They traveled for days until they reached a large city. The kid got himself a lush place and started to party. It was great watching him. This kid didn't let any grass grow under his feet. Within a week, he had a following and numerous friends. They partied all night, drinking and taking whatever women they could lure with the money. Bobby was impressed with the wild times the kid and his newfound friends were having.

As the wine and women flowed, the nights grew in experimentation and debauchery. Bobby was having a great time watching. He only wished he could participate. He called out to God to remove him but there was no response. He was starting to wonder if he was dead. The only thing he could do was enjoy watching the kid have fun.

Bobby watched as the parties started to wane as the kid started to run out of money. Bobby suspected that many of the kid's new friends had been robbing him. Each night, when he was drunk or conquering some new woman, his so-called friends would claim they needed more money for food and wine. They knew he wanted to keep the party going so they pocketed as much as they could. The kid was too drunk to realize he was being scammed. Before long, much of the kid's money was gone, and his so-called friends started to disappear. Soon the kid was all alone and penniless.

Bobby watched as the kid was kicked out of his digs. On the street, he found out, for the first time, just how much the city was suffering. It was in an economic crunch. The crops the people depended on had failed for the last two years and the larders were empty. People who couldn't find work were starving in the gutter. Bobby had never seen anything like it. Didn't they have a welfare program? It was every man for himself and the weakest were just plain out of luck. The strong survive, Bobby had always accepted that reality, it was just strange to see it in action. Strange to see the sick, the young, and the elderly left to die. Lucky for the kid he could work. He found work on a pig farm.

Bobby thought it was disgusting. The pigs smelled so bad that both Bobby and the kid were nauseous for the first few days. After a few days, they got used to the smell. *Probably because they smelled just like the pigs,* he thought. The kid was paid so little he could barely buy enough food to stay alive. His stomach ached with hunger and in a few weeks it was easy to see that his body was just wasting away. When his hunger became stronger than his pride, he decided to ask the farmer for help.

He begged, "Can I eat a little of the food that you give to the pigs? It is better than the food I can buy on the street."

The farmer roared with laughter. "Well kid, the pigs deserve the food they get. They're worth more than you are. In this famine, my pigs are worth four times their usual price. The fatter they get the more they are worth. The rich will pay dearly for a fattened hog. You on the other hand are worth nothing. There are dozens of strong men who will take your job for less. Count your blessings and if I catch you eating any of the pig's food you are out of here. That's when you'll find out what true hunger feels like!"

Bobby was disgusted as he watched the kid started to cry.

As he wept, he talked aloud, "How many of my father's hired workers have more food to eat. Yet here am I, dying from hunger. I shall get up and go to my father and I shall say to him, "Father, I have sinned against heaven and against you. I no longer deserve to be called your son, treat me as you would treat one of your hired workers."

Bobby was disgusted. A kid he once admired was going home with his tail between his legs. He was going to beg the old man for mercy. Didn't he have any pride?

Besides, Bobby was sure the old man would be so angry

the kid had squandered half of his holdings on false friends, booze and loose women that he would be quick to reject him.

The walk home took longer than the trip to the city. The kid was weak with hunger and his steps were slow. He sped up when he saw the oasis filled with tents and herds of sheep. Bobby knew the kid was wasting his time. His father wouldn't help him. His father had another son who stayed faithfully by his side. Why would he want to take back this ungrateful son who lost all his money? The kid himself seemed a little afraid. What would he do when his father told him to leave? Bobby figured the kid would die on his own. There wasn't much strength left in him. Still, the kid kept moving toward the oasis as he struggled along the rough narrow road.

He was still a long way off when his father caught sight of him. Filled with compassion, he ran to his son and embraced and kissed him.

"Father, I have sinned against heaven and against you. I no longer deserve to be called your son."

Nevertheless, his father ordered his servants, "Quickly bring me my finest robe and put it around my son. Put a ring on his finger and sandals on his feet. Take the fattened calf and slaughter it. Then let us celebrate with a feast, because this son of mine who was dead has been found."

Bobby was stunned. Even though the kid had rejected his father, ridiculed him and wasted away his inheritance, his father forgave him and took him back. Before Bobby could give it much thought though he found himself in a new situation. Suddenly, Bobby was back on the road. He was dressed in the same dirty smelly clothing the kid had been wearing. He felt faint and weak with hunger. He could see the road was narrow and rough before him. Bobby walked ahead, confused over what was happening to him.

Suddenly Bobby saw someone running toward him. The man had his arms out to embrace him. As he got closer, Bobby recognized the man. It was Jesus! The kingly Jesus who had sat on the golden throne now ran toward Bobby with his arms open and his face full of love. Bobby almost fainted. He almost repeated the words the kid had spoken to his father.

Luckily, he caught himself. As Jesus came closer, Bobby stopped walking. He wasn't about to beg. He wasn't about to say he was sorry for what he had done. The kid had no pride! Bobby was stronger than that.

When Jesus reached Bobby, he took him in his arms and repeated the loving words the kid's father had said, "Quick bring the finest robe and put it on him; put a ring on his finger and sandals on his feet. Take the fattened calf and slaughter it. Then let us celebrate with a feast, because this son of mine was dead, and has come to life again. He was lost, and now he has been found."

With burning rage, Bobby pushed Jesus away, "Leave me alone. I don't want Your mercy! You want me to be sorry for what I've done? Well, I'm not!" Bobby could feel the hatred he felt for Jesus fill every muscle of his body. "You're just like my old man. Weak, weak with your mercy! I don't want to be like you! You're just like him. You want me to love You, well, I won't! I'm my own man!"

Bobby pushed Jesus further away and ran away. He could feel the presence of Jesus standing behind him as he ran. What a fool! Just like his old man. This Jesus would never give up. It enraged him. Bobby could feel the veins in his neck pulsing with anger. His face felt hot with a fury that rose from inside him.

Bobby couldn't contain it. He turned and spit out the anger, "Leave me alone! I will not serve!"

And as quickly as the whole thing started, it ended. A little disoriented, Bobby found himself back in the little church. Everything appeared the same. It wasn't possible. Bobby felt as if he had been gone for years. He knew he had spent a few months in the city with the kid. Looking at the clock on the back wall of the church Bobby was shocked. Only an hour had passed. It made him angrier. Another trick! Another trick of the bleeding heart God! Resentment surged through him. Bobby hated Jesus.

Father D'Angelico could feel the soul return, this time even blacker with sin. Jesus had not saved this soul and he would never force Himself on a soul. God's gift to man was freewill. Father D'Angelico prayed knowing it was far from over. As long as Bobby lived Jesus would reach out to him with love and forgiveness. For now, his soul reeked of sin and darkness. A smell of decay, hatred, and sin filled the air. It called to the evil that lay bound at the foot of the altar. The evil spirits were released.

Spinning though the air, the burning demons screamed with glee. Attracted to Bobby's dark soul they spun through the air toward him. Attaching themselves to his hatred, Bobby couldn't feel the evil spirits as they swirled around him. Whispering evil in an ancient tongue, the spirits of murder, hatred, and pride consumed Bobby's mind and spirit. Evil whispered to Bobby's spirit and it listened.

Unaware of the evil spirits, Bobby's disdain for God grew. He would wait until the others left. He wanted to smash the Eucharistic Lord before him. Bobby would smash the host underfoot and steal the gold surrounding this weak God. He could hardly wait until the others left.

Bobby hated the priest. He would get him, too. Looking at the elderly priest who sat at the back of the church, Bobby chuckled. Looking at the frail priest, overcome with the spirits that whirled around him, Bobby fingered the cold metal of the switchblade in his pocket.

Twelve

And how does this happen to me, that the mother of my Lord should come to me? For at the moment the sound of your greeting reached my ears, the infant in my womb leaped for joy. (Luke 1:43-44)

Patricia Walsh couldn't believe her ears. What was this doctor saying? Trembling, she quickly reached out and held David's hand. Warm, and secure, David sat beside her in front of Dr. Puglisi's desk. The doctor kept talking but the only word Patricia heard was "coma." Megan was in a coma, and no one knew if or when she would awaken. She wanted to scream but held steadfastly to a lifetime of manners. She nodded at the appropriate times and kept her eyes on the doctor as he continued to explain the situation. The doctor's voice droned on but Patricia couldn't listen. Her heart and soul was in the hospital room on the third floor. Her little girl lay there in a coma from which she might never awaken, and at that moment, that was more than Patricia could absorb.

"It's a mystery to medical science, although recently much research has been done into comas," Dr. Puglisi continued, directing his words to David, as Patricia seemed to be in shock.

Suddenly Patricia broke in asking the doctor, "What can

we do? How can we pull her out of the coma?"

Dr. Puglisi looked with pity at the young couple before him. They were so full of hope, hanging on to his every word. Their child had been in a coma for over a month now. He had hoped that when the swelling subsided she would awaken. Instead, it seemed that as her body healed Megan's mind slipped further away. Megan's body was healing still she never awoke. What could he tell this young father and mother? He prayed for the right words.

"Stimuli. That is the best thing for now. We'll be doing stimuli therapy. You'll see the therapist come to her and apply hot and cold to her skin. She'll play music. The therapist will even apply pain to stimulate a response. Don't be upset when you see her do it. Pain is sometimes the best way to pull someone out of a coma. The therapist will come twice a day. Nevertheless, everyone must do their part.

The nurses will get Megan up in a chair. They'll talk to her and sit her in the hall or in front of a television. Megan will probably have to be tied to the chair in a vest restraint so she doesn't slip and fall; don't let that upset you. It is best if she is around a lot of action. You never know what will reach her. And you have to do your part. Talk to her. Read her favorite books to her. Touch her. People who come out of comas have remembered hearing people. They have repeated stories of things that happened while they were in the coma, so they understand on some level. Do you think you can do that? It will take a lot of time and effort on your part."

The short speech had just the effect he had hoped for. Megan's mother smiled for the first time, sensing there was hope and even better, something they could do.

Patricia spoke first, "David has to go back to work. His company has been very good but it has been a month. I can spend time at the hospital. Is it all right if I bring some of Megan's books and toys here?"

Dr. Puglisi was pleased—Patricia now had a goal. He

just hoped she wasn't going to be disappointed. He had heard of people coming out of comas after years of being in one but had never seen it personally. "Yes, yes!" he answered. "Go and get her favorite toys and books. Since David is going to be away, maybe you can spend some extra time with Megan. Talk to her, a mother's voice is the best thing. She will be drawn to it. Remember to stay upbeat. We don't know how much she can understand."

The doctor watched the young couple as they left his office with a determined air. He prayed that the effort would work.

Patricia Walsh spent her last hour with her husband picking up toys and books to take back to the hospital. David ate slowly. He was worried about her. She seemed so forgetful and scattered. He had bills stacking up, but would Patricia be able to handle the strain of caring for Megan alone? He wasn't sure. She still carried a sense of guilt about the accident. Even now as she picked up the new stuffed monkey he gave Megan for her birthday David could see the confusion.

Patricia asked, "Do you think I should bring JoJo?"

David heard the tremor in her voice as she asked and answered, "Yes Pat. It's just a stuffed monkey but she loves it. She was trying to save the damn thing when she was hit. It may be just the thing to pull her out of the coma."

He took his wife in his arms. If only he could stay with her, he thought.

"Are you going to be all right?" he gently kissed her cheek.

Patricia melted in his strength, drawing courage from his strong hands and warm eyes. She needed him for sustenance and she wasn't sure how strong she would be once he was back on the road. The thought of a lonely dark apartment filled her heart with fear, but she couldn't tell him. It would only make him guilty. They both knew the financial situation was dismal and he had to go back to work.

Pulling up a smile Patricia said, "No, of course I'll be fine. I'll be very busy with Megan. I'll probably spend most of my day at the hospital. Stimuli, isn't that what the doctor said. I plan to give her all the stimuli she needs. My baby is going to get better. My baby is going to wake up!"

He walked her to the bus that would take her back to the child they both loved.

Looking deeply into her eyes, David said, "Pat, spend as much time as you want with Megan. But don't forget to take care of yourself. Make sure you get enough rest. I'll call you every night to make sure you're getting enough sleep."

Yet as the bus door closed, he knew she would wear herself out trying to arouse Megan from her sleep.

David was right about one thing: Patricia didn't plan to spend her nights alone in the apartment. The bed they shared since their wedding would be empty. She planned to spend all of her free time — day and night — at her daughter's bedside. Patricia could do nothing else.

The pediatric wing was located on the third floor. Festive and bright, it was painted in warm lively hues of red, yellow, and green, with a mishmash theme of school and recess. Pictures of chalkboards and monkey bars depicted a conventional schoolyard of healthy classmates, but the promise of a future of school and friends would remain just a dream to many of the children on this floor.

Patricia walked out to the hall from the crowded elevator with renewed hope. She couldn't help but notice that the hall seemed almost cheerful. Parents brought balloons and stuffed teddy bears to children coming home minus their tonsils. Colorful casts decorated the arms and legs of the most active and vibrant children.

Patricia walked past the laughter and joy to the back end of the floor. Here the mood was one of quiet desperation. Parents paused to apply false smiles before they pushed the door open. Beyond that door hope died. Children, thin from the ravages of cancer, raised hopeful eyes to the parents they trusted. A doctor stripped of the corny jokes he saved for the homeward bound held a tearful mother racked with sobs. This end of the floor was solemn by contrast as these children had little hope of going home. Megan looked like Sleeping Beauty as she lay silent amidst fresh white sheets, unaware of the pain that surrounded her.

Patricia pulled the curtains around Megan's bed to afford the family next to her some privacy. The young girl who shared the room with Megan was waiting for surgery. Her parents hovered, unable to sit still. The father tried to smooth the sheets on the bed of his only daughter. He talked non-stop, as if he could chase the fear he felt away with endless distraction. Perhaps he thought that by acting as if everything was normal, the situation would become so. He prayed that the surgeon's skilled hands would get the entire tumor. Patricia prayed for them also. She pulled the plastic chair close to the head of Megan's bed.

With renewed courage Patricia talked, "Megan, its Mommy. I brought your favorite book. Let me read it to you."

Remembering what the doctor had said, Patricia touched Megan's cheek. Megan never moved but Patricia continued. Opening the hard and worn cover of the book, she started to read one of Megan's favorite books.

Patricia stopped as the stretcher bearing Megan's little roommate passed to take the child to surgery. Touching Megan, she continued reading *Alice In Wonderland.*

Patricia Walsh fell into a routine. Early in the morning, she would arrive to be greeted by the now familiar day shift nurses. Settling in, she would sit and talk to Megan, as if Megan were listening and hanging on to her every word. She'd help the nurse bathe and dress her. Megan would then be placed in a chair that resembled a high chair. Propped by pillows and tied in a vest restraint, a tray was locked in place before her. The chair was high in the back to support Megan's head. It had wheels so Patricia could push Megan around the hall. Patricia wheeled Megan around at least three times a day. Stopping to talk, Patricia became familiar with the other parents who shared her days. She listened as they spoke about children who would go home to die and of those who did not make it. Day after day moaned on and melted into endless monotony.

Dark circles appeared under Patricia's eyes as fatigue took its toll. Anxiety caused her to lose ten pounds off her already thin frame. The only time Patricia got rest was when David was home. On those occasions, she would stay home in the evening to be with him and he would come with her to the hospital during the day. Unfortunately, those visits were infrequent as David worked all the overtime he could wrangle. The medical bills were high, even with his insurance coverage, so his visits became less frequent and of shorter duration. The daily stress was crushing Patricia.

Megan slept on despite the therapy. Patricia tried to maintain the belief that Megan would wake up, but she was starting to forget. Forget what it was like to have a healthy child. Even worse, she was starting to forget how Megan acted before the accident. Moreover, as the memory of a healthy laughing child faded, so did Patricia's hope. She had no real conversations anymore. She spent her days talking to the memory of a daughter who never responded. Each day tore off a piece of her soul. She tried to remain upbeat but day after lonely day the hours piled heavy on her heart.

The grinding of aspirations is a slow and painful process. Dreams that fade are fragile yearnings of the heart. Like ghosts, they are hard to see in the light of reality. As the light of that reality penetrated, hope faded and her heart, sitting alone in a hospital room, finally broke. She wept. Alone in the cold night, Patricia's hope collapsed.

In tears, she shook her only child, "Wake up, Megan. Why don't you just wake up? Wake up and come home."

Still there was no response from the sleeping child and Patricia dissolved into tears. Sitting in the bedside chair, she bent over in tears. With the bedrail lowered, Patricia laid her head on the small, immobile arm of her daughter.

Patricia called, "Wake up. I can't take any more! Megan, please can you hear me!"

Still there was no answer. The silence was overwhelming to Patricia. Weeping, she lowered her head to the child of her lost dreams. She wept the pain of forgotten hope, lost in broken dreams. Grieving in an empty room, her tears fell upon her child's arm. The arm that lay immobile above the tucked, cotton blanket. Patricia released the pain she had held hidden beneath a veneer of cheerful expectations. She wept for what seemed an eternity. That is, until the evening nurse entered to check on her young patient.

"Mrs. Walsh, come on." The young nurse placed her arm around the sobbing woman and guided her. "Mrs. Walsh, I think you need to go home. You've been here all day. Please, go home and get some rest."

Patricia, embarrassed by her breakdown, nodded and wiped away the tears. She did need to get away. She felt as if a heavy weight was pulling her down. Depression overshadowed her. Reaching for her winter coat, she sighed.

"Mrs. Walsh," the young nurse said, "please stay home tomorrow. You need to take a day for yourself. It doesn't do you or Megan any good to wear yourself out. Megan will still be here the day after tomorrow. And you need to renew your strength. Not just for yourself but for her."

Patricia panicked, "But the doctor said we need to stimulate Megan all the time!"

The nurse was strong in her insistence, "Stay home tomorrow! If you do, I promise that all of the nurses will work with Megan. And I'll call the therapist and book an extra therapy for her."

Patricia felt relief. Broken, it was easy for her to let the nurse take control. She did need a day off. Her emotional breakdown was proof of that. She left the room and walked down the darkened hall with a new determination. She would take tomorrow off and renew herself for the task ahead. She would regain her strength.

The student nurse, who had accompanied the evening nurse on her rounds changed the young girl's sheets and repositioned her after a quick backrub.

Finishing, the student nurse looked up and asked, "Do you want me to call occupational therapy and schedule that extra session?"

The nurse rolled her eyes and answered, "No, don't be ridiculous! It would be a waste of time! I've never seen one of these head-cases get better. I just felt sorry for the mother. Someone should tell her the truth!"

The student nurse was stunned as she put the lotion in the bedside drawer and picked up the dirty sheets. "What do you mean? What truth?"

The nurse shook her head as she answered, "This little girl will never get better. She'll be in a coma for the rest of her life. All of this is a waste of time. Someone should have mercy. They have more sympathy for sick dogs. For people, they have no mercy. They'll let her lay here and suffer. Worse, they'll let her parents suffer as they drain them dry. By the time they get through with them they'll be broke. And for what? That little girl will never wake up. She'll lay there for months or years until she mercifully gets a bad infection. Eventually she'll die anyway. They should put her to sleep now!"

The student nurse, a devout Christian, was shocked. She said a quick silent prayer for the patient but kept her mouth shut. This nurse would be writing a report on her nursing skills to the clinical instructor. That report would determine her final grade in pediatrics. It was senseless to disagree with someone who had the power to destroy her nursing career. Especially for a child who couldn't even hear the negative things this callous nurse was saying.

Megan's arm felt wet and she felt drowsy. She felt like she

had been asleep for hours. Still, she was in the same room. The wetness of her arm woke her. Was something leaking? Was something upstairs coming through? Then she heard it, her mother's voice! Megan wanted to run to the stairs. She was sick of this room. She looked at the white mist that rose from the floor. She knew, from the last time, that quick moves attracted it. She would lose her way in the mist if she rushed. The mist was quiet now. Megan could see the stairs and the upper door. The dark door was still there, but it seemed to have grown smaller as Megan slept. The statue lady still stood guard at the door. It seemed like she was keeping something from getting out. Megan couldn't see anything now, but she had seen something moving there before and it frightened her

She heard movement upstairs.

"Wake up! I can't take any more. Megan, please can you hear me!"

Megan smiled. Her mother was there. She was calling her just like in the morning. Megan was sick of being alone. She had never been alone for so long before.

She would have to go slow. She needed to fool the white smoke that seemed to respond to any movement or sound. Her mommy sounded so sad. Megan wanted to answer her, but she knew better. The mist would hear her and surround her. She would lose her way like the last time. No, Megan learned quickly. She sat up slowly. Her muscles felt stiff. *I must have been sleeping for a long time*, she thought as she slowly untangled her limbs. Her left arm was asleep and Megan dreaded the "pins and needles" that would soon follow. She took a few breaths and waited as the feeling returned to her numb arm. She was quiet. The stairs were not that far away. If she was quiet and moved slowly, she was sure she could make it. Once up the stairs, she could open the door and call her mommy. Megan wanted her mommy. She was afraid of this room and the dark door that lay on the other side.

She started to crawl, making slow gentle movements. The mist responded in kind. It moved toward her and gathered around her. But not too fast, and not too much. Megan was right—the mist responded to sound and movement and if she went very slowly it wouldn't notice. Megan moved in extended, deliberate motions. When the mist moved, she stopped. It was like a game and she was determined to win. Crawling as slowly as possible, Megan almost reached the stairs. Some mist had collected around her but not enough to make it hard to see. She looked at the dark door. She could see movement in the darkness and it scared her. As more mist seemed to come, Megan looked away and decided not to look at the black door. She kept her eyes on the stairs. She was almost there. If she didn't have to move so slowly she could actually stretch out and touch the bottom step.

Megan knew that once she reached the step she'd be home free. Even if the mist came and blinded her she would be able to feel her way up the stairs to the door. She was about to make another move toward the bottom step and freedom when it happened: Megan heard voices. Voices of women muffled through the mist. Megan didn't know who it could be, but she knew it wasn't her mommy. She strained to hear and could barely make out the muffled voice. Suddenly she heard a few words. "Never wake up," and "put to sleep." Megan didn't understand the words or what they meant but the words were bad and they woke something bad up.

Megan sat frozen as the wisps of black smoke seeped through the door at the top of the stairs. It wasn't much smoke but it really stood out against the white mist. The black smoke was drawn in the direction of the other door. It flowed through the crack at the bottom of the door and was drawn to the left. It was as if it was being sucked in by an unseen power. It was as if the smoke was just being sucked into a black hole. Megan was afraid to move. Then she heard it.

A deep guttural growl, low and menacing, Megan started to sweat and her hands started to tremble as the evil moaning grew. She knew that the black smoke had awoken something — something really bad! As her fear grew, the white mist collected around her. It was drawn to the strong emotion of fear. But it didn't muffle the growl, which seemed to be growing louder. It just distorted the sound so Megan couldn't tell where it was coming from. The scary sound seemed to be coming from all directions. Megan's stomach cramped. She couldn't move. She didn't know which way to go and as she grew more frightened the white mist rose and collected around her. It made it harder to see.

Megan didn't want to see. She didn't want to look at the source of the horrible growls.

Megan didn't have a choice. She could no longer see the stairs because of the white mist collecting around her. She had to look at the other door. The black hole had doubled in size. Megan could see a quick movement within the blackness. What was worse, for just a moment, she could swear she saw two shining red eyes looking back at her. She knew that she shouldn't, but she couldn't help herself.

Megan screamed, "Mommy! Mommy, help me!"

Afraid to move, the small girl strained to hear any response. Megan thought she heard a door close. It was muffled and sounded far away. The black door was like a big dark hole now. The horrific moaning and scraping seemed louder. Megan started to cry. As she cried the black hole grew larger. She couldn't stop sobbing. Then the growls grew louder, hurting her ears as the white mist collected around her, leaving her unable to see.

Suddenly, a light started to glow! A warm light cut through the mist. It was the statue lady. Only she wasn't a statue anymore. She looked like she had been in the street. She turned away from the wall and faced the deep black hole. The hole seemed to grow silent as the beautiful lady with the shining sword in her hands turned and faced the opening.

As the lady moved, the mist that had collected around Megan flowed toward the beautiful lady's movements and swirled around her. Now that it had left, Megan could see again. The stairs that led to the upstairs door now seemed far away. The black hole had tripled in size and was now much too close. Megan started to move back, keeping her eyes on the black hole. She was too afraid to remain close to whatever evil lay beyond. The warm light of the lady was now muted by the white mist swirling around her. It gave enough light for Megan to see, so she made her way back to the wall. She pressed against it for safety. The black hole seemed to be shrinking. The growling stopped the minute the statue lady had come alive. Megan felt that the statue lady was protecting her. She watched as the black door shrunk to its original size.

The beautiful lady turned again in the now silent room. She smiled a beautiful warm smile at Megan. The small girl wished that the lady would hold her in her arms again. Megan felt so alone. The lady just took the stance she had taken before. With her back to the black evil door, she held the sword with the tip facing heavenward. Holding the shining dagger in front of her as if ready for a fight, the beautiful lady again took on the appearance of a plaster statue.

The room looked just as it did before Megan heard her mother's voice calling her. The dark door was its original size, no bigger than the other door. Megan could see the stairs and the upper door. She wondered if she should try to reach the upstairs door again. No, she was too afraid. She didn't want the black wisps of smoke to come and wake up the evil again. Megan didn't know what to do. She was so afraid. She curled up in a ball in the far corner of the room.

The nurse who closed the door on the comatose child never knew the harm her negative comments had done.

Thirteen

For my thoughts are not your thoughts, nor are your ways my ways, says the Lord. As high as the heavens are above the earth, so high are my ways above your ways and my thoughts above your thoughts. (Isaiah 55:8-9)

She had trouble with the cold icy steps that led into the church. Heavy-laden and burdened by the extra hundred and twenty-five pounds it had taken a lifetime to accumulate, she took one-step at a time. Pulling on the cold metal banister, she used all her strength to propel herself upward. The others had already reached safety and warmth. A young man brushed quickly past her almost knocking her down. Father D'Angelico waited patiently.

The stabbing pain of arthritis in her knees was sharpened by the penetrating cold. Anna took a deep breath and braced her self for the next wave of pain. Normally a few aspirin controlled the throbbing and allowed her to walk without trouble. However, when the cold weather came, the ache intensified, and her gait slowed. Still she pushed on through the pain and the cold, up the stairs that would lead her to the warmth of the church. She took a step at a time, determined to reach the door.

Slowly, carrying the heavy weight of the past, Anna

finally reached the vestibule. Grateful for the warmth and the end another struggle she kissed her hand and touched the icon of the black Madonna. Anna had given Father D'Angelico the icon forty years ago, carrying it reverently from the Polish church that was closing just two blocks from Holy Rosary. Our Lady of Chestahova closed its doors because the Polish community had dwindled to a precious few.

Anna loved the little parish and cried for two weeks upon hearing the news. The old Polish priest who was being transferred to the suburbs recognized her grief with a gift. He gave her the icon she was so devoted to. Anna promptly brought it over to Holy Rosary. The Italian church would now be her church. That was ages ago. So many things had happened over the years. Yet here was Anna, still faithful and now struggling to spend the night with her Jesus.

Anna Grubowski never missed a Friday night with her Eucharistic Lord. For as long as Father D'Angelico opened the doors to the Eucharistic worship, Anna would come. A deep unseen inner strength propelled her through the storm and illness to the church. That inner strength had been Anna's gift throughout her life.

Her worn cloth coat was little protection from the cold. However, Anna was used to the biting winds. The nor'easter reminded her of her childhood home in Poland. She untied the babushka that protected her ears from the howling winds, releasing the white curled fluff that her formally blonde hair had become. She slowly struggled up the aisle to the front of the church. Her heavy legs moved slowly and each bend of her knee brought spasms of pain. Anna was so used to the pain she barely noticed it. Even pain can become accepted as normal. Still, she was glad to sit down. It took her a few minutes of warming up to gain the resolve to kneel on those swollen knees. The pain returned quickly, but Anna didn't care. She was with her God.

Her round cheeks were reddened from the cold and the effect gave her the look of a doll whose head was carved from a dried apple. Anna had a doll like that as a child. Her papa had carved it for her and Anna had treasured it. She lost the doll when the Nazi's came. At the time, it was all she had to remind her of the papa she adored. Anna took time on her knees to pray for her children. She always prayed for them even though she had not seen any of them in years. She prayed that they were all right and healthy, but mostly she prayed that they would find faith in Jesus. Scattered across the continent, Anna told herself it was too hard for them to visit, but she knew it was a lie. Anna didn't often lie to herself but this was a lie that brought her comfort. With a quick closing prayer for all the people in the church, Anna pulled herself off her arthritic knees and onto the smooth wooden pew. Pushing her black purse to the side, she looked at the golden monstrance and sighed with peace. This was her favorite night of the week. She would rest here with Jesus until it was time for her to walk to the hospital.

She was much too old and sick to be working but the money she got from social security was not enough. The small check she collected each month barely paid for the tiny apartment she called home. The government allowed her to supplement her check up to a certain amount and so Anna worked one shift a week as a cleaning woman at the local hospital. During the night as the patients slept Anna would sweep and wash the floors to a shining glow, taking pride in her work. The little amount of money she made paid for her food. It was just enough to keep her in flour and kielbasa and that was good. It was enough, she didn't starve and was grateful.

Anna baked her own bread and made her own noodles and pierogi. Anna was a talented baker. Her father had been a baker and had taught how to bake as a young child. The first day papa brought Anna to the bakery was one of the happiest and yet one of the saddest days of her life.

Anna was just eight the morning her Papa woke her, "Come. Wake up little one. Today your wish is coming true.

You are coming to work with Papa from now on. I will teach you how to make bread. A trade you should have, unlike your silly sisters. Come, wash up and get ready. You have been asking to be with Papa and a baker has to wake up early to get the bobka and rolls in the oven."

Anna leapt out of bed. As the youngest daughter of four, she had been begging Papa to take her to work with him. She dreamed of long happy days helping him as he molded the white flour into the soft sweet bread that filled the window and display cases of the small family bakery. She couldn't be happier. At home, her mama and older sisters ignored her. Her blond, blued-eyed sisters found little use for her. Mama made them spend each morning teaching Anna to read and do figures and her sisters resented it. Ava was the most vocal of the sisters. Her insults were never tempered with kindness. Each morning she would let her resentment show in cutting words.

As Anna struggled over her primer, Ava would angrily comment, "Stupid Anna, you're so dumb you will never learn to read."

Anna tried but it was as if they were speaking another language. She couldn't understand enough to read a full sentence and her sisters were impatient. Beautiful and so much older than Anna, they were anxious to get out to market. At the market, they would meet their friends and gossip and they would catch the admiring glances of the boys. To her older sisters teaching Anna was a bore. Anna's head hurt trying to understand. She hated it.

The morning papa woke her it was a dream come true. It meant no more struggles with the books. Anna would learn to make bread and spend her days with Papa. She rushed to the bowl to wash up and had to break the thick ice that had formed overnight. Washing her face and hands quickly in the icy water, she dampened the dark blonde curls that covered her head. Smoothing her hair, she carefully braided it.

She was dressing when her sisters awoke. Giggling they

preened themselves in the mirror. They spent hours looking at themselves in the mirror that hung in the bedroom of the small house. Laughing they recounted yesterday's conquests as Anna, so much smaller, struggled to check herself in the only mirror in the house.

Proudly Anna jumped up behind her sister and shouted, "Get out of my way. I have to get ready." She felt important today. She couldn't help but brag, "Papa is bringing me to the bakery! He is going to teach me to be a baker!"

Anna couldn't see how she looked as the sisters hogged the mirror. She felt her temper rise as all three sisters ignored her.

"Papa said that I should learn a trade so as not to grow up silly and useless like the three of you." Anna reddened with the realization that she had added her own opinions to Papa's simple and loving statement.

Ava looked hard at Anna, "Oh, so that's what you think! You are so stupid, Anna!" Ava, the youngest and the prettiest of the three bent down to Anna with a look of disdain. "I heard Papa and Mama discussing the need to teach you a trade. Do you know why they are doing it? Because you're too stupid to learn your lessons. And what is worse, you are too ugly to get a husband! Papa wants you to be able to take care of yourself. You are not pretty, Anna. And you never will be!"

Anna was stunned into silence.

One of the other sisters reprimanded Ava, "You shouldn't have said such a thing!"

Ava waved her hand in defense. "I don't care. I am sick of her. She should know the truth."

The sisters laughed and left happy. Happy that they didn't have to teach Anna and could meet their friends at the market place early.

Anna was left standing alone in front of the mirror. For the first time in her young life Anna took a good long look at herself. Her hair was dark blond. It was nothing like the sparkling golden curls that crowned her sisters' pretty heads. While they had oval faces with delicate features, Anna had a large round face. Her nose was wide and her mouth weak. Unlike the almond-shaped blue eyes that her sisters liked to flash at the boys, Anna had button round eyes the color of mud. Her sisters had petite hourglass shapes. Anna's body was straight and square. Mama called her "big-boned."

Until now, she hadn't really thought about it. Anna looked with honesty at her image in the mirror. Her sisters were very pretty. They looked like Mama. Anna looked like Papa. She never really noticed before. She just assumed that she was pretty like her sisters. Now, with a pragmatic eye she knew she would never be pretty.

Anna was honest with herself. She wasn't book smart either. She had to struggle to understand the simplest lesson. Papa was right. No man would want to look at that plain face staring out of the mirror. And who would want to marry such a plain square woman? Even at the tender age of eight, Anna knew and accepted the truth. It was good that her Papa would teach her a trade.

With even greater resolve, she joined her Papa each morning, long before the sun rose. In the back of the bakery far from the eyes of the public, Anna was happy. She loved to knead the bread, adding the eggs that made the dough tender. She learned so quickly that Papa said she was a natural baker.

The priest's songs before the altar called Anna from her memories. She prayed for the souls of her Papa and Mama. She had no idea if her sisters were still alive. She had not seen them in more then sixty-five years. She had not seen or heard from any of her family since she was thirteen.

Anna could hear the homeless man moving around in the pew behind her. She and the priest were aware of Frankie the Bottle's presence each Friday. Anna, usually the last to leave the church, watched as he hid each week. It was cold outside and she was glad he would be safe and warm. He would probably freeze if he stayed outside. Anna knew most of the regulars who came each week. Tonight, because of the storm she supposed many of the 'regulars' chose not come. Many of those here tonight were strangers to Anna.

Anna decided to offer the pain in her body up for the people gathered here tonight. Why waste suffering? It was a powerful practice and Father D'Angelico could see the light of grace that Anna offered as it touched each person in the church. He thanked God for her offering and added his own. Uniting their sufferings to the crucified Jesus intensified their prayers and each person in the church received abundant grace. The heavy woman prayed the rosary. She could hear the young woman sobbing two pews behind her. As Anna prayed for her, she could feel her hands growing warm. Within a few minutes, she felt as if her hands were on fire. It was not the first time. The young girl must be praying for someone ill. Anna's hands burned whenever she prayed for the sick.

The first time had been when Mama got sick. Mama got a cold the winter Anna turned ten. It was a very bitter, windy winter and no one thought much about it until her cold didn't seem to go away. Mama drank tea with honey and stayed in bed but nothing seemed to help. The cold settled in her chest and the coughing never stopped. She couldn't sleep because of the constant, hacking cough. The doctor medicine.

He said that Mama had pneumonia and came to see her each day after the first visit. Nothing seemed to help. Anna visited Mama, as Mama coughed and burned with fever. Anna prayed. Suddenly her hands grew warm. On an impulse, she touched her mama's arm and continued to pray. She prayed that Mama's cough would stop long enough so she could get some sleep.

To Anna's surprise, her prayers seemed to be answered.

Mama fell asleep and slept peacefully all afternoon. Anna never asked for Mama to be healed. And that is something she always regretted. Mama died the following week.

Anna watched as the old priest struggled to his feet. He seemed much weaker than last week. *Age and illness gets us all in the end,* she thought. She looked to her only friend, the Lord of Bread. Bread in all its forms had always been a large part of Anna's life. She loved to watch the dough rise and bake to a golden crust. It was magic to watch and she loved to punch it down and watch it rise again. It filled her with pride to see the result of her patience and hard work. It was bread that made her father famous and filled the small shop with customers each morning. The customers became friends, but Papa's best friend was the man who spent most of his free time in the back of the shop with him. That man was the Professor.

The Professor taught at the university and was renowned for his intellect. Papa wasn't educated like the Professor, but Papa loved to read. He seemed to be able to hold his own with the Professor. They would spend hours in the back of the bakery debating social events and philosophy. They agreed on many things. Anna would listen to them as she swept the floor and washed the cases with vinegar water.

She supposed the two men were friends because they were so lonely—they were both widowers. Papa needed another male to talk to. The Professor had small children. His wife died in childbirth just a few years ago. Each evening at dusk, the two men would have tea, buttered scones, and tobacco in the back as Anna listened.

The first time she heard her Papa raise his voice it frightened her. He was passionate in his disagreement about something called *Nazis.* Papa brought a radio into the bakery to listen to the latest news about them.

Each morning, before the summer sun rose, Papa would listen to the latest news of the Nazis on the radio. He seemed very interested in a man named Hitler. Anna thought the man was very loud. She did not speak German like her Papa, but she didn't like the speeches of this man Hitler anyway. This man sounded like he was angry.

When Hitler spoke, Papa didn't pay attention to the batter. He got so upset he ruined the bread on some mornings and so Anna learned to watch what Papa was doing and take over whenever the news came on the radio. She didn't like the scratchy sound either. It had been better in the bakery before Papa brought that radio.

Papa stayed later at night with the Professor now, too. Anna grew tired waiting to lock up the store. Instead of laughter now, there was a lot of shouting. The Professor thought that this German leader was very smart. He thought that he was right about some people called Jews. The Professor even dragged Anna into the argument. One night as Anna was putting the broom away the Professor called her over to where the two men sat and smoked their pipes.

The Professor asked, "Anna, what do you think of the Jews? Have you ever met any Jews?"

Anna thought hard before she answered, "Oh yes I have, I love them!"

The Professor reddened, "Love them, how can you say that!"

"Oh because the only Jews that I know are Jesus and Mary, and they are my best friends!"

Papa laughed until tears formed in his eyes, but the Professor did not seem very happy.

The Professor shouted, "You are a stupid, ignorant girl!" Papa just laughed harder at the Professor's insult. Anna also noticed that the Professor looked at her a lot. When Papa was not around the Professor seemed to seek her out. He liked to corner her and talk softly to her. Anna didn't like it. The Professor never looked in her eyes. He stared at the bosom she tried to hide. Her breasts just seemed to grow larger each day. Anna covered them with loose tops and layers of clothing but nothing seemed to help. She didn't like the way the Professor looked at her chest all the time. She didn't know why, it just made her turn red. She was glad when Papa was around. The Professor ignored Anna when he was there.

Summer was hot the year Anna turned thirteen. Working by the oven was even warmer. Anna couldn't keep the layers of clothing on anymore. Papa seemed more agitated lately. She wished the Professor would stop coming to the bakery. Papa seemed remote, lost in thought as the Professor came more frequently. Anna could hear them arguing in the back as she waited on the late customers.

One particular day, Papa was extremely upset. The Nazi's had invaded Poland. They just marched over the border and no one was able to stop them. They hadn't reached Anna's town yet, but as the first day of September waned, it seemed just a matter of time. Papa was very worried and so Anna worked harder in the bakery. She wanted to make him happy.

Anna had just locked the glass door when Papa called her to the back.

In a soft voice, he insisted, "Sit down, Anna, sit down."

He seemed so sad. Papa wouldn't look in her eyes. The Professor on the other hand glared at her. His eyes seemed to devour her and his face seemed feverish. The look on the Professor's face frightened Anna. She was glad when he left. For the first time Anna thought the Professor looked evil.

Anna sat quietly. It wasn't like Papa to sit and talk to her. Usually they quickly went home so Anna could make dinner. Suddenly she felt afraid.

"Anna, you know about the Germans and how they have just invaded Poland. I am sure that you heard it on the radio."

"Yes, Papa," Anna was relieved. It was just about stupid politics.

"The family has to leave Poland. We cannot stay here with the Germans. You know your sisters. They will get involved with the soldiers. They are very pretty but have no common sense. You know how they are, Anna."

Still her father would not look her in the eye. He glanced around the back of the bakery as if memorizing each tray and mold. Anna was shocked. It had never occurred to her that the Nazi's had anything to do with her or her family. She had never been anywhere else but this town. The house and the bakery was all she knew and the thought of leaving it all filled her with fear.

"Anna, the Germans will be here soon. If only I had saved some money, but I was weak. I kept giving any extra to your sisters' for silly bobbles. I knew they might come. I was afraid but didn't listen to my heart. Now we must leave and I have no money. I had to make a deal with the Professor." Anna's heart froze. She prayed that her father had not done it. With fear she asked, "You didn't sell the bakery to him did you, Papa?"

For the first time her Papa looked at her. His look was tender as he reached out and gently stroked her face. His eyes were full of tears, "No, Anna the bakery shall be yours. You know how to bake the bread. You can survive. You are strong, not like your sisters. You have common sense, something that cannot be taught."

Anna started to tremble as she asked, "What do you mean Papa? Then we are not leaving?"

Papa answered without emotion, "No Anna, you are not leaving. I know that it will be hard for you to understand. Some day you will and then I hope that you will forgive me. I will give you the bakery. You will always have that."

Anna could feel her stomach cramp with overwhelming fear. Her father looked deeply in her eyes.

Papa continued, "The Professor has asked to marry you. He is an educated man. He will provide for you. He needs a mother for his small children and Anna you would be a good mother. Even he can see that. In return, he will give us the money we need to leave Poland. Your sisters and I will leave tomorrow, before the Nazi's get here. You will stay and you will marry in the morning. And you will keep the bakery. Here are the keys."

Anna sat frozen. This could not be happening. She was only thirteen and the Professor was so old. She didn't want to marry him. The thought of it made her sick, but her worse fear was of her Papa leaving her.

Frozen and afraid Anna swallowed hard and asked, "When will you come back? How long will you be gone?"

That's when her Papa rose from his chair. He took Anna in his arms and held her for what seemed a long time. Releasing her, he answered as he led her out of the bakery toward home, "I'll come back as soon as I can. You are strong Anna. You will be fine until I come." Anna didn't believe him. She noticed that he never looked her in the eye again.

That night Anna didn't have to cook dinner. Her sisters pulled out the metal tub that was usually reserved for weekend bathes. Filling it with bath oils and bubbles, they pushed Anna into the tub that sat in the middle of the kitchen floor.

"Might as well use it all, we can't take it with us." Ava poured even more of the flowery scent on Anna and in the bath water, "You will smell good for your new husband, little Anna!"

Anna swallowed hard. She didn't want a husband. She didn't want to be left behind. She loved Papa so much. Anna even loved her silly, useless sisters. She hoped they wouldn't leave her. She didn't like the Professor.

Her sisters worked on her wedding dress as Papa cooked a large farewell dinner. They heard the first bomb fall in the middle of that dinner. The Germans were bombing heavily and the aftershocks shook the house and shattered some of Mama's favorite china. Papa turned pale. He tried to remain cheerful as the sounds of war crashed around them.

Frightened, they slept on cots in the basement. All night,

the bombs reigned down as Papa tried to calm his screaming girls. Anna never screamed. She prayed the bombs would change things and perhaps Papa would keep her. Maybe things would be different in the morning. Anna secretly hoped the bombs would make the Professor run away. She must have fallen asleep sometime late that night. Papa never slept. He spent the night listening to the radio as it cried out the sounds of marching Nazi invaders.

Long before the sun rose, her sisters dressed her. Mama's lacey white dress was still big on Anna though her sisters tried to alter it. Tied with a blue silk sash, Anna's dress looked very pretty. They curled her hair with hot irons and attached little flowers from the late summer garden. Anna sat silent while she was being worked on. It all seemed surreal. She didn't face the reality of her marriage until she faced the Professor in the office of the judge. The judge seemed nervous and anxious to get out of there. Anna guessed the Professor had paid him his traveling money, just like Papa. Within five short minutes, Anna became a wife. Instead of the usual long party, the Professor paid for a small breakfast. Papa wouldn't look at Anna. Her sisters and papa were antsy, restless to start their trip. Drinking vodka in quick and numerous shots, the Professor talked too much, keeping them late into the morning.

"So you are leaving Germany!" asked the Professor. Papa nodded. "With luck, we can outpace the Germans until we reach the Russian border. From there we will see." The Professor shook his head and proclaimed, "I still say you should stay. We have nothing to fear from the Germans. They will free us of the Jews. They will set up a fair society and we will prosper."

The thundering blast from the German bomb that fell from the sky and hit the store down the street put an end to the Professor's pronouncements. Anna cried as she watched her family, the family she loved, leave Krakow. It was the last time she would ever see them.

Fourteen

When he broke open the second seal, I heard the second living creature cry out, "Come forward." Another horse came out, a red one. Its rider was given power to take peace away from the earth, so that people would slaughter one another. And he was given a huge sword. (Rev. 7:3-4)

The Professor grabbed Anna's arm roughly, squeezing it tightly as he walked Anna to his large brick house on a fashionable street in the inner village. Dragging her into the parlor, Anna saw the Professor's children for the first time.

The Professor announced sarcastically, "Vito, Klara, Jedze, this is Anna. She is the new wife I told you to expect."

Anna felt the children's eyes boring into her, examining her. Suddenly she felt out of her element. The oldest boy, Vito, scanned her up and down. Vito was as big as Anna and turned out to be just one year younger at twelve. He stared at the heavy peasant shoes beneath the lacey white dress.

Klara, a small and delicate girl stared at Anna's face, "Why Papa, she is so plain. She is not at all pretty!"

Vito's face grew tight with sarcasm as he stared at Anna and said, "Shall we call her mother, Papa?"

"Of course not!" The Professor answered in an angry tone, "She is not your mother. She is no more than a servant, here to take care of you. You will call her Anna."

The cruelty of their faces filled Anna with fear. Only Jedze, the youngest at four years old, smiled at Anna. His cheerful bright face contrasted with the anemic coldness of the others.

"I will call her Mama!" he announced as he spanned the room quickly to hug Anna's leg.

The Professor's face reddened with anger as he pulled the boy away. "Go into the kitchen Anna. Dinner shall be served promptly at six! You will find everything you need there."

Anna was glad to escape their scornful stares. The kitchen at the back of the house was the most beautiful Anna had ever seen. She quickly donned a white apron and started to prepare the meal. Stuffing cabbage comforted her. Food was something she understood. Still, as she bustled around the plentiful pantries her eyes welled with tears. Where was her family? How was she supposed to live without them?

She didn't want to give any of the people in this house the satisfaction of seeing her tears. Anna, in large bites, quickly stuffed down about half a loaf of the sweet yellow bread she had taken from the oven. As she stuffed her mouth, she stuffed her feelings down.

She figured they must have liked the dinner she served, because she heard no complaints, and they ate every crumb. Still, they complained about everything else.

Anna served them on the right instead of the left and the Professor ridiculed her, "She is a stupid girl. Look at her carefully and vow to learn your lessons. If you don't study hard, you could end up as ignorant as Anna."

The only pleasure Anna had that night was bathing little Jedze and tucking him into his crib. His joy was infectious. Anna wondered how his little spirit had survived in this house. She was singing him an ancient rhyme when the Professor came and called her to him.

He dragged Anna to the large dark bedroom at the end of the hall. He had been drinking shots of vodka since dinner, as he listened to the radio in the parlor. The Professor stumbled, unsteady on his feet. Anna looked at the large wooden bed fearfully as the Professor locked the door and placed the key out of her reach. Anna was shocked when he removed his clothes. She had never seen a naked man.

Distracted by the loud crash of the first of that night's bombardments, Anna was taken by surprise. The Professor quickly grabbed her and with his left hand pulled the back of Anna's hair with enough force to pull out the flowers her sisters had tied there. Pulling her hair tightly with his right hand, he grabbed the collar at the front of her throat. He tore her Mama's bridal dress down the front in one strong movement and forcefully threw her on the bed.

The pounding thunder of the German power raining from the night sky didn't bother him as he fell upon her. The smell of vodka choked her as his weight took her breath away. Anna felt as if she was going to suffocate. Pulling in as much air as she could, she screamed. His rough hand covered her mouth. Infantry forces drove tanks toward the city, as Anna lay trapped beneath him. She felt overwhelming pain as he brutally raped her. She closed her eyes to stop the tears and she prayed to God to die.

Then, as quickly as it started, it was over. He rolled his heavy body off her and turned his back. Covering himself with the blanket, he left Anna exposed. Naked, she shivered in the cold night air. Anna laid immobile for an eternity. The crashing sound of a blast landed just a little too close and the loud noise pulled Anna from her stupor. Anna rose gently as he snored loudly.

She felt alone as she dressed in her working clothes, afraid to wake him. She rolled the torn dress that had been so beautiful that morning into a ball. She wanted to burn it. She would burn it, in the oven at the bakery. She climbed quietly up on the wooden chair. Stretching gingerly, she reached for the key he had hidden on top of the heavy dresser. Anna let herself out. In the damp morning as the bombs continued to crash about her, Anna walked to the bakery. She couldn't believe that no one heard her scream last night. Her screams were as ignored as her needs.

She knew now that she was alone and if she was going to survive she would have to protect herself. The rape repeated itself each night for the next three nights, as the ridicule the Professor heaped upon her during the day grew more brutal. The children, especially Vito, belittled every move she made. Only here, in her bakery did Anna feel at home. On the third day as she unlocked the back door of the bakery as the Nazi tanks reached the outskirts of Krakow. That was the day that would change everything.

The Professor couldn't stop smiling as the Nazi tanks rolled through the city streets. The grin froze on his face the day that the German Colonel knocked on the door of the Professor's large house.

The Colonel was curt, "You are the owner here!"

The Professor gave his name and all the information about the family that the Nazi soldier asked for.

In a calm and steady voice the Colonel announced, "You will vacate the premises. This house is confiscated for the army of the Third Reich. You have one hour to pack and leave."

The Professor's face reddened with anger as he answered, "That is impossible! We have no place to go! We will not leave!"

The German soldier, who had been writing on a pad, looked up at the Professor. He grabbed the Professor by the collar and unsnapping his side holster he drew his gun and pointed it at the Professor's head.

In a cold and deliberate voice the Nazi whispered, "There are other ways of emptying this house. Do you want me to use those methods?"

The Professor's arrogant face quickly filled with fear as he answered, "No, no we will leave the house right away."

Deflated and filled with fear, he ignored the cries of his

children.

"Papa where shall we go? I will not leave our house." Vito cried out.

"What about our things?" Klara wailed.

The Professor was lost in thought and clearly irritated by the moaning and whining. He shouted, "Pack your things. Pack what you can carry and be quick about it!"

Anna watched in horror as the children started to pick up toys and other useless bobbles. She hurried to the kitchen, and taking two clean white aprons, she packed cans of meat and vegetables from the pantry. Returning to the living room she quickly emptied the children's satchels.

"No, these things are useless! You cannot eat toys," Anna announced to the stunned children.

The Professor was too lost in his own thoughts to pay attention. Anna directed the children to pack warm clothes and blankets. They obeyed her although the whining continued.

She packed a few gold items in Jedze's backpack. Maybe she could sell them to the Germans for money. She dressed the children in heavy winter coats despite the warmth of the day. Soon the winter winds would blow and discomfort today might just keep them alive tomorrow. Anna finished and looked around. The hour was almost up yet the Professor continued to just sit in his favorite chair and stare into space.

Vito called his attention, "Papa, we cannot do this! We will freeze on the street. We have no home and we will surely die when the winter comes!"

The Professor stared at his son. He had no answer.

Anna answered, "We will go to the bakery. There are rooms above the store that can act as our bedrooms. There I can bake bread and sell it. We will have plenty to eat and the ovens will keep us warm. Come, follow me!"

The Professor allowed Anna to take charge and carry the largest satchel containing the bulky blanket and pillow she had packed. It also contained the Professor's winter sweaters and boots. Anna led them past numerous soldiers to the small bakery that would now be their home.

The Professor had been silent until they reached the small brick building. Looking around, his memories of the evenings he spent here with Papa seemed to trigger his anger. The children turned to Anna for directions. She was the only one who remained focused on the tasks on hand.

"What shall we do now?" Klara cried.

Anna took the little girl in her arms and in a soft voice comforted her, "Don't be afraid. See there is a table and chairs in the back room where Papa and the Professor used to sit and talk. There is even a radio. And this can be our day room. We can eat in here and I can bake us plenty of bread to sell and keep. First we will go and clean out the storage rooms upstairs and they can be our bedrooms."

The children's cries softened and for the first time the Professor seemed to notice the confidence the children drew from Anna.

Anna could tell from his face that he was irritated as he shouted, "Stupid Anna! She acts as if she is so smart and so good. This is my bakery, not hers. Anything a wife has belongs to her husband. And look how lazy she is. Come children, you were not made to work like servants. Anna clean and prepare our bedrooms upstairs and do not be late with our lunch!"

Anna felt her spirit sink as she watched the four of them head for her father's room behind the ovens. She fired up the ovens and lugged the heavy bags of bedding and clothes up the back stairs. It took all day to carry the heavy boxes and supplies down the back stairs. She baked and cooked in-between and spent most of the early evening scrubbing and dusting the storage rooms. She set up the bedding on the freshly scrubbed floors and placed her bedding in the same room with the children. Anna prayed the Professor would be content to sleep in the smallest room alone.

She did not need to worry, as each night the Professor

would drink himself in to a stupor. Anna would have to hold him as he stumbled to his small room. Most nights he would pass out as soon as he fell to his bed. It angered Anna when he traded the precious gold items she had saved for a few cases of vodka. She saved them to trade for necessities if she had to. Still, the vodka served a purpose and Anna was left to sleep unmolested with the children each night.

Every morning Anna would rise gently and tiptoe downstairs before the sun rose to bake. She would open her bakery doors promptly at six each morning while the children slept. The price of the bread had come down as people had less money to spend. The little money Anna made barely brought supplies for the next day's baking. They were starting to run out of the canned meats and vegetables despite her attempts at rationing. The Professor insisted on hearty meals with bread and butter. Already drunk by dinnertime, he took little notice of the dwindling pantry and it worried Anna.

As the brown leaves that covered the sidewalk outside danced in the morning wind, a car pulled up in front of the bakery. One month to the day that Anna brought them here, fear gripped Anna's stomach as the sharply dressed Nazi soldiers entered the bakery pushing the Polish customers out of their way.

"Where is the Professor?" one of soldiers shouted.

Anna, too stunned to speak, looked toward the back stairs without thinking. The soldiers ran past her and up the stairs. After a loud scuffle, they returned dragging the red-faced Professor still in his nightclothes. The Professor struggled but the soldiers held him firmly. He screamed as they dragged him to the waiting car. The Professor looked terrified as he was forced into the car.

The people in the bakery watched in stunned silence as one of the soldiers unbuckled his gun and hit the Professor in the back of the head. As the Nazi's placed him in the back of the car, he looked back through the open bakery door and with a look of anger shouted, "Stupid girl, you better take care of my children! You hear me!"

Anna answered without thought, "I will take care of them."

It wasn't until years later that she would realize the cost of that promise. The Professor was never seen again. Anna heard that most of the university staff were taken that day. Anyone considered to be educated disappeared. It seemed the Nazi's didn't like intellectuals. Those very intellectuals who supported Hitler were the first to disappear. Anna heard rumors of the executions of those taken that first week of October. She didn't know what became of the Professor. She only knew that she never saw him again and for that she was grateful.

Anna did the best she could for the children. She fed them and kept them warm. She comforted them as they each mourned the lost of their father. Running the bakery was the easy part. It was something she understood. Rising each morning before the sun lit the eastern sky, Anna would bake as she learned to from her father. She carried the bread and pastries to the storefront, and would wait on customers for hours as the children slept. She sustained them with the small amount of canned meat she could buy. Eggs were too precious to spare. They were used in the bakery to bind the cakes and sweeten the bread.

The winter winds blew hard and cold but the ovens kept the children warm in the back room as they squabbled and listened to the radio. Anna tried to encourage them to read and study but was too busy to force them. It wasn't until the morning when Anna was starting to make the Advent cookies in preparation for the season that she first noticed a nauseous feeling. Each morning that week, her stomach felt weak and on the fourth day, she vomited.

It wasn't until Vito sarcastically announced, "Anna is eating the extra food while she starves us. Look she is getting fat!" that she noticed the chubby feel of her stomach.

Anna reddened at the accusation. It wasn't true. If anything, she had done without, giving the growing children the extra food. She looked at her abdomen and rubbed the roundness it had become. *Oh no, it couldn't be. I couldn't be pregnant!*

Christmas approached as her body belied her denial. What would she do with a baby to watch, and who would help her deliver it? Anna ignored her pregnancy. She had bigger problems.

The bread and pastries were not selling even though they were good and fresh. Anna made sure of that, but the crowd who stood clamoring in the morning for the best pick of the bread had disappeared. So many people disappeared these days. There was scarcely a family not praying in silent despair for the safe return one of their relatives. The money disappeared as well. The people simply did not have enough money for store-baked bread and delicacies. The customers instead came at the end of day to bicker for pennies over the stale bread.

Anna was worried. She did not have enough to feed the children. They complained bitterly over their meager meals. What could she do? It wasn't until a German soldier came looking for a German cake that Anna got the idea. Who had money now? It wasn't the Polish. It was the Germans.

She searched the back room for her father's cookbooks and found the two she was looking for. Silently in the back workroom, Anna practiced the recipes she found. For weeks, she kneaded the dark hearty German rye until it looked exactly like the one in the picture. Their pastries were harder. She spiced the dough and ground the nuts for the linzer tarts filling the small batch she made with the precious raspberry jam. She practiced with small batches, which she fed the children until she felt confident.

Changing to a German style of baking was a gamble but what choice did she have? Her regular customers were too poor to sustain them; the Germans had money.

A week before Christmas Anna filled each case with the rich chocolate fare. The black forest cakes looked great, and the dark seeded rye bread filled the back shelves and storefront windows where the bobka used to sit. She filled the case that used to hold the popular Javleczik with a sweet apple strudel. The linzer tarts were placed beside the dark rye in the window in hopes of attracting soldiers who passed by. Feeling fear and expectation, Anna unlocked the front door. It was Mrs. Chamanski, who was the first to complain.

"What is this? Where is the good bread?" She shook her head as she slammed the bakery door leaving.

Let her leave, thought Anna. She always haggled over the rock bottom prices Anna asked for the fresh bobka. After complaining to all the other customers, Mrs. Chamanski demanded the stale bread for pennies. It didn't matter what Mrs. Chamanski thought. What would the soldiers think? Anna didn't have to wait long. The first gang of soldiers who looked in the window purchased all of the tarts. As word spread of the German fare, Anna found Germans waiting in line the next morning for her bread. She had to close the bakery at noon because the shelves were empty. The register was full. It had been a good move and Anna treated the children to sausages that night. Each day Anna had to bake more to keep up with the demand, and the store was constantly filled with soldiers.

Throughout the winter, the demand grew as Anna refined her skills. She tried to ignore her growing belly. She wore loose clothing to cover the pregnancy. A heavy winter coat hid her shame as she traveled each evening to the store for eggs and spices. She could see the disdain in the eyes of her Polish neighbors and the way they shunned her. Mrs. Chamanski had loosed her tongue against the young girl who deprived her of cheap bread. She announced to all that Anna was a spy for the Germans.

As the bakery filled with German soldiers clamoring for the taste of home cooking, Anna's keen business sense seemed to confirm the angry woman's accusations. Many people that Anna had known all her life turned their heads as she walked by. Some of the men spit on the ground. Anna couldn't help but cry in her pillow at night as the insults grew and the treatment worsened. What could she do? She had money to feed the children. She had promised.

In the store, as Anna walked the aisles in search of dark flour and eggs, everyone ignored her. That was bad enough, but when she found out that Vito told the younger children she was a Nazi it really hurt her. She tried to hold her head up knowing it wasn't true, but as she prospered, the rumors just grew and Anna was swept along on the bitter lies of one woman.

It grew harder and harder to keep up as the infant grew inside her. The warmth of spring ended the cold winter but not the coldness of her neighbors. She had no one to turn to for help. The June sun warmed the flowers that lined the window boxes of the main street. The beauty of the city covering the ugliness of what the Poles suffered.

Fear filled Anna's heart on the morning she awoke in a sweat of pain. It was the baby. She woke Klara and sent her for the midwife. When Klara returned alone, Anna tried not to show the fear that consumed her. No one would come and help someone they thought a Nazi collaborator. Anna sent Klara for fresh towels before she could see her tears. She sent the boys down to the bakery to turn the customers away with an assurance that they would open tomorrow.

With all of that taken care of, Anna allowed herself to flow on the waves of pain, swallowed in the waters of childbirth. She bit on a rolled hand cloth to muffle the screams that rose from her agony. She didn't want to frighten Klara who remained beside her mopping up the sweat from her forehead. Anna prayed and prayed it would all end. Hours later, as the pain continued, she had a son. Anna held her son to her breast as she directed Klara in the disposal of the bloody sheets and towels. Her son was small and delicate with a weak cry. Anna named him John, after her father. How she missed her family. She felt so all alone. The infant fed greedily at her breast while Anna tried to regain her strength. Vito looked with disgust at Anna and the baby.

The next morning Anna rose and carried her newborn down to the warmth of the ovens. She kneaded the bread as the baby slept peacefully. Anna took the infant with her as she went about her work. She fed the baby at her breast when the store was quiet. The hatred Vito felt toward his half-brother wasn't evident until she ordered Vito to come and help her carry the day's supplies from the store while she carried John. The words stung at her soul as she heard her neighbors mumble "Hitler" when they saw the infant. Vito reddened when he realized the neighbors thought the infant was half-German and that Anna had slept with a soldier. It was the only explanation. Surely, this puking brat was not his half-brother.

Returning home, he quickly accused Anna of sleeping with a German. He told the others and although she denied it, Vito knew it was true. It just elevated his hatred of Anna. She was no good and here he was at her mercy. He vowed he would get back at her for her sins against his father. His family was too good for her. He would even tell little Jedze the truth.

Anna swallowed the pain of the accusations. She was too busy caring for the infant and the bakery to fight. Perhaps, she should have. Slowly Vito turned Klara and even little Jedze against her. She had allowed his insults because she thought them too ridiculous to believe. She now knew she had been wrong to do so.

The loud sound pulled Anna from her thoughts. It was the door slamming. As Anna looked back, she noticed the handsome man who entered the church. He was dressed elegantly. *Yes*, Anna thought, *even the wealthy need Jesus.*

Returning to prayer, she prayed for John. She had not seen him since he was just a few months old. She wondered if he knew that he had a mother somewhere. Did he even know he was Polish? It was hard to believe, but John would be in his sixties now. Anna sighed as she looked to the Jesus in the monstrance before her. She prayed for John as the flames of her memories consumed her.

John was such a handsome infant. His blonde curls and blue eyes reminded Anna of her sisters. His disposition was even sweeter. Lying in the basket behind the pastry case, he seldom cried. Content, he cooed and waved his arms allowing Anna to work with little distraction. The bakery was doing very well as the occupying Germans clamored for the baked goods she provided. Anna could hardly keep up with the demand, especially now. Each morning at precisely six-thirty, a car from the work camp arrived to carry her baked goods to the Nazi general who demanded her dark seeded bread.

Anna heard of the work camp the Nazi's had built. Many of the vanished were rumored to be working there. Summer melted into autumn. Anna expected the same Nazi soldier who arrived each morning for the general's bread. This day, however two soldiers arrived.

Anna's stomach cramped with fear as the Nazi soldiers shouted, "Where is the baker! We demand to see him!"

Anna answered quickly as the startled children came from the back room to see what all the shouting was about, "I am the baker."

Sarcastically one of the Germans shouted, "We do not want a shop girl. We want the baker!"

Anna could sense the fear in the children as she answered, "I am both the shop girl and the baker. This is my bakery, given to me by my father."

"You are to come and work in the camp. You will bake for the General and his staff," announced one of the soldiers as he walked behind the case to grab Anna.

Anna looked at the frightened children and answered with command and courage, "I cannot go. I have four children to take care of!"

Anna quickly spanned the length of the glass counter and picked up the little basket that held John. The two soldiers looked surprised at the infant.

"Is this your baby? Who is the father?" one of the Nazi's demanded.

In an instant that lasted an eternity, Anna realized that while the Nazi's had use for her and the older children, they had no use for a baby. Babies couldn't work. A Polish baby was of little value. Quickly, the lie rose without much thought, and she answered, "His father is a German soldier. He is one of your own."

Anna could see the look of hate manifest itself on Vito's face. Her lie confirmed all his convictions. It didn't matter. It saved her baby's life.

The German soldier's face softened as he looked at the smiling blonde baby and turning to the other soldier, he stated. "Ah yes, he is an Aryan. He should be raised as a German. Doesn't your sister still long for a baby?"

The other German looked at the handsome baby and answered, "Yes, she has been trying to get pregnant for years. She would be thrilled to raise an infant for the Fatherland."

Forcefully, the Nazi pulled the basket from Anna's hands and tossed it to his companion, "Take this boy to her."

Enlisting a soldier from the crowd who stood in line, he announced, "I will take the other four to the camp."

They proceeded to drag the children, as they screamed and cried, to the waiting car. Anna ignored their cries. She was looking out the window of the car as it started toward the camp. She watched as the soldier carried her little John away. Why had she lied? Something inside her sensed that the lie she told had just saved her baby's life. She prayed it was so. Anna never saw her son again.

Fifteen

Blessed are you when they insult you and persecute you and utter every kind of evil against you [falsely] because of me. Rejoice and be glad, for your reward will be great in heaven. Thus they persecuted the prophets before you. (Matt. 5:11)

The children softly sobbed in the back of the car, receiving no attention from the soldiers. As the 20 minute ride progressed, Anna could feel fear grip her. Her fear eased a little as the car pulled under the iron gate. The red brick buildings were new and lined in neat rows. The road was lined with trees. It looked like a university.

Nearby, a train pulled up. Shouts blended incoherently as large groups of men, women, and children were forced out of packed train cars and separated into groups by sex. Mothers and sons cried as they were separated. Husbands tried to hold the women they loved.

The cries of fear and sorrow overwhelmed Anna. Lost in the scene before her, she was pulled back to her own reality as the driver stopped the car. The tall soldier on the passenger side pulled Anna and the children out of the back of the car as the driver shouted orders to him in German. Anna and Klara were directed toward a crowd of women, while Vito and little Jedze were shoved into the large group of men.

Jedze cried, "Anna, Anna!" as he pulled away from Vito and tried to reach for her.

A German soldier headed for little Jedze as if to strike him. Anna tried to pull away to get to Jedze but another soldier gripped her shoulder so hard that Anna could have screamed with the pain. Her focus on Jedze prevented her from showing her own fear. She could see the German as he reached for the running child. Out of the crowd of men, a young, bearded Jew walked forward and scooped up the blond child in his arms. A glance was all he gave Anna. In that glance was a knowing look that connected two people. Anna could feel the tears rolling down her cheeks. The young man with a yellow star on his coat carried Jedze and held Vito's hand as all the men were led away.

The women were directed to a different building. They were silently led to a large room and left with other soldiers. The soldier who had pulled Anna out of the car spoke to another soldier and pointed to her as she stood holding Klara's hand. He quickly left the building leaving the women in the care of these other soldiers.

"Strip off your clothes!" the soldier shouted.

A beating to one of the women who protested convinced all to strip. Two soldiers handed out large cakes of brown soap as the women were hosed with cold water and instructed to wash their hair and body. Their clothes and jewelry were collected. Klara cried and shivered in the cold and Anna tried to warm her small body. They were lined up, issued rough striped dresses and made to form another line.

As Anna reached the head of the line, she could see a routine. One soldier asked questions and wrote down their answers. Two other soldiers pulled each woman's arm. One soldier would hold the woman down as the other soldier pushed the board full of needles into her left arm. Most of the woman cried out in pain. Ignoring their cries, the other soldier rubbed an inky stain into the wound. Then they were led to two female soldiers who cut their hair in uneven clumps and threw the tresses into a large bin. Each woman was handed a cloth babushka and directed to another large line.

One soldier pulled Anna away and directed her to the only black building in the camp. Klara cried as she and all of the other children, both male and female were led to a red brick building. Pulled along by the arm Anna shouted words of comfort to the children.

"You will see them soon enough!" the Nazi shouted as he dragged Anna away.

Anna was brought into the large kitchen. She was assured that she would be reunited with her children that night. Her day was spent baking and cooking. A rotund German woman who spoke little Polish showed Anna around the ovens and explained her duties. Anna would learn to cook as well as bake. The General was very fussy. Anna tried to concentrate, but worrying about the children made that difficult. The other workers in the kitchen were cruel. Clearly, her Polish nationality was disdained by the German cooks. She was threatened with severe punishment if anything was found missing from the kitchen, including food. Death was the punishment. Looking into the cold blue eyes of the housekeeper, Anna believed it would happen.

She took nothing that day or in the first few weeks. However as the children grew thin and weak with hunger she learned how to carefully hide small scraps of food in her dress and socks to feed them in the night. She would hide her own meager lunch under her cap for Jedze who needed the protein. Anna grew thin as the tiny bits of food kept the children alive.

No, she could not think of that time. It was too painful. Anna pulled her mind back from the memories of the camp. The years she spent there were hard to forget. The number tattooed on her arm was a daily reminder. Anna looked at the monstrance that contained the Jesus she depended on. A slight noise alerted her. Looking across the pew Anna saw that the old black purse she carried had popped open. Anna pulled the purse closer to her and closed the snap. Once again, she heard the soft cries of the young girl two pews behind her. Anna prayed for the young woman and again her hands grew warm.

A memory pulled Anna back to the past. Sitting in the church, she rubbed the tattoo. She was ashamed of it and often covered it with long sleeves even in the summer. Numbers that reminded her of her status as an 'undesirable' haunted her. Anna didn't trust men. She knew about hate. Hate grew out of fear and most men were fearful of anyone who was different. She had no illusions. That fear only needed a man, an opportunist like Hitler. A man willing to fan those fears into the flames of hate was all that was needed for it to happen again.

Anna looked to the Eucharist sitting on the altar. Only Jesus could be trusted. Anna knew that now. Yet there had been a time in the camp when she felt that even He had deserted her. Anna looked around the church. The same people prayed and remained lost in their troubles. Anna saw Father D'Angelico silently praying in the back. She glanced over again as he remained deep in prayer, he was a holy man, a special priest whom Anna felt privileged to know.

Looking toward the monstrance Anna thought her eyes were betraying her. In the middle of the white host sat Jesus. Dressed in a white robe, He sat on a rock just looking at her. In all her years of Eucharistic worship, Anna had never experienced the actual sight of Jesus. His eyes were so warm and gentle. She forgot her surroundings as His love drew her in. She found herself sitting on a rock before Jesus as he took both of her hands.

"Your hands are warm, Anna. Why is that?" Jesus asked in a mellow voice.

Anna was too stunned by the entire experience to answer.

Jesus smiled and looked to the ocean. They were sitting on a rocky beach and the yellow sky above held low hanging orbs. Planets unfamiliar to her hung low and large in an alien sky. The rolling waves grabbed at the beach as the two sat alone on a rock. Large narrow mountains rose up on the horizon giving the view an unearthly feel. Anna looked to Jesus as the only thing familiar in this strange place. His eyes were so compelling and Anna found herself plummeting into them.

Falling into the eternal eyes of her Maker, Anna felt as if she were flying through space. In the blackness, stars sparkled as she flew past them. The immense size of the universe made Anna feel small, yet she was not afraid. She knew Jesus was guiding her. Anna lost the sense of where she was. Her flight through the stars seemed to slow and Anna, confused, found herself in the past.

Anna was back at Auschwitz holding a feverish and thin child in her arms. She realized she was holding Jedze. It was the night Jedze died. They had been at the camp for four years. So many of the people who came after them had died, but Anna had managed to keep her children alive. The food she smuggled in her clothes had sustained them. Anna longed to help the others, but there just wasn't enough. She barely had enough to save her own children.

She had come to think of the three children as her own. Especially after John had been taken. They were all so thin. Jedze looked more like an old man than a child. His ribs poked her as she held him. There was no fat or even muscle on his small body. He had not grown since they had been taken to the camp. Anna managed to keep the children alive by starving herself. Her face was gaunt and full of worry. Now it looked as if she were about to lose Jedze. His fever was high and his breathing labored. An infection had swept through the camp and many had died in the last few weeks. Anna had seen the soldiers throwing the limp bodies in a deep trench.

After all this time she couldn't face losing little Jedze.

Anna was surrounded by death. It was in the stench of the very air she was breathing. She tried not to think about the smell of the ovens. The ashes that covered the building and grounds smelled of death. Death was all Anna had lived for the last four years. *Oh God, but not Jedze!* Anna prayed as she rocked his small body in her lap.

Suddenly and without much thought, Anna looked down into the face of the small child. Something changed. His shallow breathing had stopped. His limp body was lifeless. For so long Anna had held her feelings in check. Her only reason for living was to keep her children alive. The pain and agony she pushed down as she watched the cruelty of her captors and the suffering and death they inflicted on her fellow inmates resurfaced. A rage rose up in her soul, as she held the dead body of little Jedze.

Anna lifted her eyes to a God who seemed so distant. She prayed aloud as she covered Jedze's small chest with her now burning hands. A sense of power came over her as she willed the small boy to live. She felt the first shallow breath that Jedze took even before her mind registered it. His chest rose and fell steadily as his pale face began to fill with color. The fever that had racked his small body subsided. Anna felt the healing power leave her hands as the burning sensation subsided. Little Jedze opened his eyes and asked for a drink. Anna held the boy closer as she praised and thanked God, who had answered her prayers. Jedze not only lived but also grew stronger in the coming months. They all lived to see the Russians who liberated the camp.

"It was your gift of healing and your prayers that saved him," Jesus said in a soft deep voice. Like a magnet, His voice pulled Anna back to the beach and away from the terrible memories.

"Yes, we survived," Anna answered, "but so many others didn't."

"Yet you never used your gift of healing again. Why, when

so many others needed it? I gave you the ability to heal for a reason. Yet you were too afraid," whispered Jesus as he held Anna's hands.

"In the camp I didn't want to draw attention to myself and the children. That is how we survived," answered Anna. She closed her eyes tightly not wanting to see any more painful memories.

"Look Anna, seek and understand." His soothing voice eased Anna's fevered thoughts. Remembering the past unnerved her. It was full of pain and she did not want to remember her years at the camp. Yet, she had to obey her God. Opening her eyes, she dreaded what she would see. But it was not what she expected.

Anna saw a man in an ancient robe walking in a wilderness. When the man came to a blossom tree, he sat beneath it.

In loud cries he prayed for death, "This is enough, O Lord! Take my life for I am no better than my father."

The man lay down and fell asleep under the tree and an angel touched him and ordered him to get up and eat. He looked again and there at his head was a hearth cake and a jug of water. After he ate and drank, he lay down again to sleep.

But the angel of the Lord came back a second time, touched him and ordered, "Get up and eat, else the journey will be too long for you!

He got up and ate and drank. Strengthened, he walked forty days and forty nights to the mountain of God.

There he came to a cave where he took shelter. But the word of the Lord came to him, "Why are you here, Elijah?"

He answered, "I have been most zealous for the Lord, the God of hosts, but the Israelites have forsaken your covenant, torn down your altars, and put your prophets to the swords. I alone am left, and they seek to take my life."

Then the Lord said, "Go outside and stand on the mountain before the Lord; the Lord will be passing by."

A strong and heavy wind was rending the mountains and crushing rocks before the Lord—but the Lord was not in the wind. After the wind, there was an earthquake—but the Lord was not in the earthquake. After the earthquake, there was fire—but the Lord was not in the fire. After the fire, there was a tiny whispering sound. When he heard this, Elijah hid his face in his cloak. He went and stood at the entrance of the cave.

The voice of the angel said to him, "Elijah, why are here?"

He replied, "I have been most zealous for the Lord, the God of hosts but the Israelites have forsaken your covenant, torn down your altars, and put your prophets to the sword. I alone am left, and they seek to take my life."

Go take the road back to the desert near Damascus," the Lord said to him. "When you arrive, you shall anoint Hazael as king of Aram. Then you shall anoint Jehu, son of Nimshi, as king of Israel, and Elisha, son of Shaphat of Abelmeholah, as prophet to succeed you. If anyone escapes the sword of Hazael, Jehu will kill him. If he escapes the sword of Jehu, Elisha will kill him. Yet I will leave seven thousand men in Israel—all those who have not knelt to Baal or kissed him."

The scene then slowly faded and Anna found herself back on the golden beach holding the hands of her Lord. Together they sat looking into each other's eyes so intently the moment felt like an eternity. Anna was filled with a pure sense of peace. She had not felt that kind of peace since she was a child working with Papa in the bakery. She wanted this moment to last forever, but Jesus spoke.

"Do you understand, Anna?" he asked softly.

"No, I don't," she answered, "I don't know what this man has to do with me."

Jesus smiled. "He is one of mine, as you are. Yet great Prophet that he was, he became overwhelmed by the evil of his world. He grew afraid of the evil, and tried to run and hide. He looked for me but could not find me. Look again, Anna"

Anna was back in the desert — she was not just observing it this time. She was the person running away. She felt so tired, so frightened. The pain she felt in her heart was the same as when her father and sisters deserted her. She was running away, feeling as if she were being chased until she reached a flowering tree. Exhausted, she collapsed under it and prayed to die. Overwhelmed, she fell asleep, hoping never to awake.

An angel came and fed her. She felt a little stronger but still didn't want to live. She fell asleep and prayed for death again. The angel came back a second time. And this time his face looked familiar. It took Anna a few minutes to recall it but she finally realized the angel had the face of a priest who had been at Auschwitz. When Anna was able, she would steal extra bread from the kitchen and give it to the priest. A secret Mass would be held and to those who wanted it, Communion was given in the form of a few consecrated crumbs. Anna hadn't thought about the priest in a long time. He had been executed sometime in the second year there. The angel in the vision who looked just like the priest pulled her back by touching her and ordered, "Get up and eat else the journey will be too long for you!"

Anna obeyed. She got up and ate. Feeling strengthened, he got up and walked for a long time. After many days, she came to a cave where she took shelter. Anna heard the voice of Jesus come to her. "Why are you here, Anna?"

Anna heard herself cry, "The world is full of evil men. I have to hide from them or they will kill me. I have been faithful to you but the entire world has rejected your teachings. The world worships power and money. The world would like to rid itself of God's people. I feel so alone. They tried to kill me!"

Jesus answered, "Go outside and stand on the mountain, the Lord will be passing by."

Anna obeyed and stood, exposed and alone. A strong and heavy wind began to blow. Anna swayed in the wind. It was loud and crushing. She was afraid. As the wind whirled in the sand, it swirled into a form. As it swirled and roared the wind took the form of the Professor. She found herself back on the day of her wedding. Back in the Professor's bed, she relived the rape. Like an evil wind, he attacked her. Anna cried to the Lord, "Where were you Lord? I couldn't hear you then!

She heard the voice of Jesus answer, "No you couldn't hear me that night because the sound of his fury overwhelmed you. You couldn't hear me in the wind of his evil, but I was there."

"Where were you Jesus? Where?" Anna screamed to Jesus in anger as the pain of that night was being relived.

Suddenly the wind died down and Anna could hear a whisper in the stillness. It was Jedze's voice. Jedze was praying, "Help her Jesus. Save her from my father!" Anna was shocked that Jedze prayed for her that night, but it made her anger worse. Screaming into the silence Anna answered, "But you didn't answer his prayer either! I was still raped and beaten."

Again, she heard the calm voice of Jesus, "I did answer Jedze's prayers. I heard his childhood whispers. The Professor would have killed you that night if I had not. Instead he fell asleep and you escaped." Anna was speechless.

Suddenly the ground beneath her began to shake. Anna slipped and fell as the ground rumbled in an earthquake. The rumbling turned into a steady pounding beat. The beat hit the ground thumping like the sound of boots, boots of an approaching army. The army overwhelmed the mountain of the Lord and as they approached, the sound of the Nazi's marching hurt Anna's ears. This army of evil men overcame Anna and dragged her kicking and screaming back into the camp. Anna cried in pain as she gasped for air, "Where were you then Lord? Why didn't you save us from the camp? Why didn't you stop the Nazi?"

"You couldn't hear me over the sound of marching evil.

Evil that strong is loud and deafening, but I was there," Jesus answered.

Suddenly Anna found herself being pulled from the car. Jedze and Vito were torn away. Then Jedze was running toward Anna and screaming for her while the German soldier approached. Looking up Anna saw the young Jew who saved Jedze scoop him up as he had on that day. Only Anna could see now that the Jewish man had the face of Jesus.

"He was one of my own. I lived in his heart. If he had not reached Jedze that day the soldier would have killed him. I was there in the whispers of that man's heart."

Anna again found herself alone atop the silent mountain. She smelled the fire before she saw it. The flame rose up before her, destroying brush and tree as it approached closer and closer. Overwhelmed and afraid, she closed her eyes. She could feel the heat of the fire. As the flames came closer, she was forced by fear to open her eyes. In the flames that approached, she saw a vision of the camp. Starving and neglected people collapsed and died. Ovens burned night and day.

The smell of death was everywhere and so familiar to Anna that the potent memory overcame her. She couldn't stand to breathe death again. Anna screamed as the horrid memories she had pushed from her mind for so long flooded back. It was too much. It was too hot. The fire of evil consumed all, leaving nothing. It destroyed everything as it roared across the lives of those in the camp. Anna cried as the memories burned, "Where were you then Lord. I didn't see you there. The fire of death consumed all at the camp and across the world. Where were you then Lord?" accused Anna.

Anna, with great anger at God, stared into the flames that approached her. She could see figures moving in the flames. Suddenly she was back in the kitchen. Thin and weak, Anna found the pieces of food the sloppy German cook had left scattered on the counter. The food that kept them alive.

"What does this prove? She was one of them. She was

horrible to me. So what if her habit of sloppiness saved the children? If she had known I was stealing she would have killed me."

In a calm voice, Jesus answered, "She knew. She left the scraps of food deliberately. She shouted and mistreated you to cover up her actions. She worked you late so you would be alone to collect them."

Anna was stunned. She had hated that woman for so long.

"I was there at the camp Anna, look and see." Jesus softly whispered.

Anna stared into the flames that closed in on her. In the flames other memories came. Anna had forgotten the kindness of her fellow prisoners. She watched as mothers gave their own food to the babies of other women. She watched as children listened to whispered stories of love from women full of fear. Despite their own fear, they brought peace to others. She watched as young people fell in love despite their circumstances. Then she saw the priest. The one from whom she received Communion. He was standing in an open courtyard of the camp. He was taking the place of a man picked for execution. He was led to a painful death. He gave his life to save another.

"I was in the eyes of those mothers and the hearts of those lovers. I was in the whispered prayers of those in the camp who gave their very lives to save others. I was in the courage of the Allied soldiers who died to defeat the evil forces. Anna, you couldn't hear me because of the roaring fire of evil. You couldn't hear me in the whispers of everyday goodness and love, but I was there."

The flames disappeared and Anna found herself alone on the mountain. Overwhelmed by the pain, she hid her face in her hands. She had not seen God. Anna had been overwhelmed by the evil, and evil still existed. Evil was blowing, breaking, and burning in new parts of world. It seemed to Anna that when the fire of evil was put out in one place, it sprang up in another.

Anna cried to the Lord. "I have been faithful to you. The world has forsaken you, torn down your churches, and executed your people. I am alone, and if evil could, it would http://www.aspen-tree.com/contact.shtml even kill me now."

"Go back into your life Anna. Use the weapons and gifts I have given you. You are not alone. You have never been alone. I have been with you always. There are many others, enough of you to fight the evil of any age. You are full of my power. Find that power. Don't run and hide from the evil, face it."

"I am an old woman now Lord. What good can I do?" asked Anna as she stood on the mountain.

"Listen to the whispers of your heart." answered Jesus.

Anna closed her eyes with a sense of peace. Opening them, she found herself back in the church. She was sitting in the pew as if nothing at all had happened. Yet everything had changed. She was no longer full of fear. She could feel the heat in her hands as she prayed thanksgiving to the Lord. She would hear him now. Anna would listen to the whispers of her heart.

Sixteen

Blessed are you who believed that what was spoken to you by the Lord would be fulfilled. (Luke 1:45)

Patricia Walsh didn't feel the cold as it stung her nose and ears. The snow swirled around hitting her face in small icy bites that froze the tears that flowed from her reddened eyes. She simply turned right as she exited the hospital— the opposite direction from her apartment. Patricia made an unconscious decision not to return to its empty rooms. Those empty rooms always seemed to draw her into darkness and despair. She turned into the wind and struggled. Pushing against the cold, she stepped cautiously across the icy sidewalk as the snow swirled around her feet.

Patricia didn't know where she was headed. It didn't matter. She hoped the storm would swallow her up. She hoped the cold would numb her. If she died from exposure it would be a relief. Pushing on, Patricia managed the strength to walk three more blocks. The 20 minute struggle left her exhausted, cold, and much to her disappointment, still alive.

She was snow blind. Nothing was visible through the blowing snow. It had covered everything blanketing the city in sameness. But she saw a new light that shone through the whiteness. The church's stained glass window reflected prisms of colors on the fallen snow. It called the broken woman's attention. She could see figures bundled against the cold as they stood waiting on the steps. She struggled toward them. Patricia Walsh joined the faithful waiting on the church steps unaware of what made her do it. She flowed into the warm church as the elderly priest opened the door. The church drew her spirit against her numbed will. She would have preferred to die in the cold.

Taking a seat toward the front of the church, Patricia watched dispassionately as an elderly woman struggled to get into a pew ahead of her. She watched emotionlessly as the elderly priest placed the Eucharist in the monstrance and sang familiar songs of worship. His songs fell silent on her numbed heart. She didn't want to feel anything. The young woman tried to focus on the scene before her. It worked until the church fell silent and she could no longer keep her feelings at bay. They flooded back as Patricia reached for the tissues in her purse. She couldn't contain the sobs that wracked her body as she knelt before Jesus. Lost in pain, she tried in vain to muffle her cries.

Patricia's thoughts took her back in Dr. Puglisi's office. He had called and made the appointment last evening. Ever since the emotional breakdown Patricia had experienced in Megan's room six weeks ago, she had taken care to get a good night sleep each evening. Nothing changed with Megan anyway. Every morning Patricia would arrive to the same sleeping child. Reality choked the hope from her heart as hopeless day followed hopeless day. Patricia didn't realize how much she was clinging to an elusive hope until Dr. Puglisi added to her despair.

After waiting in the outer office for five minutes, she was called into Dr. Puglisi's hospital office at six o'clock. She wished that David could be with her. She had talked to him on the phone last night after the doctor called to make the appointment. He was in Oklahoma and it would be two days until he would be home. He promised to call her tonight to find out what the doctor said. She always seemed to be alone lately. But never felt as alone as she did when Dr. Puglisi gave her his news.

"Patricia, I am sorry for what I have to tell you. I fought with the committee but I can't put it off any longer then I already have."

Fear was gripping Patricia as she responded. "Is something wrong with Megan?"

With pain in his eyes Dr. Puglisi answered, "No and that is the problem. Nothing is new with Megan. Her leg has healed. Her ribs have healed. I am pleased with her physical healing. She has been healing from the trauma and that is the problem. The hospital can't keep her. Her care is custodial and your insurance won't cover the cost of hospital care. Frankly, I'm surprised we managed to keep her this long. She will have to be placed in a nursing home."

Patricia's mind screamed 'no' as she sat polite and silent before the doctor she had learned to trust. *They are giving up. They are giving up on my baby!*

"I don't want her moved. She is getting the best care here. The hospital is close and I stay with Megan everyday. I don't want her moved to a nursing home. What kind of care will she get there?" Patricia held the sobs back as she begged the man before her.

"I don't want her moved either. Unfortunately, it's not up to us. I know you and your husband can't afford the daily cost of hospital care. The good thing is your insurance will continue to pay until we place her in a home," he said in a reassuring voice.

Patricia wasn't soothed, "What do you mean? What do you mean by placing her? Don't we get to pick the home she is going to?"

Dr. Puglisi cringed as he answered, "No, I'm afraid not. Megan will be placed in the first available opening in the city. So you may have to travel more but you will still be able to visit her as regularly as before. As soon as there is an opening they'll make all the arrangements. If you refuse, they will drop her coverage."

The doctor could see the worry in Patricia's eyes and tried to reassure her, "There are many fine nursing homes in the city. Many of them offer better rehabilitation then the hospital."

Patricia didn't feel any relief as she asked, "Will you continue to be her doctor? Do you have any say as to what nursing home?"

The doctor skirted the desk to place his arm around the shaken woman. Medicine used to be compassionate, before the government and insurance companies started to override the doctors and nurses.

Dr. Puglisi tried to sound positive, as he answered, "No, I won't be her primary once Megan is moved. I will keep in touch and check with her new physician regularly. The nursing home will have a physician who cares for and visits each patient monthly. I will do my best to see that she gets into the best nursing home in the city."

Patricia looked at the Doctor. "You can't promise that though, can you?"

Dr. Puglisi's pained eyes gave the young mother all the answer she needed.

Patricia left the office with a sinking heart. They could move her baby anytime, anywhere. She had no say and felt completely powerless. Returning to Megan's room Patricia looked around the hospital. Before the doctor's news, she had grown sick of this floor. Day after day, the same nurses and routine had left her sick. She knew all of the nurses too well. She had longed for her daily visits to end. Now she didn't want to leave. She didn't want to leave the familiar for a scary unknown.

Patricia knew what the move meant. It meant that they thought Megan was never coming out of the coma. It meant they were sending a hopeless case to a nursing home to die.

Patricia started to sob. The pain was overwhelming.

Maybe they were right. Maybe her baby would have been better off if she had died in that accident. Patricia wasn't able to stop the negative thoughts. She couldn't stop the tears. She didn't want to cry in front of Megan. That's when she ran from the hospital room straight into the nor'easter.

The sound of the church door slamming pulled Patricia from her memories. A man struggled with the wind and the door, finally pulling it closed. He took a side seat in the back. Patricia turned forward again and found herself staring at the host. It was a long time since Patricia had been in church.

I don't really know what happened, she thought. I just got so busy and I stopped going to Mass. She looked at the Jesus she had been so faithful to in her childhood. Patricia attended the same Catholic grammar school that Megan had started on the day of her accident. Raised by faithful Catholic parents who never missed Sunday Mass, Patricia had been faithful until she married. The first time she missed Mass she was tired from a full and busy Saturday. The next Sunday it just seemed easier to stay home. Soon, it was easier not to go at all. There was no real excuse. It just became a habit to miss Mass. She still said her daily rosary, but in her heart, Patricia knew she was doing wrong. She just kept herself too busy to think about it.

Now she was feeling like a hypocrite. She was here to ask Jesus to perform a miracle for her.

I haven't got the right to ask, thought Patricia. I am a hypocrite. Why would He help me? I've got to help myself. I've got to see to it that Megan gets the same therapy she would in the hospital. I'll go to the nursing home each day. I'll make the therapist work with her. God knows I've memorized the routine. I can give her the stimuli and range of motion therapies myself. I will get my daughter well no matter what the doctors or the insurance company thinks. I don't need them. I don't need anyone. Patricia was angry. Who were they to give up on Megan? Reaching to put the tissues back in her purse, she knocked a book off the pew. She hadn't noticed it before. Reaching under the kneeler to pick it up, Patricia saw it was a Bible. *Someone must have accidentally left it here,* she thought as she picked up the open Bible.

She couldn't help but look. It was open to the New Testament. A memory of her mother whispered across the years of her mind. Mom always said that when a Bible opened, it had a message for you. *"A silly superstition,"* she thought. Still her eyes, reddened with her tears as she scanned the page before her. The Bible was open to Matthew 8, and the first bold heading on the page said, *The healing of a Centurion's Servant.*

"This is ridiculous! What does this have to do with Megan?" Patricia rubbed her eyes and blew her nose. Setting the Bible on the wooden pew beside her, she tried to pray and ask for help. She couldn't concentrate. She picked up the Bible and read the story:

"When he entered Capernaum, a centurion approached him and appealed to him, saying, "Lord my servant is lying at home paralyzed, suffering dreadfully. He said to him "I will come and cure him." The centurion said in reply, "Lord, I am not worthy to have you enter under my roof; only say the word and my servant will be healed. For I too am a person subject to authority, with soldiers subject to me. And I say to one, 'Go,' and he goes; and to another, 'Come here,' and he comes; and to my slave, 'Do this,' and he does it. When Jesus heard this, he was amazed and said to those following him, "Amen, I say to you, in no one in Israel have I found such faith. I say to you, many will come from the east and the west, and will recline with Abraham, Isaac, and Jacob at the banquet in the kingdom of heaven, but the children of the kingdom will be driven out into the outer darkness, where there will be wailing and grinding of teeth. And Jesus said to the centurion, "You may go; as you have believed, let it be done for you." And at that very hour {his} servant was healed."

Patricia gave the story little thought. Another myth shot

down. This story was about a soldier and had nothing to do with Megan. Where were the answers *she* needed? Patricia stared at the monstrance, daring God to answer. *He doesn't care!* her mind screamed. I've prayed and begged for months but there is no answer. Megan will never wake up. She will suffer and die alone and forgotten in some horrible nursing home. They've written her off, and so has God.

Those painful thoughts caused the tears to sting her swollen eyes. Lost in grief, Patricia tried to silence the small voice of her heart as it replayed the story of the soldier asking Jesus to cure his servant. What did it mean? Patricia tried to calm herself and think. He trusted. He prevented Jesus from physically coming. Why? If Jesus had offered to come off the altar and go with her to Megan, she would be elated. She would rush him to Megan's bedside and witness while he laid his hands on her and cured her. What was wrong with the Centurion? Why did he tell Jesus not to physically come?

Her heart whispered, *"Because he had true faith in the Power."* The answer that soared through Patricia's heart shocked her. Was it because she didn't have faith? What kind of answer was that? She looked up to the Eucharist. A white host, it showed nothing. Patricia picked up the Bible and read the story again. What was Jesus saying? The soldier wasn't with the servant either. Neither the soldier, nor Jesus was physically with the servant when the servant was cured. Jesus had the power to command his angels and all the dominions of heaven like the soldier commanded his underlings. The soldier had faith.

"You only believe in your own power!" Patricia's heart shouted. The power of the thought stunned her. Her mind screamed denial but visions of her hospital vigils assaulted her. Day after day, night after night, she had not left Megan's side. At first it was understandable—a mother's reaction to a desperate situation. But over time it had grown out of control. She ate and slept at the hospital leaving her husband's calls unanswered, her home ignored and her own

health perilously in jeopardy. She watched every move the staff made. She repeated the therapy when they left the room. She was determined to take control, to fix her baby.

"Determined to be God!" again the thought caught her by surprise. Patricia had never looked at it that way. She had been praying for God to cure Megan. Now she realized that she wanted to cure her. But was that so wrong? Megan was her baby. She wanted her well. Could it be that she had not allowed God the time and space to do what was clearly his job?

What had the Centurion done? He had asked and trusted. He had not asked and then, as if God could not be trusted, taken over the producing of a miracle himself. He had not questioned the power of God. What is more, he had not questioned whether the decision to cure his servant was up to him. What if Jesus had said no? What would the Centurion have done? Patricia only knew what she would do. She would take over the role of God herself. It's what she had been doing for months.

The moment hung in time. She hadn't trusted the Power of Jesus. Patricia Walsh had spent every waking moment trusting in her own power to cure her daughter. The thought hit her hard.

Looking to the monstrance, it warmly glowed as the flickering candles reflected off the gold metal. Nothing had changed and yet everything had changed. Jesus had spoken to her through the Bible in this silent church. Patricia Walsh had finally heard Him. Her tears stopped as she wondered whether He had been talking to her all along and she had been too busy to listen.

Now she knew what happened tonight didn't matter. It didn't matter if they put Megan in a home. It didn't matter if they gave up on her baby. God hadn't given up. Patricia knelt down as a sense of peace flowed through her spirit for the first time since the accident that had devastated her so many months ago. She knelt down in confidence before the

God of Power. In the silence of her heart, she found her God again. In the words of a simple Bible story, her Father spoke to her. Now she would speak to Him.

"I give Megan to You, Lord. I have no Power to cure her. If it is your will, I know that You and You alone can wake her up. Do it in Your own time, if it be your Will. If it is not Your Will, so be it. I am not God. I trust in You. I have no Power. All the Power is Yours." She prayed silently as a sense of the eternal touched her spirit.

Father D'Angelico's heart rejoiced as he felt the turning of the young woman's spirit to God. It was a powerful moment. He knew that Jesus had something special in mind for this young woman and her child.

Seventeen

The people who walked in darkness have seen a great light; Upon those who dwelt in the land of gloom a light has shone. (Isaiah 9:1)

Terrence Kinney pulled with all his might against the door. His Italian leather gloves were warm, thin, and had a good grip. The power of the wind defeated him. The shattering storm pulled the door from his grasping hands and slammed it hard against the frame of the outer stonewall. The wind was strong but died quickly. Reaching the ancient wooden frame, he pulled it roughly and it closed with a loud bang. With the door secure, he turned without embarrassment as the people in church who watched his struggle averted their eyes. The man was pure grace walking. It had always been his gift. A sense of confident presence had always been his demeanor. It made his political career a natural. People noticed when Terrence Kinney entered a room. All eyes always turned to him, drinking in his sense of knowledge and charm.

All of his life people turned to him for advice and gravitated to him just to bask in the light of his charisma. He never questioned it. Terrence Kinney found the attention he drew as natural as breathing. His father had recognized his son's gift too. He honed the gifts with the proper education and training. Terrence was a born politician, his education adding the layers of knowledge and social balance needed to promote his father's dreams. John Kinney had one dream for his son: For him to become President of the United States. He raised his son for the job.

Terrence thought about his father as he found his way to the side pew. His father longed for the day he'd just experienced. John Kinney unfortunately did not live to it. Taken by an unexpected heart attack just six months ago, he had gotten his son's career only as far as Lieutenant Governor. In one night, with one scandal, Terrence Kinney would fill the suddenly vacated governor's seat.

It began late last night. The Governor was about to be exposed in the news. A reporter discovered that the pimp who supplied him with prostitutes had been given a government position. The position was so undemanding that the pimp never had to report for work, while his hefty paychecks were directly deposited into his bank account. Naturally, the governor's supply of call girls continued to be generous, as the taxpayers subsidized the cost. The scandal was going to be front-page news in the morning and the house of cards the governor had built would come tumbling down.

In the three and a half years he served under the Governor, Terrence had solidified his base. His strong moves to protect the environment culminated in a wetlands protection act that was a model for other states. His rousing speech given at the convention drew even more national attention. He was on his way. His father was elated. But, years of stress had taken its toll. Leaving his office one night, John Kinney collapsed gasping for air in the middle of the parking lot. His employees waited while the piercing screams of the sirens sang through the air only to arrive too late. John Kinney died with the hopes for his son yet unfulfilled. Terrence knew his father would have loved today.

Terrence hadn't been in a church for Eucharistic worship in many years. His mother, Rose, was a devout

Catholic. The small dark-haired woman never missed daily Mass. Taking her small son by the hand and bringing him to church, she taught him faith. And the faith she imparted was a generational gift from her loving heart. She was a quiet, gentle woman, quite the opposite of his father.

Opposites attract, thought the handsome politician. And no couple was as opposite as Rose and John Kinney. Their love was the only glue that held the marriage sacred. The love they felt extended to and included their only son. But they held different truths. They held completely different dreams for their son. Rose hated the public attention Terrence's political career drew. His father basked in his public acclaim. While his father dreamed of the Presidency, Rose dreamed of a marriage and grandchildren. His father's dream had won out.

The silence of the church was a welcome relief. It had been a day of hurried meetings and whispered crisis management. The governor resisted. The medium-built grey-haired man with piercing blue eyes tried everything to save himself. His eyes struck the very core of Terrence's soul as he looked to him for help. Terrence had remained silent. It was just a matter of time. It would be in the morning papers. The secrets the Governor kept were going to be public knowledge within a few hours.

The man was desperate. It took all day for the party officials to convince him to resign. They argued that for the good of the party he needed to give up his seat. Terrence Kinney would take the Oath and finish off the last six months of the Governor's term. Naturally, the party officials hoped he would run for another term as governor and as the incumbent, his chances of winning would be better. Yes, his father's dream took a huge step today. Now the only question was this: Would Terrence be able to use this to his advantage?

Lost in the whispers of political intrigue the State House took little notice of the storm that raged outside. The winds of political change were stronger right now than the snowy winds that blew with the nor'easter.

The long day had left Terrence with a splitting headache. He directed the limo driver to stop for some Excedrin. Leaving the store, he noticed the lights of the church. He directed the driver to the front of the church and told him to return in an hour. The sign outside announced the Eucharistic worship. It had been years since he had attended worship. Somehow, he knew this was just what he needed.

It was a beautiful little church. Pre-Vatican II and filled with ornate carvings and statues just like the church his mother attended. He loved the statue of Mary on the right side of the church where he found an empty seat. The statue's face had an expression of kind acceptance. In fact, the face reminded him of someone very familiar. He just couldn't place who it was. Thoughts bubbled through his mind like white-water rapids, crashing against rocks and pushing on. In the silence of the little church he took deep breathes to pacify his soul.

All day his spirit had been in turmoil. Conflicting feelings of sorrow and pity for the sitting governor mixed with elation over his own fortune. He had always been divided between his spiritual life and his ambition. He did want his father's dream. He was drawn to the power—a desire instilled in him by his father. His mother and her spiritual teachings drew him to the need to do good works. He wanted to help the poor, and protect the environment. His desires fit perfectly with most of the party's platforms. His family had belonged to the party for generations and he remained devoted even though he struggled with differences between his Catholic beliefs and some of the party's positions. So far, the discrepancies were not a part of his work. Now the platform of the party had come home to roust.

Terrence pulled his thoughts away from the hectic day. He had come to this church to find serenity. His afternoon with Alan Lennon, the party boss had his spirit in an uproar. Terrence didn't like Alan and his father had often warned Terrence about him. John Kinney didn't like or trust the party boss but he respected his power. He advised Terrence to do the same.

Alan Lennon had been in the State House all day. He spent most of the day pushing the governor to resign before the stories came out in the papers. He was a little weasel of a man. Bald headed, small, and chubby, he was a hardnosed fundraiser with a Napoleon Complex. His greatest joy seemed to be browbeating the powerful. It gave him pleasure to be the real power behind the scene. After Alan had pushed the governor into signing the resignation letter, he turned his attention to Terrence—leaving the past to mold the future.

Terrence pulled his thoughts away from his upsetting afternoon with Alan. Looking at the monstrance brought him as sense of peace. The golden branches that surrounded the white host reminded him of the quiet peaceful times he spent with his mother. He attended daily mass as a child before school each morning and never missed Sunday Mass with his family. His father attended to socialize and to network. He preferred the cathedral while his mother preferred her little parish church. On Sundays, his father won out. It was always that way. The gentle woman always capitulated to her husband's wishes, even when it came to her son. Terrence always wondered what would have happened if it had been the other way.

It wasn't that he didn't love his political career, he relished it. It fit him like a glove even though he sometimes wondered if the stress was worth it. An afternoon as he had today triggered dreams of a less hectic life. Being pushed around by the little party boss had tired him.

"This is your big chance Terrence. I always knew your

day would come. Too bad the old man isn't here to see it. You're the new governor. At least for the next six months and those next six months should cement you as governor for the next term. It all depends on you," Alan said with a menacing look in his eyes.

Terrence was wary. He knew Alan had an agenda and was careful with his answer, "You know I'll do my best. I have no hidden secrets or scandals to embarrass the party. I'll make the party proud. Of course, I would be interested in running for the full term. I would like to do a lot of good for the state."

Placing his arm around Terrence's shoulders, Alan patted him hard on the back and said, "That's the attitude! You have a great career in front of you if you learn to play the game. Your position on abortion isn't a problem right now. It shouldn't even come up since it's a federal issue. We will have to deal with that if you run for President." Terrence could feel the screws tightening already, "Let's just deal with governorship right now. One step at a time as the old man used to say."

"And your old man knew his stuff, didn't he?" Alan snickered. "Keep that in mind Terrence. The thing to be concerned with now is public opinion. The state is in a get tough mood. There are fourteen men awaiting execution on death row. I don't want you to do anything stupid. Let the executions go though. I know your personal opinion and the Catholic Church's position on capital punishment. Even the party is soft on the death penalty, but don't give your opponents the fuel to defeat you in the next election. Don't do anything to rock the boat! Do what you are told, Mr. Governor! The crime rate is rising and you need to look tough on crime to win."

Terrence felt the screws again. Who gave this man the right to be arbiter of another's conscience?

His answer was framed carefully, "You know my belief on the death penalty. I think that it is wrong. It's barbaric and reduces society to the level of the murderer that they want to eliminate. My personal belief tells me that only God has the right to take human life. Only in self-defense may we take a life. I feel that since society is able to protect itself from harm with life sentences it is unnecessary to have a death penalty."

The sarcastic smirk on the little man's face annoyed Terrence. He knew Alan had no morals—he had proven that in the past—the only thing that mattered to this man was power and he would easily sell his soul to obtain it.

The smirk grew as Alan answered, "The key word in that syrupy tirade is *personal*. Your beliefs are personal and you should keep them to yourself. No one in this state wants to spend money supporting murderers. The taxpayers won't stand for it. Your challengers will rip you apart if you try it. What you believe is between you and God. What you say in public is between the party and you, understand? Just so we're clear: God may own your personal life but I own your political life. In your political life, I am your God!"

Terrence could feel his jaw tighten and it kept him from speaking. His face blanched with the need to swallow what this man was saying. It was a bitter draught, because it was true. This man could make or break his political career with one word. He was not lying about his power. He wondered how much he could swallow to realize his personal ambition.

His silence spoke volumes to the arrogant man who took it to mean Terrence was in tow and magnanimously said, "If you feel the need to ease your sensitive conscious and let someone off with a pardon, let that rich white boy go. But don't do it until you've won re-election. His rich friends and relatives will be grateful enough to make many contributions to the party."

Terrence's stomach turned. He could keep his silence no longer, "That's exactly why I think the death penalty is wrong. Not only is it taking a life but the life taken is usually poor and black. We all know he killed his girlfriend for his own amusement. His only defense was that she wanted it. He doesn't have a conscience, he's a sociopath and he's the one I have permission to save. Right now, there are fourteen people on death row. Ten are poor blacks, two are Hispanic and two are white. Only one of the white prisoners comes from money and he's the one my belief can save."

Alan snickered, "Well you can fry him too for all I care. It's up to you."

The little weasel of a man rose and slapped Terrence's back just a little too hard, reinforcing his victory. Terrence kept his mouth clamped shut. That's what his father taught him. Politics was full of compromise. You had to pick your battles. And right now, Alan had all the cards. Swallowing his beliefs left a sour taste in his mouth.

And as if to add insult to injury Alan turned at the door and grinned, "Remember what your old man always said, it's all about the polls. As long as you jive with the polls your success is assured. The polls say the people want justice and revenge. Don't interfere with that."

With a laugh, he slammed the door. Terrence was glad to see him leave. He disliked any man who had the nerve to compare himself to God. He hated his arrogance, his conceit and his callous attitude. The worse part was he hated himself for acquiescing, but what choice did he have? His own ambition left him no time to figure that one out.

Disgusted with everything he decided to leave quietly by the side door. He'd had enough of the seedy part of politics.

The fresh winds surprised him. Wrapped up in themselves, most of the people in the State House had ignored the storm brewing outside. The cold biting winds hit him hard. He called his limo driver on his cell phone to pick him up. Terrence saw him rounding the circular drive that led to the front of the Grecian-style State House. The fresh cold wind felt good. Maybe it would blow away the concessions he had made for his career. Somehow, he doubted it.

Rubbing his graying temples, he unbuttoned his topcoat.

It was warm in the church. He felt comfortable. He came in here to forget about today. Leaving the past day behind, he looked around at the present. The church was scattered with various people. A young attractive woman wept softly up in front. The elderly priest slept in the back pew. It suddenly dawned on Terrence that once he took his oath all of these people would be in his care. Would he do right by them? Only time would tell. The quiet of the church eased his headache. A few deep breaths relaxed his tense muscles. It was a wise decision to come in. Looking to the monstrance, he prayed for guidance. As the ache in his head subsided and his body relaxed, he felt a sense of peace. He could have fallen asleep. The warm candlelit air smelled strongly of incense.

Catching himself, he opened his eyes. Looking at the statue of Mary, he realized it looked so familiar because it had her face, the beautiful face of his first love, Susan. The memory of Susan's face full of love and laughter washed over him. He hadn't thought of Susan in ages. Susan and Terrence grew up together. She was the blond, blue-eyed daughter of one of his father's associates, a rough man from the old neighborhood, one of the few his father trusted.

Susan and Terrence spent many days together. They both worked after school in Terrence's father's office. The two grew first to be friends then found themselves shyly falling in love. Their attraction grew until Terrence actually asked Susan out on a date.

That's when John Kinney got wind of the budding romance and quickly decided to squash it, "She's from the old neighborhood. That would be fine if you were just another boy, but she's not good enough for the future President. You have to marry up boy. Don't waste your time thinking of love. Becoming President is going to involve sacrifice!"

Terrence succumbed to his father's will. Susan cried softly in the office without looking at Terrence. His heart was broken as he watched the gentle tears fall from her eyes. He wanted to hold Susan and comfort her. He wanted to tell her everything would be all right and that he still loved her. He didn't. He obeyed his father and watched her sorrow change to anger. He watched in silence as she turned to other boys for comfort. Two years later Susan became pregnant by the roughest boy in the high school.

He knew Susan was unhappy but it was too late. He missed his chance many years ago. She hated him now. He listened to his father and it cost him dearly. He never married. His father paraded a barrage of eligible women in front of him like horses at an auction, but none of them interested him. Eventually he knew he would have to marry. Voters preferred a happily married man as President. Looking to the soft face on the statue that so reminded him of Susan, he knew he would eventually marry. He also knew that it wouldn't matter much.

Eighteen

And no wonder, for even Satan masquerades as an angel of light.
So it not strange that his ministers also masquerade as ministers
of righteousness. Their end will correspond to their deeds.
(2 Cor. 11:14)

T errence tried to break away from the memory of Susan.
It was too painful and it served no purpose. Looking to
the monstrance, he tried to find the tranquility he longed for in
the Jesus before him. The white Eucharistic Lord glowed from
the flickering candles that cast their magic on the white carved
altar. He felt the peace that his faith always brought him. The
peace of this dark little church was more than an oasis in a
storm. The winds of the nor'easter battered it outside, but
the church stood strong and tight against the pressure. He
wondered if he could be like this church, able to resist the
pressure and keep his faith strong.

Suddenly Terrence realized he could see something
moving in the middle of the Host. He strained his eyes. The
white host started to deepen, looking as if it was no longer
flat. It seemed to spiral into a cavernous deepness. He could
see a large tunnel, a spinning kaleidoscope of colors that
drew him in. Terrence found himself pulled into the vortex.

His vision blurred as he spun around. The sound of static

filled his ears. It was so loud it caused ear pain but he had no time to think, as unfocused scenes twirled around him. He tried to center himself but was too dizzy from all the spinning. He lost all sense of time and space. He felt nauseas. His feet had no place to plant themselves. He didn't know up from down. The eerie sensation of being propelled through the tunnel overtook him. He saw visions, like scenes from a movie—blurred visions of different people from a different time glowed and then faded. It left him feeling vulnerable and he felt the fear rising in him. And as he became aware of his racing heart, the spinning slowed. The flickering visions became clear. The panorama was focused and revealed ancient landscapes. Greeks played sports. Romans marched.

The static softened. He heard loud sounds he distinguished as voices. Slowly he entered the last vista. Terrence found himself standing in a courtyard where he stood in a large mob-like crowd. Above the crowd stood a balding man dressed in Roman attire and flanked on both sides by Roman soldiers. He had a disgusted look on his face as he gazed out at the crowd.

It took Terrence a moment to compose himself. He looked down at his feet, now planted firmly on the sandy soil of the courtyard. He was still wearing his polished leather shoes. His designer suit remained crisp and unwrinkled. All of these people were dressed in robes and sandals. Didn't they see him?

Terrence reached out and touched the bearded man beside him, "Where am I?" he asked but the man ignored him.

He grabbed the shoulder of a teenager beside the man, "Can you tell me where I am?" The boy didn't seem to feel or see him. Terrence was invisible to them. He screamed loud enough to penetrate the rumbling crowd, but no one responded. They couldn't hear him. He stood alone, unseen and unheard as he tried to calm himself. Why was he here? What was Jesus trying to show him?

Terrence felt shaky. He was weak. He sat on the ground despite being surrounded by angry people. He held his head in his hands as he rested his elbows on his knees. He heard the mob grow louder. He felt the throng sweep past him as they surged forward to the platform that held the Roman Soldiers. It was a miracle he wasn't crushed. It was as if he had a bubble of protection around him. He stayed on the ground as the scene played out before him. In time, he composed himself. He took a few deep breaths and raised his eyes despite the bright noon sun. Terrence was surprised by what he saw.

A man in Roman dress went out on the platform above the crowd and said, "Look, I bring him out to you so that you may know that I find no guilt in him."

Terrence watched in shock as Jesus was led out on the platform, his hands bound.

The man in Roman dress waved at Jesus, and said to them, "Behold, the man!"

Men dressed as chief priests cried out, "Crucify him! Crucify him!"

The man that Terrence now recognized as Pilate said to them, "Take him yourselves and crucify him. I find no guilt in him."

Pilate then summoned the chief priests, the rulers, and the people and said to them. "You brought this man to me and accused him of inciting the inhabitants to revolt. I have conducted my investigation in your presence and have not found this man guilty of the charges you have brought against him. Nor did Herod, for he sent him back to me. He committed no capital crime. Therefore I shall have him flogged and then release him."

The sight of the bound Jesus horrified Terrence. He knew the horror of the suffering Jesus was about to experience as he was beaten and crowned with thorns. He screamed at them to stop until his throat was raw. They could neither see nor hear him. Terrence followed Jesus in total frustration.

The soldiers led him away to the praetorium. They clothed him in purple and, weaving a crown of thorns, placed it on him.

They began to salute him, "Hail, King of the Jews!" and kept striking him. They knelt before him in mock homage.

Terrence could not stand to see the God he loved being beaten and mocked. He ran to the courtyard only to meet an unruly mob. It was only a few minutes before Jesus himself was pushed back onto the platform, as the crowd shouted insults.

On Passover, it was a Jewish custom to release one prisoner. Pilate allowed the mob select a prisoner of their choice. Pilate had the notorious prisoner Barabbas brought forward.

Pilate shouted to the crowd, "Which one do you want me to release to you? Barabbas or the Jesus called Messiah?

Pilate sat on the bench, and received a message his wife sent to him, "Have nothing to do with that righteous man. I suffered much in a dream today because of him." His wife had experienced a dream telling her Pilate should not condemn Jesus to death.

The chief priests and elders persuaded the crowds to ask for Barabbas. Terrence could see them pan through the mob with directions to leave Jesus and save Barabbas.

The governor said to them, "Which of these two men do you want me to release to you?"

They shouted, "Barabbas!"

Pilate said to them, "Then what shall I do with Jesus called Messiah?"

They all shouted, "Let him be crucified!"

Pilate said, "But why? What evil has he done?"

The chief priests answered, "We have a law, and according to our law he ought to die. He made himself to be the Son of God."

Now when Pilate heard this his fear grew. He went back into the praetorium with Jesus and he asked, "Where are you from?" Jesus did not answer him. So Pilate said to him, "Do you not know that I have power to crucify you?"

Jesus answered, "You would have no power over me if it had not been given to you from above. For this reason the one who handed me over to you has the greater sin."

Pilate again tried to release him but the crowd cried out, "If you release him, you are not a friend of Caesar. Everyone who makes himself a king opposes Caesar."

When Pilate heard these words, he brought Jesus out and seated him on the judge's bench in the place called Stone Pavement. It was about noon on the preparation day for Passover. He said to the Jews, "Behold, your king!"

They cried out, "Take him away, take him away! Crucify him!"

Pilate said to them, "Shall I crucify your king?"

The chief priest answered, "We have no king but Caesar." So Jesus was handed over to the Roman guard to be crucified.

Terrence sat stunned. He knew the gospel, but this was real.

It was hot, and it was loud and bloody. The dust from the feet of the surging crowd rose to choke him. He had to stand to escape it. He could see the soldiers lead Jesus away as a group of women wept. He could not believe his ears. Pilate found Jesus innocent, yet he listened to the mob and let him be crucified. Terrence began to follow the crowd who followed Jesus. Feeling disorientated he walked but he seemed to be going in the wrong direction. Despite his intentions, he could only watch as the crowd followed the Messiah, while he walked to the platform where Pilate had stood. Terrence stood there for what seemed like an eternity. He watched as Pilate sat upon the stone bench watching the innocent man carry his heavy cross toward Calvary.

Terrence could not describe the look of disgust in Pilate's eyes. Terrence had seen that look before. He had seen it in his own eyes—today, after Alan left him, Terrence spotted his own reflection in the mirror.

Pilate rose and left with a defeated air. Terrence who was left alone on the platform heard the crowd as it wound its way to Calvary. He watched silently as the first two crosses rose against the horizon. Terrence cringed as the sounds of hammers traveled through the air. Watching the Cross of Jesus rise between the others, Terrence wept. He had been unable to do anything to save Jesus. Moments froze as he stood alone in grief. The sky suddenly darkened above the scene of Calvary. As Terrence looked toward the death of Jesus, a flash of lightning seared the sky. He had to cover his eyes as the flash of lightning stuck the earth. When he opened his eyes, everything had changed.

Now he stood in the center of a stage. The crowd before him was a mixture of Klansmen and skinheads. It frightened him. He could also see sweet-faced grandmothers and blue collar laborers. The crowd before him grew rowdy and surged toward the stage. He was dressed in the same spotless suit and polished shoes. The dust had disappeared.

Terrence sensed the presence of others on the stage. Looking around he saw most of the party leaders sitting on metal chairs with open notebooks and programs. They looked as if they were at a convention. Terrence realized he stood behind the podium with two lines of seven men beside him. He recognized some of the people beside him and in that recognition grew afraid. They were the men on death row. A frightened black teenager stood beside him and shook with fear. Tears streaked down his face. Across from the boy was the Preppie Killer who had strangled his girlfriend because he claimed she liked to be roughed up. The smirk on his face was so evil it made the hairs stand up on Terrence's neck.

Nevertheless, the presence that most frightened him stood just behind him and sent chills through Terrence's soul. He was afraid to look, but more afraid not too. In the back and just to the side he saw the party boss. The afternoon Terrence spent with Alan in the Governor's mansion now seemed so far away. It was Alan, but he looked different. Small and twisted, his features were distorted in evil contortions. His eyes had no pupils and glowed with a burning red. On his back flapped leathery bat-like wings. His claw-like hands reached up and slapped Terrence on the back as he had that day in the library. His voice, low and guttural, growled, "Listen to the people. Don't deny them their blood!"

Terrence instinctively pulled away. He moved to the front of the podium and toward the surging crowd. Raising his hands in the air, he tried to quiet them. Used to crowds he took the mic and announced, "Please quiet down now, if you want me to hear you. Tell me what it is you want from me."

The shouts were reduced to a low murmur as Terrence used his skills to handle the crowd. He pointed to a mild looking man in the second row, "Tell me sir, what is it you want from me?"

The man rose amid a clamor and shouted, "I want them executed! I want revenge. I want the death penalty!"

The crowd roared with approval. Terrence stepped back, grabbed the young black teen by the arm and pulled him forward, "Suppose I told you this young boy is innocent. Would you still want the death penalty?"

The crowd rose and surged toward the stage screaming and shouting, "Execute him! Execute him!"

The power of their hate pushed Terrence back to the podium as he dragged the weeping teenager with him. Looking to the side, he could see the Preppie Killer laughing as he waved at the crowd to come forward. Terrence almost tripped in his effort to place the podium between himself, the teenager, and the mob. Suddenly he felt the touch of a claw as it grabbed his shoulder. Then Alan's voice whispered in his ear, "Crucify him!"

In an instant, Terrence was back in the church. Gasping for air, he fell to his knees. Kneeling and shaking before the

Eucharist, he started to weep. He understood now. It was all so clear. Pilate was a politician, a great politician. He had made compromises to promote himself in his political career. He had given the people what he thought they wanted despite his own feelings and became the most hated man in history.

Terrence shook as he knelt before the silent monstrance. He could not control his thoughts as they raced though his mind. The revulsion he felt when he thought of Alan slapping him on the back overpowered him. The man was evil and yet Terrence had allowed him to touch and influence him. He disgusted himself with his own ambition. Terrence felt completely shaken. Jesus had shown him the truth. Jesus was, as the Bible said, the way, the life, and the truth. It was clear to Terrence now as he knelt in this beautiful church. Pilate had condemned himself for not following his heart. Pilate had taken a poll.

Nineteen

Consider this; whoever sows sparingly will also reap sparingly, and whoever sows bountifully will also reap bountifully. Each must do as already determined, without sadness or compulsion, for God loves a cheerful giver. (2 Cor. 9:7-8)

The harsh winds no longer blasted the little church in their mad dash to the sea. The stain-glassed windows no longer rattled with the storm's rage. The sky, which had cleared of the low gray clouds, now opened to the light of the full moon. The moonlight shone through the stained glass window illuminating the pieces of colored glass that formed a scene of the Visitation of Mary. The window displayed Mary and Elizabeth as they hugged in greeting.

The Bible story it depicted told the tale of Mary traveling rough terrain to help her older cousin in spite of her own troubles. It regales how John the Baptist leapt in Elizabeth's womb at the nearness of the unborn Christ Child that Mary carried. The lunar light gave a special glow to Mary's act of charity. The bells in the tower of the church chimed eleven as the nightly worship continued. Seven people knelt as the rest of the city slept beneath an ivory blanket of snow. Father D'Angelico dozed as the time for closing the worship and the church drew near.

The monstrance glowed like the moon as the two candles that flanked it on either side of the altar burned. Melted drops of white wax cooled and remained on the gold candlesticks. Flickering flames glowed in a reddish hue against the jeweled monstrance that held the Body of Christ. In the dim light threads of incense smoke remained to ease the hearts of the sojourners.

Peter Caine was not feeling mellow. He was restless and antsy, anxious to start his new life in the mountains of West Virginia. His longing was palpable. He wanted to see his old home. He could taste the cool morning breeze that flowed around the mountain. He could hear the whispers of the people as they seemed to call him home. It was as if a part of his heart had been sealed with hatred and now the hatred was gone. His heart overflowed with love, and a longing to give that love back. Most of all, he longed to love the old couple he had ignored for so long.

His father was a quiet man who had spent his life loving others. His patients depended on him. He was like family. For a long time, the mountain people and his wife were Dr. John Caine's only family after his son abandoned him for a life of money and comfort.

Peter Caine was ashamed now of how he ignored his parents. He was the only family they had. He hadn't visited them in years. Now every minute of separation seemed a lifetime. Peter longed to hold his father in his arms. He wanted to beg his forgiveness and tell him everything. Now he couldn't wait to see the old man.

Looking to the Eucharist on the altar Peter bowed his head in thanks to Jesus. He could still see the Lord, though now only in his heart. Peter knew he was a changed man from the one who had entered the little church just a few hours ago. It was another hour to the end of the service and Peter couldn't wait. He quietly left his seat and genuflected at the end of the pew.

The street outside the church was muffled in white. No

footsteps marked the sidewalk. The night was quiet. Peter headed toward the hospital. *My timing is perfect,* he thought as he strode the deserted streets. *The shifts will be changing and I should be able to collect my things without being noticed.*

His things were in the cardiology conference room, papers packed in a box in the closet and ready for pick-up. He had been so angry when his practice closed that he allowed the office girls to take care of everything. It seemed strange that ten years of his life fit in a small cardboard box that lay at the bottom of a dusty closet. He would need his diplomas when he applied for a medical license in West Virginia.

The warm antiseptic air hit Peter's nostrils as he entered the hospital through the employee door. Hoping to slip in and out of the hospital unnoticed he walked through the employee locker room. On the other side he opened the door to the main hallway. Not seeing a soul, he decided it was right to leave the church when he did. Everyone would be in the report room at the change of shift and he could walk around unnoticed.

Peter took the elevator up to the cardiac wing on the fifth floor. A lone nurse guarded the beeping monitors, which sat on the nurse's station. No alarm warned of any trouble and the young nurse was absorbed in something. She didn't notice Peter as he entered the hall. The sound of a cardiac unit is unique. The beeping and pulsing lights of the heart monitors give a certain rhythm to the unit. The beats pulse and blend until the floor seems to have a beating heart of its own. Peter was drawn to the pulse. His own heart beat in rhythm to the sounds of the floor. Excitement filled Peter's veins as adrenaline entered his system.

Peter spent many hours on this floor, handling emergencies here with skill and wisdom. Pride welled up in Peter and wrapped itself around his heart as he slowly walked past the patient rooms. He saved a life in every room on this floor. His talents had shone in the ten years he spent here, garnering him a reputation of respect. His honor had grown as he taught interns his medical skills. How he longed for that respect.

It's not too late, he thought, *I could open my own practice again. I could build it up. I'm sure that many of my patients would be glad to come back to me. I could develop a larger and more successful practice then Vinny's.* As the thought occurred to him, he grinned with satisfaction at the idea. The smells of the hospital floor invigorated him. A pulse of energy ran through his veins.

Peter stopped in his tracks. *"What am I thinking?"* He was shocked at how fast his old train of thought returned. In less than an hour, he had almost forgotten the lesson Jesus had shown him in the church. *"I am no longer that man. I was never meant to be him,"* Peter thought as he reached the outer door of the cardiac conference room. The memory of Cain and Abel returned as he shook thoughts of revenge away. Peter pushed the key into the lock on the office door and tried to turn it. It wouldn't budge. *Oh God, the lock's been changed.*

Peter trembled as he realized he would have to ask one of the nurses for help. This was the last thing he wanted to do. He didn't want to see any one who knew him before this trouble. He could feel sweat break out on his forehead. He was about to swallow his pride and seek help when he heard a soft voice.

"Can I help you, Dr. Caine?" asked a female voice in a soft whisper.

Turning he noticed Valerie, a night-shift nurse standing behind him. She had assisted him many times. Peter greatly respected her skills.

Unable to open the door, his face reddened as he answered, "I've come to collect my things."

Valerie smiled and taking the large key ring from her belt unlocked the door and continued, "I'm so happy to see you Dr. Caine. We've missed you so much. Are you going to open a new office? So many of your patients ask for you and all of the nurses miss you."

Peter stumbled over his words as Valerie opened the closet door and removed the box that contained his possessions, "I plan to start over somewhere else. I have plans to go home and open my new practice with my father."

It was the first time Peter had announced his intention aloud and somehow it seemed so right once he said it. Valerie's face fell as she handed Peter the box. She turned back and locked the room up again.

"I'm sorry to hear that. We were hoping you'd come back. We'll all be disappointed to hear that you're leaving. I hope you knew we were rooting for you. I think it is a shame what happened. Are you sure you won't change your mind?"

Peter was surprised. So there were people who still believed in him. Apparently, his former associates weren't laughing at him. Maybe he could start over here. Peter could feel the old longing for acclaim rising in his spirit. He could rebuild his practice if there were others who believed in him.

Valerie could see the emotions that played across Peter's face and was encouraged.

"You should reconsider and stay here. Your father will understand," she said hopefully.

The mention of his father called Peter back from his musings. No, he had made up his mind. He was going home to West Virginia.

"I'm sorry, Valerie. I'm leaving tonight. Please thank all the nurses for me. It's gratifying to know that I'll be missed," answered Peter as he turned and quickly left. He was being tempted and so far, he was resisting.

Reaching the elevator, Peter felt a tugging in his heart. He realized he would never again see this hospital again. This medical center was once the core of his life. If he followed through with his plans, he would be closing this door forever. It would be so much easier to stick with what was familiar. Perhaps he should wait a year before he made such a drastic move. Peter could feel the envelope with the

$10,000 in his jacket pocket. With it he could get started. He could open a new office. *"No, I won't go back to that old life. I'll trust in God,"* Peter decided with resolve. Putting the box down, he reached into the envelope and removed five hundred dollars. Shoving the money into his wallet he thought, *"Five hundred will be more than enough for my trip home and the money will be safer this way."* Peter picked up the box just as the elevator reached the main floor and headed for the exit. He spotted a homeless man on the icy bench just outside the main entrance.

The ragged man turned to Peter, "Do you have a dollar for a cup of coffee?"

He moved quickly toward Peter with his hand extended. Beneath the clear starlit sky, the man seemed so alone in the cold. Peter impulsively made up his mind. He acted without much thought. He walked off quickly before he had a chance to change his mind. Somehow he felt lighter, his step quicker as he headed toward the train that would take him to the mountains of West Virginia and his new life.

Francis had left the church because he swore he heard the voice of Jesus tell him to start his new life tonight. It made no sense at the time. It made more sense for him to sleep in the warm church as he did every Friday night until morning. What could he do until the light of day? Stepping outside, he looked at the starlit sky. It was a bitter cold night. Francis could go to the subway station and spend a warm night there.

Instead, he turned to the left and headed for the hospital. No matter how good or bad the weather, Francis was always able to beg money there. They were always generous to him there. Maybe they wanted God to see their act of generosity in hope that He would answer their prayers. Maybe they thought He would answer their prayers if He saw them help the less fortunate. Whatever the reason, these do-gooders always gave him money when he panhandled in front of the hospital. With that in mind, Francis traded the warmth of the subway platform for the cold wooden bench at the entrance of the hospital.

He thought if he could collect enough money, he would get a room at a cheap boarding house. With a little luck, he might get enough for a new set of clothes from the thrift shop. Francis was anxious to start his new life. With a shower and new clothes, he could go down to the union hall. He could renew friendships and ask for work. With a job, he could get an apartment. A new apartment to share with his daughter. That was his plan as he reached the hospital.

It wasn't long before he saw someone leaving.

With his hand, extended Francis approached the man and asked, "Do you have a dollar for a cup of coffee?" The man put down the box he was carrying, reached into his jacket pocket, and squeezed something into Francis' hand. Picking up the box again, the man headed quickly away.

The homeless man watched as the well-dressed man disappeared into the darkness. Opening the envelope, Francis collapsed on the bench. After a few deep breaths, he sat up and counted the money. *$9500, I can't believe it,* Francis could feel the hot tears roll down his cold face.

Twenty

Probe me, God, know my heart; try me, know my concern.
See if my way is crooked then lead me in the ancient paths.
(Psalm 139: 23-24)

Anna Grubowski struggled to her feet. Her knees were swollen and sore from prayer. She hated to leave her Lord but she had to catch the eleven-thirty bus. She donned her coat, grabbed her black purse and bowed as she left her pew. Anna couldn't bend her inflamed knee enough to genuflect. Slowly, she reached the door of the church and opened it. A beautiful winter scene greeted her. The radiant snow glowed unmolested beneath a clear, bright moon. The beauty didn't fool Anna. The sparkling ice held danger. One fall and she could break a hip that could leave her crippled for life. Anna hoped the bus would keep its schedule in spite of the storm. She watched from the church steps as a city plow pushed its way down the street and continued past the church and down the road in the direction of the hospital. Anna smiled her way was now cleared, and she whispered, "Thank you Lord."

She took a deep breath and held on tightly to the metal banister. She didn't have to go far. Once safely down the icy steps she only needed to walk a few feet across the slippery sidewalk to the bus stop. She was just in time. The bus arrived at the stop with her.

Reaching into her worn black purse for the bus fare, Anna rummaged around for her wallet. She found her wallet, but it was empty. Anna could have sworn she had put a ten dollar bill in there before she left home. She must have forgotten it in her rush to get to church. She reddened as the bus driver, not the usual driver but a stranger, fidgeted with impatience.

She sheepishly looked up at him and softly said, "I'm afraid I don't have the money."

Pulling on the latch that closed the bus door the driver announced with disdain, "No money, no ride."

Anna watched in sorrow as the bus started down the road. It would reach her destination in just a few minutes. She wasn't surprised at the cruelty of the driver. She had known cruelty often in her life. She didn't have time to dwell on it. She had to decide what to do now. She could see the hospital just three blocks away in the shining light of the full moon. But Anna wasn't fooled — it looked close but she knew that between her and the hospital laid snow-covered sidewalks and hidden patches of ice.

Looking back to the church, she thought of asking Father D'Angelico for a loan for the bus fare. He would be glad to help but he was probably reciting the closing benediction prayers by now. *No, I'll just have to walk carefully,* Anna decided.

As the bitter cold started to chill her, Anna walked tentatively toward the hospital. She had gotten 15 feet down the sidewalk and was just starting to feel a little confident when she hit her first patch of ice. She could feel her right foot slipping as she extended her arms in an attempt to regain her balance. Her left foot then started to slip behind her. In the split second that it took Anna to realize that she was going to fall forward, she extended both her arms in front of her to break the impact.

As she started to fall, someone grabbed her arm.

Clinging to the sudden help, Anna braced herself and regained her balance. Taking a deep breath and looking up to her rescuer, Anna found herself looking into the face of the young woman who had sobbed all night in the church.

Patricia Walsh held the elderly woman's arm as she found her footing and steadied herself, then asked, "Are you all right?"

Anna smiled at her pretty helper and answered, "I am now, now that you are here to catch me."

Patricia nodded in acknowledgement and inquired, "Where are you going, anyway? Maybe I can help."

Anna pointed to the medical center as she answered, "I'm on my way to the hospital. I work the night shift as a custodian. It's only three blocks but it seems like three miles tonight."

Patricia smiled, "Well, that's great because I'm headed to the hospital myself. Just hold on and we'll make the three blocks."

Anna put her arm in Patricia's and the two women started slowly up the sidewalk together. Anna took a good look at the young woman who had come to her rescue. She was tall and extremely pretty. Dark caramel hair curled around her face and highlighted her large green eyes. Anna wondered what was causing her suffering. What would make this young woman cry all night in a dark church? She could feel her hands grow warmer, as she looked at the young girl. *It must be someone she loves, yes, someone who is sick. Why else would my hands be so warm on this bitter night?* she thought as they walked arm in arm.

Patricia was the first to introduce herself. She spoke easily and freely about her life. Anna listened with interest.

"My husband is a truck driver and away much of the time," Patricia continued as they walked carefully toward the hospital, "His job requires it. Sometimes I feel so alone."

Anna looked at the young woman beside her and asked, "Do you have any children?"

Anna noticed the catch in Patricia's voice as she answered, "Yes, I have one daughter, Megan, she is gravely ill and in the hospital."

"I'm sorry to hear that," Anna answered softly.

A single tear fell down Patricia's cheek as she continued her story, "Megan was hit by a car. She's been in a coma for months. My little girl has been asleep in a bed on the third floor of this hospital since her accident. Now the doctors have given up on her. The insurance company won't pay for her hospital care, and they want to put my baby in a nursing home. Somewhere far away I guess, out of sight and out of mind."

Patricia sobbed as she verbalized her pain for the first time, yet there was something freeing about telling this strange woman her troubles. Looking into Anna's soft brown eyes Patricia sensed that somehow this woman understood loss. Anna tightened her grip on Patricia's arm as if to confirm her understanding.

They had finally reached their destination. Standing at the front entrance of the hospital, Anna who had just been listening finally spoke, "Are you going to visit your daughter now?"

Patricia was about to nod in the affirmative when something stopped her. A memory quickly rose to her mind. Patricia suddenly remembered the Bible story of the soldier, the soldier who while kneeling in front of the Lord had enough faith to trust that Jesus could heal at any distance. A spark of hope rose from her soul.

She surprised herself by answering, "No, I think I'll go home and get a good night's sleep. My husband is supposed to call. He'll be home tomorrow. I'll visit Megan in the morning before I go grocery shopping. Then I'll go home and cook David a good dinner."

Patricia was shocked by her own resolve. She had not planned any of this.

Anna smiled and answered the young woman with a

hug, "Yes, that is best. Take care of your husband. Jesus and His angels will watch over your child. What room is she in? Perhaps I will take a peek at her during the night, that is, if it is all right with you."

"Of course," answered Patricia with a smile, "She's in 312, bed B."

Turning the corner for home, Patricia felt a sense of peace. She found trust in Jesus. *I will turn Megan over to the Lord*, she thought as she reached the door of her apartment. Getting to her door the sound of the ringing phone greeted her. Patricia just knew it was David calling.

Anna decided to start her cleaning on the third floor tonight. Taking her cart up the elevator she mopped the hallway as she looked around. All of the nurses were busy. The hallway was dark and empty as she reached room 312 at the end of the hallway. The door of the room was hidden behind a wall. Anna looked around, and seeing no one, pushed open the door to Megan's room.

"Poor little baby," exclaimed Anna as she pulled aside the curtain that hid the little girl. Megan looked tiny in the fluffy white sheets of the hospital bed. Pillows were propped to position her slightly on her right side. Rolled up washcloths had been taped and placed in her hands to prevent atrophy. *She looks like a little angel,* Anna thought as she watched the gentle breaths of the sleeping child. Long eyelashes fluttered on Megan's rosy cheeks. But the eyes never opened.

Anna emptied the wastebaskets in the room and set up the yellow cones that read, *Caution Wet Floor*. Anna wanted the room to look like she was cleaning it in case any of the nurses came by. Listening, she heard no one coming so she gingerly walked over to Megan's bedside. Anna started to pray. She laid her hands on the child's chest and forehead. Anna's hands burned as she lifted the child up to Jesus. She could hear the breaths the child took deepen and become more rapid as she prayed. Slowly, Anna's hands cooled as the heat seemed to enter the little girl. It felt just like what she experienced when she prayed over Jedze the afternoon he had come back to life.

Anna lifted her hands and opened her eyes. She could see the little girl stir slightly against the pillows and she knew that God had answered her prayers. She quickly stacked the cones and pushed the cart out of the room. Anna was thrilled. At this late age she finally recognized her gift of healing. Praising God she steered the cart onto the elevator and pushed the first floor button. She had to clean the Intensive Care Unit next. *That teenage boy who was hit by a drunk driver is on a respirator,* thought Anna. She realized God's grace as the elevator surged downward. Smiling alone in the elevator, she felt joy rise in her soul.

Megan's head and chest felt hot. The rest of her body felt cold. The heat woke her up. She didn't remember falling asleep. Her legs were numb and pressed hard against the wall. Looking around she could see that nothing had changed. The white room was still full of mist. The statue lady stood in the same spot and hadn't moved.

She hated to move her legs. Megan dreaded the 'pins and needles' as her daddy called it. Megan looked at the stairs that led to the upper door. *Should I try it,* Megan thought as fear rose in her heart. *I want my Mommy,* she cried silently as she realized once again how alone she was. Looking at the other door she cringed in fear and her legs returned to normal. She was still afraid to move and wondered what lay beyond that dark opening.

The white mist rose and surrounded her. She had to make a try for the stairs and the upper door. Her mommy was behind that door, she just knew it. Megan had heard her voice calling her, but that was a long time ago. Looking up at the door, Megan was about to try when something unexpected happened. The door, at the top of the stairway, jolted and then started to creak open.

Twenty-One

There is nothing concealed that will not be revealed, nor secret that will not be known. Therefore whatever you have said in darkness will be heard in the light, and what you have whispered behind closed doors will be proclaimed on the housetops. (Luke 12: 2-3)

Father D'Angelico rose from his pew at the back of the church and walked up the aisle to kneel before the altar. Now fully alert after his night of prayer, he rose up in prayer before his Savior.

> "Tantum ergo sacramentum, Veneremur cernui
> Et antiquum documentum, Novo cedat ritui
> Praestet fides supplementum, Sensuum defectui
> Humbly let us voice our homage
> For so great a Sacrament
> Let all former rites surrender
> To the Lord's New Testament
> What our senses fail to fathom
> Let us grasp through faith's consent
>
> Genitori Genitoque, Laus et jubilation
> Salus honor virtus quoque, Sit et benediction

Procedenti ab utroque, Compar sit laudation
Amen

To the everlasting Father,
And the Son who reigns on high
With the Spirit blessed proceeding
Forth from each eternally
Be salvation, honor, blessing
Might and endless majesty
Amen"

The three people remaining in the church knelt in their pews. Only two of them sang with the priest. Maisie Johnson and Terrence sang softly knowing the Latin by heart. Bobby knelt silently with his eyes closed as the others worshipped the God he hated.

Father D'Angelico rose and circled the altar. Wrapping a stole around his shoulders and hands, the priest faced those who waited for the closing prayers. Lifting the Eucharistic Lord high above his head, Father D'Angelico made the sign of the cross with the monstrance, blessing all in the church. Returning to kneel in front of the altar he loudly recited the Divine Praises as Maisie and Terrence joined in the prayer. The tired priest then ended the prayer, "May the heart of Jesus, in the most blessed sacrament, be praised, adored, and loved with grateful affection, at every moment, in all the tabernacles of the world, even to the end of time. Amen."

Father D'Angelico felt weak as he pushed himself up from his knees. Again circling the altar he bowed and removed the Luna containing the Eucharist from the monstrance. As he returned the Host to the tabernacle he could feel a sharp shooting pain run down the length of his right arm. It grew worse as he returned to his seat at the back of the church. He gasped for air. He couldn't get enough in his lungs. He shivered in the cold dampness. *Perhaps I should sleep in tomorrow,* he thought as the worshippers rose and donned their coats.

The next pain tore thought his chest so deeply that his breathing stopped completely. The priest's body slumped forward in a kneeling position against the back of the pew in front of him. Suddenly the pain ended and Father D'Angelico found himself standing in the middle of the aisle. A bright light glowed warmly in front of him. Falling to his knees, he saw Jesus standing in the light. Dressed in glowing gold and shining white, Jesus reached down and placed his hand on the priest's bowed head. In a soft and loving voice, Jesus announced, "Well done, my good and faithful servant."

"Is it finished then?" asked the priest looking back at the body he had left behind. He no longer felt any pain.

Raising his face to look into the eyes of his Savior he saw Jesus smile, "No my friend, it has now begun."

Maisie passed the priest thinking he must be deep in prayer. He remained kneeling with his eyes closed and his head bowed for such a long time. She was quiet as she did not want to disturb him. Dipping her hand in the bowl of holy water by the church vestibule, Maisie noticed the distinguished-looking gentleman by the door.

Terrence held the door open for Maisie as they both left the church. He instinctually took her arm and slowly helped her down the icy stairs. Maisie could see the limo driver waiting by the curb to open the door for the man. *He must be very important,* she thought as he walked her carefully toward the bus stop. The night was shimmering white and as quiet as the church as they walked cautiously. Maisie was grateful for his help and turned around to thank him.

Bobby waited until the two slow-assed worshippers left, pretending he was deep in prayer. Hearing the door slam shut he looked up to the now empty monstrance on the altar. He would steal the golden candles and monstrance right from the altar. Now that the old man placed it back into the tabernacle, he would have to retrieve the tabernacle key from the old priest's pocket. *No problem! I'll smash the old man's God under my feet after I kill the old man,* Bobby thought. He shivered with excitement. He fingered the knife in his pocket as he headed toward the back of the church. *No sense tipping off the priest,* Bobby smiled as he pretended to leave the church with the other worshippers. He passed the priest and the old man didn't move. It was all too easy! Rounding the last pew, Bobby pulled the knife out of his pocket and popped the switchblade open. It made a snapping noise, but still the old man didn't move. *He must be deaf!* Bobby laughed as he raised his arm and without a second thought, plunged the knife into Father D'Angelico's back. Bobby was so thrilled to see the body slump to the side that he didn't notice the lack of blood spilling from the wound. Pulling the body over, Bobby fumbled around until he found the pocket that contained the tabernacle key.

Bobby couldn't stop grinning. Everything was working out great. He would open up the box that contained the God who ridiculed him. He would dump all of the Hosts on the floor and smash them with his feet. He felt energy pulsing through his body. After he crushed the so-called God who had tried to crush his spirit, he would steal God's gold. He could probably get good money for it even though he'd have to hide them for a while. At least until the heat was off.

Next, he would head for home. His father and stepmother were probably asleep in their bed. They didn't know it when they went to sleep, but they would never wake up. Bobby was about to fulfill his dream. He knew now that he could kill.

Looking up toward the altar, Bobby stopped in shock. Standing before him was the old priest he had just stabbed. The priest held his arms out to his side and the vestments he wore seemed to glow in the dark church. Unable to move Bobby's mind raced. *This isn't possible! He's dead!* Looking slowly behind him, Bobby saw that the body of the priest remained slumped on the back pew.

This isn't real, Bobby decided as he turned around expecting to see an empty church. The spirit of the priest remained standing before him. Father D'Angelico's spirit reached for Bobby as it announced, "I forgive you and your Father in Heaven will forgive you also, if you just ask."

Bobby screamed as he dropped the tabernacle key and turned. He ran holding the bloody switchblade and quickly exited the church. He didn't want to see any more. Bobby was sick of this church and this God. Running down the icy steps he clung to the knife. Without much thought, he headed toward the waiting limo. The driver held the back door open as a rich-looking man was about to enter. Bobby decided that he would take the man's place and force the driver to get him out of here. He unconsciously positioned the knife to stab the guy getting into the limo and headed toward him.

Maisie stood frozen for just a second as the young boy sprinted out of the church. The knife glinted in the light of the full moon. Instinctively and in an instant, without thinking she moved quickly to place herself between the angry youth and the man who had just helped her down the church steps. She saw the boy raise the knife to stab the man's back as he was getting in the car. He stood frozen. Maisie reached the man just in time.

Bobby didn't see the old black woman. He was focused on the man as he plunged the knife, but a blur caught his eye. The knife hit flesh. Bobby could feel it and he pushed the knife as hard as he could to drive it further. It tore deep into Maisie's shoulder. Warm blood gushed forward soaking her old cloth coat. In an instant Bobby realized he had stabbed the wrong person. Everything had gone wrong! As the man he intended to stab turned in shock and horror Bobby pulled the knife out of Maisie's shoulder. He wasn't about to leave his only weapon behind. Turning quickly, he ran off.

Bobby ran down the block. He was headed for the alley

when the ice caught his foot. Spinning, he lost his balance. Falling toward the sidewalk, Bobby instantly realized what was happening, but not in time to move the knife. He could feel it tearing into his chest. It severed an artery in an instant. Bobby lay on the sidewalk bleeding as his life pumped out of him. His warm blood melted the red snow. Bobby cursed his bad luck as his spirit stood up and watched his body die on the sidewalk.

Looking up, he saw Jesus. Jesus reached out to Bobby just as he had in Bobby's vision of prodigal son. Once again Bobby cursed God. The image of Jesus faded sadly. Darker entities rose from the sidewalk and surrounded Bobby's spirit. Bobby screamed as their flaming hands pulled at him. His plans had gone all wrong. The entities pulled him down and Bobby's spirit melted through the sidewalk as his body lay dead above.

Maisie could feel herself fainting as her blood soaked the front of her coat. Just as her knees started to buckle beneath her, Terrence lifted her small frame up in his arms. Maisie could hear him shouting to the driver as he carefully carried her into the back of the limo, "Hurry, there's no time to wait for the ambulance. The hospital is only three blocks away! Let's go!"

The driver gunned the engine as Terrence slammed the limo's back door. The police arrived in four screaming cars and cops with guns drawn surrounded Bobby's dead body. One car followed the limo as it sped down the street to the emergency room. Terrence took his scarf and wrapped Maisie's shoulder, attempting to stem the bleeding. Maisie took a deep breath although the movement, which accompanied the breath, caused her great pain. Looking up into the blue eyes of the man who held her, Maisie sighed.

"You know you saved my life, don't you?" the man asked softly.

Maisie gave a weak smile in response.

"Anything you want? Anything I can do for you? You

just need to ask," Terrence announced with conviction as he applied pressure to Maisie's shoulder wound to stem the bleeding. The limo was turning into the emergency room entrance.

Maisie opened her mouth to answer. She almost said, "No, you owe me nothing," but a thought stopped her. Maisie suddenly thought of Esther. This man did look important. Perhaps he knew important people. Perhaps he had influence like Miss Mona.

Weakly, Maisie answered before she passed out, "Maybe, maybe you could help me."

That was all Terrence needed to hear. He stayed with the woman as the doctors stitched, cleaned and dressed her wound.

He was by her bedside when she awoke. Slowly she told Terrence her story. Terrence was riveted. She asked him for her purse. Following her instructions, he pulled the photo she asked for out of her wallet.

Maisie spoke softly, "That's my Johnny. That's my great-grandson. They are going to execute him tomorrow at midnight. Can you help?"

Terrence Kinney sat spellbound starring at the photo. His spirit silenced by shock. Maisie's grandson was the young black youth in his vision, the young man who cried for mercy while the crowd screamed for crucifixion. It was too mysterious, more than Terrence could comprehend. Maisie again passed out in weakness before Terrence could answer. The doctors assured him that she would recover fully with time and rest.

Terrence arrived at the statehouse two hours late to take his vows as the new governor. Alan was red with anger. Terrence didn't care. It no longer mattered what the party boss thought. It no longer mattered what the polls said. Pilate had taken a poll. What was right mattered more than politics or polls.

Despite his anger, Alan smiled and posed with

Terrence as the photographers snapped pictures for the front page of the morning newspapers. As quickly as he could, Terrence pulled away and performed his first act as the new governor. Terrence Kinney called the prison and stayed the execution of Johnny, Maisie's great-grandson until further investigation.

Epilogue

You, my child, shall be called the prophet of the Most High for you will go before the Lord to prepare his way, to give his people knowledge of salvation by the forgiveness of their sins. In the tender compassion of our God, the dawn from on high shall break upon us, to shine on those who dwell in darkness and the shadow of death and to guide our feet into the way of Peace. (The Canticle of Zachariah)

Father D'Angelico watched Bobby run out of the church. Bobby had free will. The priest had work to do for the Lord before he could enter eternal Glory. He now knew that Eternal Glory was not Eternal Rest. St. Therese of the Roses claimed that she would spend her time in Heaven doing good on the earth. She had been right. Until all souls came to judgment at the end of time, no Christian, alive or dead could rest. There were souls to be brought to Jesus. There was work to be done. Glory laid in doing the work of the Lord. With this thought, the priest, no longer in pain, left and went to the door. It was time to turn the knob. Father D'Angelico opened the door.

Megan pushed back against the wall as she heard the door creaking open. Would it be something bad, something dark? Megan assumed that opening the door at the top of the stairs would be good. She thought so because she thought she heard her mother's voice come from behind that door. Now she wasn't so sure. She closed her eyes tight. Megan was afraid. She heard the opening of the door at the top of the stairs.

Then she heard nothing. It seemed an eternity and yet she heard nothing. Megan was afraid, but she couldn't stand the suspense any longer. She had to look. She opened her eyes and as they adjusted to the light she was shocked to see an ordinary man standing at the top of the stairs.

He was an old man with a kind face and he smiled at Megan. Suddenly she felt good. She no longer shook with fear. The man beckoned her to come to him by waving his hands. His smile seemed to light her way. Megan noticed that the white mist parted forming a path up to the man. She could see him clearly now. He was dressed as a priest. Megan had seen a priest once at church. Megan took a step and nothing bad happened. She took another and another and her way stayed clear. Soon, Megan found herself running. She ran up the stairs and into the arms of the priest who picked her up and carried her through the door. Looking over his shoulder, Megan could see the statue lady come to life and follow. Megan understood now. The statue lady was her angel. Mommy had told her about angels. Now Megan understood her angel would be with her for eternity.

Once through the door, Father D'Angelico set Megan down. When Megan turned around to look at the priest both he and the door were gone. Megan found herself alone in an empty space. She was afraid. Megan closed her eyes. What was happening? Why was she always alone? Why had the priest left her? She held her eyes tightly shut, afraid of what she might see.

Megan's body shook with fear. Afraid to move, she listened. Suddenly she heard voices that seemed close. Megan heard the bustle of the hospital floor without knowing what it was. She heard the sound of an elevator door opening in the distance. She had to open her eyes. Instantly Megan forgot the mist-filled room even though she had been there for so long. She forgot the lady who carried her from the accident. She forgot the priest who saved her. She only remembered running in the street after JoJo. She opened her eyes and found herself in a bed. Megan didn't know where she was or how she had gotten there.

Patricia Walsh enjoyed her walk to the hospital. The full moon was just starting to wane and the streetlights glowed dully. She felt refreshed after the first deep and peaceful sleep she had enjoyed in months. She felt rejuvenated after she took her shower and dressed. Her light breakfast did not tire her. Despite the early hour Patricia decided to head to the hospital.

David would be home this evening and the thought of seeing him made her heart beat faster. How she missed him! Since the accident she was so focused on Megan that she spent little time thinking of David. How lucky she was to have him.

Patricia headed out the door. She would visit Megan for a few hours before going shopping, but she was determined to spend the day with her husband. They could both visit Megan together tomorrow. Patricia felt as if a weight had been taken off her shoulders. The story she had read in the church last night had been meant for her. Patricia was sure of that. God was telling her to let go. She couldn't control what would happen with Megan. She never had control. She had to trust Megan to God.

Patricia's step was so much lighter. The sidewalks were not as slippery as they were the night before. It was warming up. Looking at the sun rising, Patricia supposed the warmth of the sun would melt the rest of the ice. Taking the elevator up to the third floor she quickly made it to Megan's room. The night shift was still working, preparing their reports for the day nurses who would start to arrive at six-thirty. Pushing open the door to Megan's room, Patricia was awed by the spectacular sunrise that framed the hospital window. Golden streaks lightened the morning sky as the sun reached the horizon. A sudden movement caught the corner of Patricia's eye. Before her mind could register the meaning of the movement she heard a voice. A low voice that was so familiar.

Megan turned and announced, "Look, Mommy, the sun is risen!"

Patricia stood still and stared at her daughter who smiled and pointed to the window. Patricia started to tremble and quake as reality hit her. Megan was awake! It astounded her. Unable to stand as the shock of Megan's recovery tore through her mind, Patricia fell to her knees.

Looking up into the blue eyes of her daughter, Patricia's own eyes filled with tears. Reaching up to touch the small girl she loved with all her heart Patricia whispered, "Yes, Megan, never forget, the Son is Risen!"

About Author
Karen Kelly Boyce

Karen Kelly Boyce was born in Jersey City, New Jersey. She learned her faith and love of reading at the hands of the Sisters of Mercy. Only a few blocks away from the Barron Library, she spent most of her summer days and weekends lost in the stories and biographies of famous people. The turbulent sixties led her away from her first loves of church, reading, and writing. The only part of her faith that remained was the belief that we were made to help others. That belief led her to graduate as an RN in 1974.

Karen married in 1975, and raised two children. After going through a Life in the Spirit Seminar, she found peace and eternal love in the faith that would sustain her. In 1990, she became very ill and was eventually diagnosed with end stage Lyme Disease and was unable to work as a nurse anymore. As a disabled person, Karen's love of reading was rekindled and her love of writing born again.

Karen is the author of two other books - *According To Thy Word* and a *Bend in the Road: A Year's Journey Through Breast Cancer*. The book you are holding and *According To Thy Word* have received the esteemed Catholic Writers Guild seal of approval.

All books can be purchased on line at :

www.queenofangelsfarm.com or
www.jacksonwritersgroup.com/boyce.html

Made in the USA
Columbia, SC
05 July 2018